By MUTUAL CONSENT

TRACEY RICHARDSON

Bella
BOOKS
2016

Bella Books, Inc.
P.O. Box 10543
Tallahassee, FL 32302

Printed in the United States of America on acid-free paper.

First Bella Books Edition 2016

Editor: Medora MacDougall
Cover Designer: Linda Callaghan

ISBN: 978-1-59493-475-9

Other Bella Books by Tracey Richardson

Blind Bet
The Campaign
The Candidate
Side Order of Love
No Rules of Engagement
The Song in My Heart
The Wedding Party
Last Salute

Acknowledgments

Thank you to Bella Books, their staff and authors, for their professionalism, their talent, their support, and for producing such high quality work. Bella does put out the best lesbian novels in the world! Without exaggeration, my editor, Medora MacDougall is also the best! I would also like to thank readers everywhere, along with my fellow writers, for their encouragement and support...without you guys I wouldn't be doing this. Thank you to my partner Sandra for her ongoing patience and support as well. Oh, and my dogs love having a stay-at-home mom/writer!

About the Author

Tracey is the author of eight other Bella Books novels, including the popular *Last Salute*, *No Rules of Engagement*, *The Candidate*, *The Campaign* and *The Song In My Heart*. She has been a winner or finalist for several lesbian fiction awards, as well as newspaper awards. Among her accolades, Tracey is a two-time Lambda Literary finalist. Tracey worked as a daily newspaper journalist for more than two decades and lives in southwestern Ontario with her partner and two very busy chocolate Labrador retrievers. Besides reading and writing, she enjoys playing ice hockey and golf, and playing guitar. Please visit www.traceyrichardson.net, and on Twitter @trich7117.

CHAPTER ONE

"What you need, dear, is a wife."

Joss McNab gaped at her mother and immediately lost her ability to speak. Madeline McNab—a socialite with almost unheard of clout, arbiter of all things prim and proper, Southern gentlewoman and purveyor of, until now, sensible and practical advice—was suggesting something so utterly outrageous that it took a full minute for the shock to yield to anything resembling rational thought.

"Mama, are you having a stroke?" Joss said upon finding her voice. She wasn't even seeing anyone, for Christ sake. And if she was, well, it would be a disaster just like every other relationship she'd ever had. Joss and her mother never—*never!*—talked about her dating life, mostly because it simply didn't exist. But marriage? *What the fuck?* "Because I swear you just mentioned me and the word *wife* in the same sentence."

Thick-skinned and with a sense of humor as dry as her daughter's, Madeline's smile brimmed with amusement. "I hope that's not your clinical diagnosis of me, or I might actually be frightened right now. And yes, since you seem to have developed a hearing problem, I said you need a wife."

For all of about four seconds, Joss pretended to consider the idea. "I see. You want me to marry some poor woman so she can sit at home waiting on me while I'm off working my sixty-hour weeks. Plus there's all those out-of-town conferences. Throw in my routine functions, and it'd almost certainly be a marriage of one."

Her mother's blue eyes were laser beams. Clearly, she was insulted by Joss's dismissal of her idea. "Your father wouldn't have been half the doctor he was without me. I won't pretend either of us was perfect, but we had a common goal, and I think we achieved it rather marvelously."

Joss rolled her eyes, because she was quite sure most women wanted much more from a relationship than what her mother had settled for.

"I don't think," Joss said evenly, "it works that way anymore."

She'd never fully understood, or approved of, her mother's eagerness to adopt her husband's goals and achievements so fully as her own. For that amount of selflessness, she must have loved him more than Joss could truly fathom. Joseph McNab had certainly been a magnetic, charismatic man—a giant of a figure in their lives. Indomitable, brilliant, big and good looking, filling up a room with his knowledge and with his physical presence. She didn't appreciate until she was in high school that he'd been one of the South's top heart surgeons in the 1970s and 80s. His name graced Vanderbilt University School of Medicine's department of cardiology, a fitting tribute considering all the time he'd spent teaching there, not to mention all the money he'd bequeathed to the school upon his death almost five years ago. Joss missed him, but she never understood how anybody could so thoroughly give up her own dreams for someone else.

She certainly hadn't. In many ways, she'd become her father, exactly as her mother had triumphantly predicted many years ago. When she was a kid, her nickname had been Daddy's Little Double or L.D. Their identical blond hair, sea-green eyes and square jaw rendered them near carbon copies of one another,

but more notably Joss resembled her father in personality—
she was a perfectionist, a high achiever driven to the point of
exhaustion and obsession, someone who was happily unaware
of everything peripheral. She lived in her own world and was
completely fixated on her own needs and interests, which meant
romantic relationships were doomed to failure. Within about
three dates.

Joss sighed and took a sip of her coffee, which had finally
cooled to a tolerable temperature. The mother-daughter
Sunday morning brunch ritual always took place at Madeline's
six-bedroom colonnaded mansion in Brentwood, a wealthy
enclave south of Nashville. Madeline had been left a wealthy
widow, and Joss, a cardiac surgeon like her father, also wanted
for nothing. He had left her his pied-à-terre—a million-dollar,
three-bedroom condo conveniently located mere blocks from
Vanderbilt, and he had left Joss's mother plenty of money to see
her through her remaining years.

The McNab women were not imperious about money nor
did they obsess about it. A foundation in Joseph's name took
care of the family's charitable donations, and if either woman
wanted something, they simply bought it without any drama or
preamble.

"As wonderfully as marriage might have worked for you
and Daddy, I don't have the time or inclination for a wife," Joss
said, determined to put an end to the discussion. "Or even a
steady girlfriend. You know that, Mama. When was the last time
I brought someone home for you to meet?" It had been years—
since college, actually. That was when Joss still bought into the
romantic misconception that she could have both a career and
love, like most normal people. Like her father had apparently
managed. But reality had inserted itself in the years since, as
Joss began to realize she had little left to give after a long day
in the operating room or teaching or schmoozing at the endless
functions required of Joseph McNab's only offspring.

Joss's mother, never one to sit for long, was at the sink wiping
down the counter for about the fifth time in the last hour. "I
realize this sounds like it's coming out of left field. Although,

come to think of it…" She spun around, pointed a wet finger at Joss. "Your father was your age when we got married."

Joss's eye rolling began in earnest again. "I don't need you reminding me I'm pushing forty, you know. Or that I'm going to die an old cat lady or something. Did we just time-travel backward a hundred years or what?" The truth was, her mother did often remind her she was becoming middle-aged, but this was the first time she'd ever suggested Joss should get serious with someone. And to skip right to marriage? "Next, you'll be pushing me to produce a grandchild," she mumbled around the rim of her coffee cup.

"Oh, don't be silly, dear."

But Madeline had that faraway look in her eyes, and her lips were pursed in deep concentration. She was thinking. Scheming. And that meant trouble.

"Oh, Lord, Mama. What did you do?"

"Nothing yet." She threw the wet cloth on the counter, picked up the dry towel. "And I don't mean you need a *real* wife, of course. Not while you're married to your blessed work."

"So there are other kinds of wives? Is that what you're saying?" This definitely ranked as one of the weirdest conversations Joss had ever had with her mother. "Blow-up dolls? Mail-order brides? A computer avatar? What, exactly?"

Madeline threw the towel at Joss, her aim as accurate as ever. "I won't even begin to try to figure out what a computer avatar is. Look, I mean a wife in name only. A companion."

Oh, sweet Jesus. "I knew this conversation would devolve into sex. And I do *not* want to talk about sex with my own mother."

"Oh, settle down, child."

Madeline returned to their table, which offered a straight shot view through large sliding doors that led to the expansive backyard. The leaves, in full transition now, were a searing red and orange, and both women's glances continually strayed to the bursting trees and their blazing carpet of leaves below.

"I'm not talking about sex," Madeline continued, her expression mercifully blank. "Although, I do worry…"

"Mama!"

"All right, all right. Fine. What I mean is, you need someone to take to all these functions you're required to attend. A woman who can ease some of your social burdens. A woman who can set *you* at ease before these crowds you despise so much. She could help, you know, smooth things out and do all the unsung but indispensible things a wife does at these events. Believe me, I helped your father in a million different ways in his career. And you're even more of an introvert than he was."

I know exactly what would put me at ease before going to one of those rubber chicken dinners, Joss thought mischievously. *An orgasm and a glass of bourbon!* A fuck buddy was what she needed, not a wife, she thought wickedly. Then she looked at her mother, not a strand of silver hair out of place, lipstick perfectly applied, hands folded neatly on the table, and felt a prick of guilt for making fun of it all.

The two women were close; Joss told her mother almost everything. But now she regretted complaining to her last week about the new demands the school's cardiology department had placed on her. As deputy chief of the department the past two years, she'd been largely able to buzz around in the background teaching a couple of second- and third-year classes on top of her surgical duties at the Vanderbilt University Medical Center and her consults with patients. But the department's chief had confided in her that he'd recently been diagnosed with prostate cancer and that he was going to have to hand over to her most of what she characterized as the ceremonial portfolio. It was unfair to label it ceremonial, she knew, because it was a lot of damned hard and vitally important work—graduations, recruitment of students and instructors, sponsorship courting, conventions, galas, speeches, receptions, fundraisers. It meant being the public face of the school's cardiology department. She abhorred the idea of publicly waving the banner, but she'd given in rather easily. Partly because it wasn't poor Stan Chalmers's fault that he had prostate cancer. But mostly because the department was her father's legacy, and she had to agree that her taking a higher profile was good for the Joseph P. McNab Department of Cardiology. It was her duty to help the school to continue to succeed and thrive.

"Mama, even if you have a point—and that's a big if—you don't just dial up a wife like ordering takeout, you know."

"Of course not. You have to be discreet about the whole thing. Why, you remember the dean of the school in the late 1990s? Jim Hart? That wasn't his wife who accompanied him to all those dinners and functions, you know."

Joss vaguely remembered the couple from her own time as a medical student at the school, before she'd gone off to Stanford to further her surgical training. "All right. So that woman he dragged around was his mistress?"

"No, no. Not his mistress. His wife had died years before that. Karen was his friend, his platonic friend, who was always at his side when he needed a woman's help. A social escort. He didn't care what people thought, and of course, most people assumed they were a couple. But they weren't. They were pragmatic companions."

"Oh, pfft. He was probably screwing her six ways to—"

"Joss! Jim was our friend. Don't be churlish. And they were not lovers. Their relationship served a specific purpose."

Whatever, who cares, Joss thought. *If I ever have a wife, even if it's a pretend wife, I'd better be getting something out of it between the sheets.* "And what does all this have to do with me again?"

"It would be the perfect arrangement for you. A socially adept woman who could accompany you to this heavy load of functions you said you're going to have to take on. She'll have to be brilliant at conversing with people, of course. And she'll need to be stylish, clever, witty—"

"Mama, please. You can stop with your Dear Santa list, because it's never going to happen."

"Just think about it, honey. She could make things so much easier for you at these events, and then at the end of the night, you simply go your separate ways. Most people are enlightened now, and it won't matter in the least that you're both women. And besides, you've been out since before college." She rubbed her hands together with what Joss concluded was a little too much glee. "It's simple, don't you see?"

Joss didn't subscribe to her mother's elementary conclusions, because nothing was truly that simple, but she didn't want to be here all day. "And what's in it for Ms. Make Believe?"

A triumphant smile burst onto Madeline's lips. "To be on the arm of my gorgeous, brilliant, talented daughter, of course."

Joss took her mug to the Keurig machine and popped in another K-Cup. "Yeah, that'll sure have them lining up down the street." She couldn't dam up her negativity. Mostly because it was one of the craziest ideas her mother had ever suggested. In fact, it was a shocker, and for a moment, she worried her mother was suffering from early onset dementia. Not that she'd have the guts to muse about something like that out loud. Not if she wanted to live to see tomorrow.

"Well, all right, I suppose those things are not enough," her mother conceded. "I'm not sure what Jim Hart gave Karen in return."

"Probably about six inches of—"

"Joss!" The ice in her mother's eyes told her she'd gone too far.

"Sorry."

"Perhaps you could take her on some nice trips or something. Take her shopping now and again. Let her drive your BMW. Give her a nice allowance. I don't know what else."

"Okay, enough. You make it sound like I'm trying to attract a candidate who's about seventeen years old! For God's sake, 'let her drive my car'?" Joss returned to the table, her temper as hot as the fresh coffee in her mug. "This idea was ridiculous to begin with, and it's getting more so by the second. I'm not interested. End of subject." It was insane to think that some normal adult woman out there would actually be pleased to be Joss's trophy, a kept woman who would be little better than a mistress.

Madeline sighed unhappily. "Fine. What would you like to talk about?"

"Want to go to the Titans game with me a week from Sunday?" Joss had been given two tickets by a fellow surgeon who'd forgotten it was his fifteenth wedding anniversary. His wife was not a football fan, which meant he'd had to get rid of the tickets in one hell of a hurry.

"Hmm. That's the twenty-sixth of October. Don't you have that birthday party to go to? For Jack Pritchard?"

Joss rubbed a hand over her face and groaned. "Oh, damn. I forgot about that." Now she was definitely grumpy. Dr. Jack Pritchard was professor emeritus at the medical school and its longest-serving faculty member, even though he no longer practiced medicine or even taught anymore. A cramped office and a title had been given to him for life. He was surly and ill-tempered at the best of times, and Joss would rather pull out her hair one strand at a time than attend a seventy-fifth birthday party for the old coot. But all the department heads and sub-heads had been ordered to attend. "Why don't you come with me, Mama? Pritchard at least tolerates you."

Madeline had the audacity to laugh. "You couldn't pay me to spend an evening with that old so-and-so."

"You know, you could actually use a swear word once in a while. It won't turn you to stone." Madeline McNab was a genteel Southern woman—strong, fierce when she needed to be, polite to a fault—who belonged in the antebellum era. Swearing, or doing anything that resembled letting her hair down, was a rarity.

"Oh hush. You young people more than make up for my failure to swear. But you see what I mean? A companion could help make Pritchard's party much more tolerable for you. Maybe even enjoyable."

Joss buried her head in her hands. She should know by now that arguing with her mother was futile. If the idea of a trophy wife provided Madeline with a harmless little fantasy or some sense that she was helping Joss, then so be it, but Joss would never allow it to become a reality. She wasn't that desperate. Or that much of a loser.

CHAPTER TWO

Sarah Young glanced worriedly at her chest, then her lap, then her tidy heels. No spillages, no wardrobe malfunctions, nothing wrong that she could see. So why the hell was her father giving her that scowling, judgmental look across the table as though she'd missed curfew or had forgotten to clean her room?

The petulant twelve-year-old in her wanted to challenge him, tell him to mind his own business, but it was far too late for that. Sarah had swallowed her pride a long time ago, starting when he'd bankrolled her undergrad degree at Chicago's Institute of Fine Arts and then her two-year master's degree in fine arts at Boston University. Four years later, he was still subsidizing her to the tune of about a thousand dollars a month—money she needed to augment her meager salary as a part-time instructor to freshmen in Vanderbilt U's art department.

She understood the trade-off all too well. If she was going to take his money, she had to take his crap too. Only tonight, she wasn't feeling so philosophical about it. Annoyance and guilt mixed with the acid of the garlic and red wine in her stomach. It was a lousy way to spend her twenty-ninth birthday, and she resolved that her thirtieth would be a hell of a lot different. *Next year at this time, I'll have sold a few of my paintings, maybe commissioned something, and I'll be paying my own freight. And I can tell Daddy to go to hell if I want.* She didn't want to think about how many times she'd given herself the exact same speech— every birthday and every Christmas for the last six years. Maybe longer. It was goddamned depressing.

A birthday card sat in the center of the table, the evening's coup de grace. When she was a kid, Sarah had looked forward to her present being a surprise. One year it was a compact car. Another year it was a pearl necklace. The last ten years, since she'd gotten serious about her education and career as an artist, her birthday present consisted of an envelope containing a healthy check from her father's personal account. It was a good chunk of her living expenses for the remainder of the year, and now it sat as a visible reminder of Sarah's inferiority and weakness.

"Shall we order dessert?" her stepmother Linda asked helpfully. She often played the mediator between them, and over pasta she had tossed little warning looks at Sarah. Which were well intentioned but of absolutely no help.

A waitress armed with a smile so fake it threatened to crack her face in half carried a candlelit cake to the table. Sarah dutifully blew out the candles one at a time, the same as she'd done at every birthday dinner, including her childhood ones at the neighborhood Chuck E. Cheese. By the age of eleven she'd rebelled, threatening that she'd celebrate no further birthdays unless they took her to grown-up restaurants.

As sternly as if she'd forgotten to genuflect in church, her father said, "You didn't make a wish, Sarah."

"Yes I did," she lied, resisting a good eye rolling, but barely. Every birthday, she wished for her paintings to sell or for a worthy gallery to come calling, and every year her wish was another catastrophic letdown. There was no point in paying lip service to this wishing business anymore.

Sarah's father cleared his throat and nodded severely at the envelope. "I feel I must warn you first, Sarah. You're not going to like what you see in there."

Linda's gaze strayed to her hands, the floor. Anywhere but at Sarah.

Sarah opened the envelope, quickly scanned the card and looked at the check she'd pinched between her fingers. It was for less than half as much as usual—enough to keep her going for four, maybe five months. She smiled as politely as she could manage, thanked them and ignored the ominous voice in her head that told her she'd better start looking for a *real* job.

"Don't you want to know why the check is smaller this time?"

Sarah didn't want to talk about money with her father. She hated the way he always framed the discussion in a tone that characterized her as lazy, unmotivated, wasting her time with her paints and canvases and her "useless degrees."

"It's fine," she said. "I'm grateful. Thank you."

She could see he wasn't going to let it go, that the check was his way of initiating a serious discussion. Well, not a discussion. A lecture. He'd squared his shoulders in that courtroom posture he was so well practiced at, and his jaw was set in that uncompromising way that indicated it would strictly be a one-way conversation. "You'll be thirty in a year, Sarah. It's time you grew up and took a proper job. It's time I stopped supporting you."

In theory he was right, but there was no reasonable way to discuss the subject with him. He wanted her to abjectly agree with him. He wanted her to take an office job—his law firm could help her he'd told her so many times she'd lost count. His other standard suggestion was that she teach elementary or high school students full time. But she'd sooner choose the office job than teach kids who weren't serious about art, who only took the courses because they could goof off in class. Nothing appealed to her but what she was already doing, and she wasn't yet ready to "grow up."

"Sarah, darling." Linda stood up, placed her napkin neatly on the table. "Come to the ladies' room with me and help me get something out of my eye, would you?"

At the sink, Sarah grumbled, "Thanks for the rescue." They were alone in the large, marble tile washroom.

"I wish I could have warned you, but I only learned of the amount this morning."

"It's okay. I don't blame him." He was never going to respect her work until it provided her a living wage because that was the way he measured a person's worth. And she *would* make a living from her art one day. She was getting better at it every month, every year, and she was making strides selling a few small pieces here and there the last couple of years. A couple of galleries in town and one in Memphis had shortlisted her as a candidate for sales and exhibitions, and while they'd ultimately passed on her, she was sure that with a little more time, she could convince them.

"You know, if it was up to me…"

"I know." Sarah patted Linda's arm. She liked Linda and had never been one of those bratty teenagers who gives nothing but grief to the woman her father marries. At least Linda was loyal— something her biological mother was definitely not. Sarah had essentially been raised by her father from the time she was ten, after her mother decided living in Tennessee was holding her back from what otherwise would have been a spectacular acting career. California was calling her, she'd said in the terse, one-page note she'd stuck to the fridge. Since then, Sarah had seen her mother on television once, in a Ford commercial driving a minivan full of kids. What a joke that was, pretending to be a soccer mom. She was a mother from hell, and Sarah had no intention of ever having a relationship with her again.

"I want to help, Sarah."

Sarah shook her head. "No, I don't want you going against Daddy's wishes and sneaking me money." Linda had already helped her over the years by convincing a few of her wealthy friends to buy some of her paintings. Linda had, in many ways, been more supportive of her career than her father.

"Well, there might be another way."

"Like the lottery?"

"No, not the lottery. Do you know who Madeline McNab is?"

"The name vaguely rings a bell. Isn't she one of your luncheon ladies?" Sarah winked. "Or should I say, a member of your mint julep club?" There were eight or nine influential Nashville ladies who got together monthly on the pretense, Sarah guessed, of discussing philanthropic missions. Linda had once confessed that the lunches usually stretched to an afternoon of mint juleps made with Tennessee's finest whiskey and discussions that ranged from books to celebrity gossip to politics. Oh, and charitable causes, of course, but they were almost an afterthought.

"Part of Vanderbilt's medical school is named after her husband."

"Oh, right, that's where I've seen the name." Sarah tapped her temple. "Wait, I get it! I can donate a kidney or some other organ for cash. Is that your idea?"

Linda threw her head back and laughed. "Where do you come up with these wild ideas?"

"Buy me one of your famous mint juleps and I'll come up with more."

"Oh no, not a chance. I suspect some of your wild ideas would get me arrested. Or divorced."

The specter of her father and his dim view of her tightened her stomach. "Daddy is certainly immune to my ideas."

"Don't you worry about him. There might be another way. A part-time job, so to speak."

"I already have a part-time job. If I take another one, there'll be no time for me to paint."

"But this would only be a few hours a week."

"And it pays well?"

"I think it could potentially be very lucrative. If you play your cards right."

"And what would I be doing, exactly?"

Linda hushed her voice, even though all the stalls were empty. "Madeline's daughter needs a…you know, an escort from time to time."

"You want me to be a call girl?" Sarah felt her eyebrows pop straight into her forehead. Escort was one of those icky words that really meant prostitute. It also meant that the only thing you were good for was sex. "And you think *I'm* the one with the wild ideas?"

"No, not a call girl. Not like prostitution, for goodness sakes. Her name is Joss McNab, and she's a heart surgeon like her father was. She's involved in the medical school too, and she needs an escort to take to receptions and functions. Someone who looks good. Someone smart and fun. Someone *exactly* like you." Linda reached out and touched a few strands of Sarah's long, lush red hair. "You're really gorgeous, you know. And you're a great conversationalist."

"Wait a minute." Sarah shook her head to clear it. "This Joss woman wants a trophy wife to take to boring, stuffy dinners and receptions? No thank you."

"It's only every once in a while, according to her mother. And you like people and socializing. And it could help you work up potential clients for your paintings."

That got Sarah's attention. Socializing with doctors and other professionals could be exactly her ticket to selling more paintings. People like that had money, connections, and they'd need art for their elegant mansions and fancy offices. "Is this woman willing to pay me to do this?" Sarah still couldn't quite fathom what Linda was suggesting.

"Yes. I'm assured there would be some sort of mutually beneficial arrangement."

Sarah removed her lipstick tube from her bag and began touching up her lips. "I don't know, Linda. It sounds strange. I mean, do people actually pay other people to be their friend? Or to be their pretend girlfriend? It's damned weird, if you ask me."

"Apparently in some circles, yes."

"This Joss McNab. She's not some pervert or serial killer, is she?"

Linda frowned at her, but Sarah could tell she was trying not to laugh. "No, she's not some crazy person."

"Does she have hygiene issues? Hairy ears? Bizarre social habits?"

Linda raised an eyebrow at her.

"Okay, fine. I'm just wondering why she has to pay someone to attend functions with her, if she's a doctor and all. And probably richer than Daddy."

"Her mother says she doesn't have time for a proper girlfriend, that's all. And that she hates all this schmoozing and small talk that's expected of her. She's an introvert. Exactly what you are not."

Sarah sighed. "Well, growing up with Daddy, I'm certainly used to being a social butterfly." After her mother's departure from their lives, she was often her father's escort and sometimes even his stand-in at parties and dinners until he hooked up with Linda.

"You'd be great it at, and I told Madeline as much."

"Hmm, I swear this is sounding more and more like some kind of arranged marriage."

"Well, it is the South, after all." Linda grinned. "Shall I tell Madeline you're interested?"

"If this woman wants me as her escort, I'm assuming she's out?" Sarah had come out the minute she left Nashville for college and had never looked back. She wasn't about to pretend she was straight for anyone. Or for any amount of money.

"She is, although Madeline says she hasn't had a proper girlfriend in years. So, you'll do it?"

Sarah thought of her father back at the table, the stern and unforgiving expression on his face, his eagerness to remind her of her bleak prospects for the future. What the hell. Flitting around on the arm of a wealthy doctor couldn't be as bad as a job at her father's law office. Nothing was that bad! "Fine, I'll try it once. That should be enough to convince both of us that it's a stupid idea."

"Great, I'll email you the details. Now let's get back to our table before Peter sends a pack of dogs after us."

CHAPTER THREE

"I've got to hand it to you, Joss. You sure do know how to keep your success with the ladies a secret around here."

Joss gaped at Rob Spalding as he stuffed olives into his mouth like a man who hadn't eaten all day. Which he probably hadn't. Rob was always running in a million directions, absent minded to the point of sometimes forgetting to eat, grabbing an apple— grabbing someone else's apple, more like—while rushing to the lab, to the OR or to teach his next class. He was a genius with Vanderbilt's new left ventricular assist device implant, but he couldn't organize his way out of a wet paper bag when it came to things more mundane. Like eating.

"What are you talking about, Rob?" Joss shouldered him out of the way so she could reach the shrimp platter. The only good thing about this dreadfully boring birthday reception for the grouchy old Jack Pritchard was the catering. She wouldn't have to worry about throwing together a meal tonight or mooching off her mother.

"I'm talking about your girlfriend, of course. Who else?"

Joss's shrimp slid off her suddenly unsteady plate and plopped unceremoniously onto the table's white cloth. "Sweet Jesus. My what?"

Rob stuffed another olive into his mouth, then tilted his head in the direction of the guest of honor, who was talking with a flaming redhead with dancing blue eyes and an elegance of movement that was bewitching. She was dressed conservatively in a blue, thigh-length dress, but the way it clung to her, revealing every smooth, full curve, suggested that her sexiness could not be camouflaged by such simple attire. She smiled graciously at the guest of honor, and, most shockingly of all, she was making the old bastard laugh.

"Wow," Joss muttered. "I don't think I've ever seen Pritchard laugh before."

"Laugh? How about smile?"

Her attention drifted back to the mystery woman. Joss had never seen her connected to the medical school in any way. Or to the Vanderbilt Medical Center, where Joss spent even more of her time. The hospital employed thousands, but she would have remembered the gorgeous redhead. *I would remember that hair and its threads of gold and copper. I'd remember those hands and the way they move so artfully when she talks. And that thousand-watt smile that's kind and curious and hinting at an impatience to get on with life.*

Beauty and confidence and sincerity seemed to intersect in a stunning package, and if Joss weren't such an introvert, she would beg someone this minute for an introduction.

"So," Rob said, his thick eyebrows raised in challenge. "I overheard someone saying that she's your date. Aren't you going to at least introduce me to her?"

Joss nearly choked on her shrimp. "My...*date*? Introduce you?"

"Okay, look. Obviously she's taken. And doesn't play for my team. But I've absolutely got to meet the woman who can wrap Pritchard the Prick around her little finger like a ribbon. And you, for that matter."

"Whoa now, hold on a second. Where did you ever get the idea that—"

"C'mon, let's go. Pritchard's just been hauled away by his wife."

Rob tugged her toward the red-haired beauty, who settled a dazzling smile on them that all but sparkled. It was almost hypnotic and it embraced them, as though she'd been waiting just for them. The effect it had on Joss nearly made her knees buckle.

"Joss, hi," the woman said sweetly, touching Joss's arm as though she'd done it a thousand times before. When she stood on tiptoe to peck Joss's cheek, a ripple of dizziness washed through Joss. "I'm sorry I was a little late getting here."

"Oh…I…ah…" *What?*

"Oh, I'm sorry." The woman directed her attention to Rob and the loss of it to Joss was as jarring as a spotlight being turned off. "How do you do? I'm Sarah Young. I'm Joss's…" Blue eyes darted to Joss, then back to Rob. "Friend."

"I'm well, thank you. I'm Rob Spalding. A colleague of Joss's both here at the school and the hospital."

"I'm very pleased to make your acquaintance, Rob. Can I prevail upon you to find me a glass of champagne so I can have Joss all to myself for a moment?"

"You most certainly can." He leaned closer to her, lowering his voice conspiratorially. "But first. What in hell did you ever say to Pritchard to light him up like a Christmas tree?"

"You mean that nice elderly gentleman? I just wished him a happy birthday and told him he didn't look a day past fifty." Her smile turned sheepish, and she batted her eyes with eyelashes so long and thick, they reminded Joss of Tennessee Indiangrass. "And there might have been something to the effect that if he'd been my doctor, I would have kept finding reasons to visit him."

Rob laughed and nudged Joss's shoulder. "I think you need to bring Sarah around this place more often. I can give her a long list of people to charm."

Joss felt dumb, unable to produce a witty response. Or any response, for that matter. Coming up with small talk was a chore for her. Torture, really. Her social awkwardness was what had propelled her toward books and schoolwork from such a young age, because she could immerse herself for hours and not have to speak to anyone.

"Oh, right," Rob said. "The champagne." He winked at Joss, as though he wanted to say more but didn't dare. "Excuse me."

"Certainly. Thank you," Sarah said, lightly resting her hand on Joss's forearm again, instantly imprinting Joss's skin with a warm tingle. "I really am sorry I was a few minutes late. I can assure you, I don't make a habit of it. My car wouldn't start, except I kept trying, and I think I wore down the battery. I finally took a cab."

Joss had the disorienting feeling that she'd been thrust on stage without a script in the middle of a play. "I'm sorry. I don't understand. Was I expecting you?" *And who the hell are you, Miss Sarah Young?* She'd speak if she could, but those soft sky-blue eyes made it nearly impossible to form full sentences. Or to ask questions that didn't make her sound like a third grader.

"Our arrangement today," Sarah continued, her smile faltering briefly, her face paling a shade to reveal faint freckles. "You…Oh, no. Your mother didn't tell you about it, did she?"

Her jaw quickly turning to cement, Joss tried to keep her voice level. "I see. My mother put you up to this. I sincerely apologize for her actions. She was misguided in whatever arrangement she made with you."

"Actually, your mother and my stepmother made the arrangement. I'm just following instructions to be your escort at today's birthday celebration for Dr. Pritchard."

Heat shot to Joss's face and a few choice curses stormed through her mind. "Well, that's just perfect." She'd been clear with her mother about this crazy idea, and yet Madeline had defied her. And made a fool of her. Annoyance threatened to flare into full-blown anger.

"Why don't we try to make the best of the situation?" Sarah suggested coolly, her eyes as inviting as a swimming pool on a hot summer day. It was damned tempting to dive in. "Start over again?"

Joss couldn't seem to open her mouth. Which was just as well, because she was still pissed off at her mother and feared that if she did try to speak right now, she'd sound like a horrible daughter—all petulant and self-absorbed.

Sarah's smile somehow maintained its charm and warmth. It made Joss want to say yes. To anything. "What do you say, Dr. McNab?"

The longer Sarah's gaze stayed on her, the more Joss melted from the inside out. This woman, she thought with puzzled admiration, knew exactly how to win people over. She still chafed a little, but already her anger toward her mother was beginning to fizzle. "All right. I'm Joss McNab. It's a pleasure to meet you, Sarah Young. And please, call me Joss."

"Thank you, Joss, and the pleasure is all mine." She snaked her hand possessively through Joss's arm as Stan Chalmers and his wife approached. "And to the public, we're friends, right? Or is it special friends?" She lifted her eyebrows in mild flirtation, making Joss's heart skip a beat. Transitory mild tachycardia brought on by sudden stress, Joss decided, the self-diagnosis giving her momentary comfort. And a steadying distraction, because she did not—ever!—fall for women who came along batting their eyelashes and flashing million-dollar smiles.

"Joss, my dear, you're looking handsome as always." Stan's wife Elizabeth kissed both her cheeks, European style. Stan shook her hand warmly before the couple turned expectantly to Sarah.

"I'd like you to meet my, er, friend, Sarah Young."

Joss watched them smile warmly and shake hands with Sarah. How strange it felt that these people now assumed Sarah was her girlfriend. She'd never been closeted, not even when she was a medical student, and for the past three years she had sat on the medical school's LGBT MD committee. But she'd never before brought a date to a work function. And while it felt foreign to be presenting herself as part of a couple, it mildly surprised her that it didn't actually feel all that bad. The truth was, having Sarah by her side made her stand a little easier. Especially when Stan and Elizabeth Chalmers began engaging Sarah in animated conversation about everything from the Titans to last week's symphony concert to the upcoming political election. Joss let Sarah do the talking while she tuned out and let her mind wander to the valvular stenosis she'd diagnosed late yesterday in a fifty-seven-year-old patient.

"Your champagne, madam." Rob handed Sarah a glass, then handed one to Joss. He finished with a little bow to Sarah, an elegant show of respect Joss had never seen him make before. She'd been skeptical until now that her friend was at all familiar with formal manners.

"Well, I'm very impressed," Elizabeth Chalmers whispered to Joss after a cluster of others had joined their little group.

"Excuse me?"

"With your date, Sarah. She's a lovely young woman. I'll make sure to include her on our Christmas guest list."

"Um, I…You don't have to do that." Surely, Joss thought, this little charade was a one-off that would be a distant memory by Christmas.

"Oh, don't be so modest. I was just saying to Stan last week that you need to find yourself a nice lady friend." She squeezed Joss's forearm. "And it seems you have. I'm so glad."

The reception flew by, Joss's self-imposed deadline of leaving after the first hour having long expired. Nearly three hours later, the crowd having thinned, she took Sarah's elbow so they could take their leave.

"I think we should talk about today's little arrangement," Joss whispered. "It's either that, or I'm of a mind to string up my mama by the toes."

Sarah laughed. "I don't think stringing up your mother is a viable option. But talking certainly is. We could go somewhere for dinner?"

Joss glanced at her watch. It was five o'clock. A bit early for dinner, and besides, she wasn't hungry after munching her way through the buffet table. "How about coffee?" She'd had two glasses of champagne and didn't need any more alcohol.

"Coffee it is. I know a great little café not far from here."

"The Mixed Bean, by chance?"

"Yes, that's the one. Best coffee anywhere near campus."

"You work on campus?"

"I teach two freshmen classes for the faculty of art."

Damn, Joss thought. She'd have remembered if she'd ever seen Sarah around campus, although the medical school and the art department were at opposite ends. "I'm surprised I haven't run into you before."

"I'm not. Art and medicine aren't exactly bedfellows around here."

"True." The med school was extremely insulated. It wasn't that it was the sun with everything else revolving around it, but rather that it was alone in its own galaxy.

They set out on foot in the direction of the café, the late afternoon warm and breezy, and Joss realized the day had gone much better than she'd expected. She'd been dreading attending Pritchard's birthday reception. She didn't think anything would trump that unpleasantness until she'd discovered her mother's manipulations. But now as they passed a handful of people on the leafy sidewalk, Joss felt an unfamiliar tickle in her belly and a buoyancy to her mood that she could only attribute to the presence of the woman beside her. Her shoulders relaxed, and she caught herself nearly smiling as she held open the door of the café for Sarah.

Oh, this was *so* not good. Because nothing this good, this easy, ever was, in her experience. She could only compare herself to an animal that had walked into some kind of trap, not yet realizing the severity of its situation.

Oh, Mama, what did you do!

CHAPTER FOUR

As they took their seats in the café, Sarah watched Joss's face harden to a deep scowl in a matter of seconds.

"I'm sorry my mother's devious plan wasted your time today. I'll certainly compensate you for it, and I can assure you this won't happen again."

The rapidity with which Joss had turned cool and distant surprised Sarah. She had been a little stiff at the birthday reception, a tad detached and somewhat impatient, like she didn't want to be there. She had had the good manners to be polite about it, however, and had even found a modicum of humor about it. Sarah couldn't really blame Joss for being less than pleased about the afternoon; clearly she wasn't a fan of Dr. Pritchard and, worse, she had been caught off guard by Madeline and Linda's machinations. Sarah expected that Joss was very much the type who did not suffer fools gladly and abhorred being publicly embarrassed.

But there was no reason now for her frostiness, unless perhaps she was still feeling embarrassed by Sarah's ambush at the party. Sarah had taken satisfaction in the easy way they'd managed to camouflage Joss's surprise and discomfort, with Sarah smoothly working the room and Joss following along as though they were an actual couple making the social rounds. Things had gone as well as they could. *Hadn't they?*

Joss stood. "I'll go place our order. What can I get you?"

"Cappuccino, please."

Joss's long strides to the counter appeared hurried, impatient, angry. Sarah could see that the arranged date was continuing to rattle her, though if she were to be honest about it (she wouldn't!), the whole thing was actually kind of amusing. No harm had been done, and their little performance at the birthday event gratified Sarah because they'd pulled it off as if they'd rehearsed it a dozen times. Or as if it wasn't a performance at all.

Moments later, cradling her cappuccino on the table in front of her, Sarah considered how to be delicate with her words. "When I was in high school, my dad went behind my back and arranged for the son of one of his law partners to take me to my prom. I didn't realize what he'd done until the end of the date, when neither of us was interested in making out." Sarah smiled at the memory of her and Tom Whitfield sitting in his car, both of them embarrassed, both of them not wanting to admit the truth at first. "Turns out we were both gay, and our dads had set us up."

Joss's answering smile fell short of the mark. "I don't need my mother setting up dates for me. And this isn't high school. These are my colleagues. This is my *profession*, and my mother had no right to do what she did. To either of us."

Was it really that bad? As far as Sarah could see there was nothing to be embarrassed about, because nobody else needed to know the truth. But clearly Joss was in no mood to be mollified. "Okay, look. Let's figure this out together."

Joss had closed up tighter than a furled flag, and it wouldn't have surprised Sarah if she bolted right now, good Southern manners or no. But instead, her fingers slowly relaxed their grip on her cup of black coffee, and she leaned back in her chair. It was a good sign that she seemed willing to hear Sarah out.

"First, let's get something straight," Sarah said. "You don't really have a problem getting your own dates, right? I mean, if anyone has left a blazing trail of broken hearts behind them, it's probably you."

As soon as the words were out of her mouth, she knew she'd made a tactical mistake. That square, handsome jaw of Joss's clamped down so hard, the ropey muscles of her neck began to bunch up. If her coffee cup had been someone's neck, they'd be strangled about now.

"What I mean is…" *Oh God.* Heat shot up Sarah's throat and into her face. This was not smoothing things out at all. "You're smart. And nice, of course. And successful. What I'm trying to say is, you're a good catch. A great catch, I'm sure. And you must be, like, going on dates all the time, right? Not that I mean, like, that you're breaking hearts left and right…Oh dammit!" Coffee sloshed over Sarah's cup and onto the table. She sopped it with her napkin, which quickly became saturated.

"Here." Joss wiped up the rest with her own napkin.

"Thanks," Sarah said, her face still hot, and she knew it was splotched with red patches. It was the worst thing about being so fair-skinned—she couldn't hide her emotions worth a crap. "I didn't mean—"

"I know you didn't." Joss smiled for real now. "But it was amusing watching you try to walk it back."

Sarah's temper sparked. "Well, I'm glad I can at least provide you with some entertainment."

"Hey." Joss awkwardly placed her hand on Sarah's, then quickly retracted it. "Let's start this conversation over, all right?"

"Fine. I didn't mean to insult you. I know you don't need anyone making dates for you."

Joss looked away, her fingers tapping an ardent beat on the tabletop.

Sarah's hand flew to her mouth. "Oh my." She lowered her voice to a whisper. "You *do* have trouble getting dates."

The truth of it was written all over Joss's face, and yet the idea of it was unfathomable. She was a doctor, a successful surgeon. She came from a wealthy family, and she was very good looking, even if it was in a starched, conventional way. Her blond hair was functionally short but stylish. Her green eyes were clear, intelligent, a little mysterious in their skill at hiding all those emotions. She was tall and had a runner's body. She was everything other women would find attractive.

"I don't have time to date," Joss countered.

"Okay. But you'd like to go out with someone once in a while, would that be fair to say?"

"It would be helpful for my work, I suppose."

"Then maybe your mother was simply trying to help."

"And what about your stepmother? Was she trying to help you?"

"Yes, I suppose she was." Sarah sipped her cappuccino and decided to be honest. "I'm basically your starving artist, and she was fixin' to set me up with a part-time job, so to speak."

Joss paused for a long moment, her thoughts unreadable. "What kind of starving artist?"

"I paint. Landscapes mostly, but some abstracts as well. As I said, I teach part-time on campus, but it's not enough to make a living. And my paintings, well…they're not exactly in high demand. Not yet, anyway."

"I see."

Under Joss's scrutinizing gaze, it was like she was a specimen under a microscope—a feeling she wasn't unfamiliar with—but she didn't much like it. She didn't want to seem pathetic. Or desperate. She mentally counted to five and returned Joss's gaze. Perhaps it was the certainty in those eyes or the strong angles of her broad shoulders, but she seemed to be the kind of woman who could handle the truth. "My father—he's a corporate lawyer in town—has been my benefactor, but he's made it clear he thinks I should give up this painting 'silliness' and get a real job."

Joss frowned. "He calls your work silly? As in frivolous?"

"Yes, mostly. Although 'hogwash' is usually his word of choice. I think he was willing to indulge it through my college years, probably because he thought it was some kind of phase that would pass. Now, he's…" Sarah's voice faltered as her thoughts drifted to the uncompromising look on her father's face at dinner last week, when he'd told her she needed to stand on her own two feet. His financial withdrawal hadn't been the painful part. What hurt was that he didn't believe in her talents, in her determination to be successful at what she loved to do. He'd never truly believed in her—something she typically tried to downplay to everyone but her stepmother and her roommate Lauren. Joss was the first stranger she had confided in about her father's disapproval.

"I'm sorry," Joss said. The warmth in her voice, the understanding and quiet self-possession in her eyes that said everything would be okay made Sarah fall apart inside for a moment.

"No," Sarah answered, finding her voice again. "I'm sorry. I don't want you to think I'm a charity case. Because I'm not. I'll find a way to keep painting, no matter what my father does or doesn't do. Or what he chooses to believe. So it's really not your problem, okay?"

Joss's grin was like a needle in Sarah's heart, until she realized Joss was not making light of her situation at all, but rather the opposite.

"Then I think you should show him that you will not be discouraged. And I think maybe we can help each other after all."

* * *

Joss offered to walk Sarah home before she had time to question what the hell she was doing. Or how the offer might be perceived.

She was not trying to be chivalrous, she told herself as the evening light faded and porch lights began to wink on. Nor was she trying to come on to Sarah. She was simply doing the polite thing in walking a woman home, because the truth was, she had little experience at romancing women and hadn't the first clue how to do it. Hookups usually came at the end of a long conference day in a perfunctory and efficient acknowledgment over a drink in a hotel lounge. She didn't know how one went about the dating dance, other than trolling the Internet dating sites and joining those speed dating events she heard the nurses regularly chatting about—things she wouldn't be caught dead doing. In any case, none of it mattered. She wasn't romancing Sarah or even flirting with her. And while what they were doing might resemble a date, it absolutely wasn't. In fact, there was no mystery about their arrangement. No worrying about whether Sarah expected a kiss or flowers or more at the end of the night. No. As much as it pained her to admit her mother might be right, this actually was kind of perfect. Act as a couple at an event, then go their separate ways at the end of it. Sarah would be doing nothing more than providing a service, for which Joss would be compensating her.

And yet. The way she'd felt at the birthday reception with Sarah at her side—smelling like wildflowers in a cedar forest, looking elegant, charming people with witty and intelligent conversation, using her soft, graceful hands to emphasize a point or to touch someone in a friendly, almost intimate acknowledgment—had ignited a tiny spark inside Joss that she instantly recognized as something she thought she'd never feel in the presence of another woman. Next to Sarah, she'd come alive—slowly, but profoundly. She'd felt attractive, likeable, engaged—as though she too, by extension, was charming and witty and sociable. Sarah's relaxed, genial demeanor had been contagious, to the point where others had remarked in knowing whispers how sweet and right they seemed as a couple. At the time it had horrified her, made her angry all over again at her mother. But now? Now she felt ridiculously pleased, although she wasn't ready to admit it yet.

"You're awfully quiet," Sarah said beside her.

"Just thinking about the logistics," Joss lied. Sarah—or rather, the feelings Sarah kindled in her—confused her. She needed to ground herself, get back to her comfort zone of clinical detachment. She was single for a reason, she reminded herself. She enjoyed an uncomplicated and regimented life that revolved around her work. She could and did come and go as she pleased, answering to no one.

"We don't have to, like, sign something or be too formal about this, as far as I'm concerned," Sarah offered.

Joss didn't pretend to know how all this was supposed to work. She'd Googled the subject of paid escorts after her mother had first suggested it, but the search produced only ads for prostitution and porn sites. She'd need to improvise.

"How about this?" Joss said, the boldness in her voice a fabrication. "I'd like to pay you a retainer. Four hundred a week. If I require you more than twice in a week, I'll double your fee. All your expenses will be paid...cabs, drinks, meals and so on. Clothes too if you need them."

"That's extremely generous." Sarah stopped beneath a streetlight and eyed Joss. "Are you sure about all of this?"

Joss wasn't at all sure about any of it, in spite of the ease with which she'd spouted off the details of the arrangement. But the idea of it made sense. Sarah clearly needed the money to support her art, and her presence at events like today's would make Joss's professional life a lot easier. Sarah would be able to divert much of the agonizing spotlight from Joss to herself at these things. Which would be a godsend, because the only place Joss wanted to be the center of attention was in the operating theater. She took a deep breath and let it out slowly. It wasn't like she was asking Sarah to marry her. Or as if hiring Sarah was going to cost her her inheritance. "Yes. Are you?"

"I suppose so." Sarah spread her hands out, and Joss had the urge to capture one of them with her own.

"Does it make you uncomfortable in any way? Because if it does—"

"No, it's just...I've never done anything like this. I guess I expected it to feel a bit icky, but it doesn't. It feels almost deliciously illicit." Sarah's eyes turned playful. "Like our own version of that old movie, *Pretty Woman*."

Joss laughed, picturing herself as the debonair and smooth-talking Richard Gere, albeit much less of a self-important jerk. "Unlike the Julia Roberts character, you don't have to sleep with me. And I'm no white knight in shining armor." *And I'm certainly not going to marry you at the end of it all*, Joss thought.

"Hmm," Sarah said, turning and walking again.

Joss waited for her to say more, but she didn't and her mind strayed to thoughts of extending their little agreement to include sex. What would it be like to conclude one of their little functions with a good roll in the sack? *Hmm*, she thought, arousal unspooling inside her. What would Sarah be like naked? And what would she be like in bed? Had the other guests at the party concluded they were sleeping together? Yes, she decided, they undoubtedly had, and the thought secretly thrilled her.

"You okay?"

"Yes, fine, thank you. Sorry. How old are you, by the way?"

"Plenty old enough to be your…" Sarah's forehead furrowed in confusion. She looked, Joss thought, adorable when she was flustered. "What exactly am I, anyway, since I'm something quite a lot less than your mistress?"

Joss thought about that. Something rebellious inside her quietly relished the idea of Sarah being her mistress, like in some old-fashioned romance novel where the shirtless man is leaning over the scantily clad, bust-thrusting woman. Not that Sarah seemed like the kind of woman who wanted to be dominated—sexually or otherwise—by anybody. And Joss wasn't the controlling, domineering type anyway. But she liked sex as much as the next red-blooded lesbian, and the idea of no-strings, relationship-free sex with Sarah was a definite turn-on.

Oh hell, she thought. Who was she kidding? She'd never pay for sex, even if Sarah was the type to offer it up on a plate—which she undoubtedly wasn't. Joss would never bring herself to allow their little arrangement to become that distasteful. Or that dishonorable. She would never put herself and Sarah in that predicament, fantasies aside. Her moral code and breeding were a definite libido killer in this instance.

"How about my professional companion?" Joss finally suggested.

"All right, that sounds okay. A damned sight better than paid companion. Or escort." Sarah shivered at the word *escort*. "Ugh, that makes me think of fat, hairy men going to massage parlors. And I'm twenty-nine, by the way."

Twenty-nine. That was a good number, Joss decided. Sarah looked young—her eyes were unlined, her skin as smooth and unblemished as porcelain—but she didn't act young. She was poised and possessed a composure that suggested she was closer to Joss's age.

"And you?" Sarah asked.

"Thirty-eight."

"Wow. You don't look that old, but being a surgeon, I guess you would be."

"Old?" Joss laughed. "I don't think I've been called old before." If anything, in her world of teaching and performing complicated cardiac surgeries, she was young.

Even in the twilight, Sarah's face noticeably colored. "Sorry, I didn't mean that the way it sounded. I just meant…You're very attractive—"

"For an old person?"

They both laughed until Sarah stopped in front of a three-story walkup. They were only a few blocks from campus. Joss's condo was also within a few blocks of Vanderbilt, but at the opposite, more moneyed end. This part of the neighborhood was clearly inhabited by students and probably some of the lesser-paid staff of the university.

"My apartment's on the second floor. I share it with a roommate."

Joss walked with her to the front door. Simultaneously they pulled out their cell phones and exchanged numbers. "I'll call you tomorrow. Then we can figure out what's going on next."

"All right."

Joss awkwardly stuck her hand out because she didn't know what else to do, but Sarah ignored it, stood on her toes and kissed Joss's cheek. "Good night, Joss McNab."

CHAPTER FIVE

"So, that's your sugar mama?"

Lauren Douglas, Sarah's roommate and best friend dating back to high school, was all over her the second she walked in.

"I wouldn't quite put it that way. And what were you doing, spying on us?"

"I saw y'all out the window. Pretty sweet, walking you home and all. Do tell!" Lauren's eyes shimmered with curiosity. She was an incurable romantic who had shelves full of lesbian romance novels and had watched *Notting Hill* seventeen times. Twenty-one times for *Imagine Me & You*.

"It's not sweet. We were walking, that's all." Sarah stepped out of her heels, strode to her bedroom and, with the door slightly ajar so they could talk, stripped out of her dress and into jeans and a light sweater.

"She's kinda hot from what I could see. Why didn't you bring her up?"

"Because I didn't want you to scare her away. Especially if you're going to call her my sugar mama."

"Aw come on. I wouldn't do that. But I would like to know if she has a sister. Or a best friend who's also a rich lesbian. God, I'm so jealous, Sarah."

Lauren was a struggling musician and songwriter, trying to make it in Nashville along with the thousands of other aspiring young singers and songwriters who clogged the streets and honky-tonks with their beat-up guitars and their shiny enthusiasm. Unfortunately having talent was only loosely linked with achieving success around here. In Sarah's opinion Lauren and her friends all seemed so talented, and yet few of them were able to make a living from their music. That was something to which she could totally relate. And just as she was doing part-time work to keep herself in paints, Lauren was working as a waitress at the Wild Horse Saloon to fuel her music dreams.

"Well, don't be jealous. It's going to be boring most of the time, all these stuffy receptions and dinners." Sarah emerged from her room and sat down on a worn chair across from Lauren, who'd plucked a guitar off the living room wall and began picking out a tune Sarah didn't recognize.

"So, like, is she paying you?" Lauren asked over the guitar notes.

"Yup." Sarah was still getting used to the idea. Four hundred a week was generous. Probably more than she needed. Her broom closet-sized studio in a warehouse a few blocks away cost her four-fifty a month in rent. Her supplies added up, her occasional seminars with visiting painters too. And then there was the apartment rent she split with Lauren, along with food, clothes and keeping her crappy old car going. Her teaching job provided about twenty thousand dollars a year. Now, with the money from Joss, she'd be more than set until her paintings began to pay off. No more handouts from Daddy. Supporting herself was something she'd hoped to do with her art, but what the hell, at least now she was supporting herself, and that was worth celebrating.

Lauren stopped playing. An impish smile tugged at her lips. "Do you have to sleep with her?"

"Of course not! What do you think I am, a prostitute?"

"No, but a little on the side might be fun. Especially with a hot-looking doctor."

"I'll have my hands full as it is. I don't need sex complicating things. Besides, what's important is that she seems nice. And not the type to take advantage of me in any way." She rhymed off the phrase with which she'd decided to characterize her and Joss's relationship. "We're just friendly acquaintances in a mutually beneficial arrangement."

Lauren made a face. "That doesn't exactly have a nice ring to it. It would sound much better if the two of you were sneaking away from your little obligations and getting it on in the backseat of whatever fancy car she drives."

Sarah sighed impatiently. "As much as it sounds like material for a movie or a song, it's not going to happen. End of story."

She would never admit it to Lauren, but she did find Joss attractive. She wouldn't be human if moments ago she hadn't enjoyed a fleeting fantasy about a proper kiss with Joss on the front porch, but that was all it was, a fantasy. Sleeping with her—not that it was ever going to happen!—would make Sarah no better than the young women she despised who slept with older men for the size of their wallets. No. This was a paying gig, same as teaching those eager freshmen twice a week. The only difference was the gourmet food and the expensive champagne.

Lauren began plucking the strings of her guitar again, and before long she was singing. "Sugar mama gonna make ever'thin' right. Sugar mama gonna shine in my pocket, gonna shine in my bed too. Sugar mama gonna rock me all night."

Sarah pitched a cushion at Lauren, hitting the guitar and nearly knocking it out of her hands.

"Hey, careful, or I'll use your precious paintbrushes to clean the toilet next time."

Sarah laughed, feeling more in control of her life than she had in a very long time. Her father was no longer pulling her strings. She was financially independent for the first time in her life. About all that was missing was a gallery showing interest in her work, but one thing at a time, she cautioned herself. *One thing at a time.*

* * *

The inside of the Bridgestone Arena was a sea of yellow hockey jerseys and T-shirts sporting the Nashville Predators logo. When the Chicago Blackhawks were in town, it was always a spirited tilt, and the fans were restless waiting for the opening whistle.

Joss stood in a private box more than halfway up the arena at center ice. Nathan Sellers, who owned a successful statewide chain of high-end furniture stores with his wife, had invited Joss to the game along with the dean of the medical school, the hospital's cardiac surgery chair, the director of cardiovascular medicine, six hospital board members and the chairs and co-chairs of three different hospital fundraising campaigns. The evening was for spouses too, which meant Joss had asked Sarah along. The gathering represented the blue bloods of the hospital and medical school's cardiology services, an echelon that Joss didn't truly belong to—yet. But Sellers had been a big fan of her father, who'd performed life-saving bypass surgery on him two decades ago. It was only because he was a major donor to the hospital and the medical school that Joss felt compelled to accept his invitations, even though she'd rather be doing almost anything else. At least the game provided a welcome distraction.

Sarah looked lovely in a tight taupe skirt, white ruffled blouse and a tailored, dazzling blue jacket that nicely matched her eyes. Her hair was tied back in a ponytail, revealing simple yet classic sapphire earrings. *I could buy her jewelry*, Joss thought before quickly dismissing the idea as a bad one. She was not Richard Gere and Sarah was not Julia Roberts.

Sarah had shown no nervousness or apprehension about mixing with such notable guests, which surprised and pleased Joss, who at this moment wasn't far from upchucking her dinner. She never knew what to say to these people that didn't involve talk about work. She'd welcome a discussion about the latest advances in heart valve replacement, but this was not the time or place. The occasion was mostly for Sellers to brag about his business and his latest six-figure donation to the hospital and medical school. He was a self-centered, pretentious bore, but everyone tolerated him because they adored his money.

The hockey game started, giving Joss something to concentrate on—when she wasn't keeping half an eye on Sellers and the lecherous attention he was showering on Sarah like confetti. He long had had a deserved reputation as a skirt chaser, which was probably why his wife stayed mostly at their Memphis property. Predictably, he'd quickly cornered Sarah and was plying her with mint juleps. Joss wasn't especially worried. Sarah seemed like the kind of woman who could handle herself appropriately, meaning she could keep Sellers in line without having to kick him in the balls. Joss imagined a core of toughness behind the magnetic smile and the intelligent eyes, but by the second intermission and Sarah's second mint julep, she decided it was time to intervene. She didn't pay Sarah enough to have to put up with the likes of Sellers, who was fluttering around her now like a moth to a flame.

"Darling, we've got a very early day tomorrow," Joss said, clamping an arm around Sarah's waist. "Perhaps we should think about saying our good-byes?"

"Oh, but your lovely companion was telling me all about her paintings," Sellers enthused, moving close enough to Joss that the reek of bourbon hit her like a wall.

"They sound spectacular," Sellers continued, fishing a gold-embossed card from his pocket. "Young lady, I'm out of town for the next couple of weeks, but I want you to contact my executive assistant." His voice turned syrupy, and a long bony finger snaked out to touch the top of Sarah's hand and lingered there. She had the good grace—and the patience of Job—not to recoil at his touch. "If your paintings look anywhere near as good as you, I'd like to acquire some of them to hang in our furniture stores. And to use for staging homes."

"Oh, well, thank you," Sarah said coolly, but her eyes had widened with surprise. "I'll be sure to do that, Mr. Sellers. That's very kind of you."

"Dr. McNab," he said, clapping Joss on the back until she wanted to grind her teeth. "Wherever did you find this gorgeous and talented specimen? You must tell me *every* detail."

Joss bristled. How dare he call Sarah a specimen? She grew hot along the back of her neck, words of admonishment tingling on the tip of her tongue. She was saved by Sarah, who leaned into her one-armed embrace. "Actually, Mr. Sellers, it was I who found Dr. McNab. Turns out our mothers are acquainted."

"W-well," he stammered, something dirty and solicitous in his moist, rheumy eyes. "I'd love to hear all the details. You know," he whispered, leaning unsteadily like a tree blowing in the wind, "about your relations. I mean, relationship," he slurred. "I love a good love story."

"Ah, but that's something precious between myself and Sarah, and I know you're a gentleman, Nathan," Joss snapped before steering Sarah toward the others so they could make a polite departure.

"I'm really sorry about that," Joss said as she opened the passenger door of her BMW sport utility vehicle for Sarah.

"You mean Nathan?"

"He's gross. I'm used to him by now, but you're not." Joss climbed into the driver's seat, started the car and slammed it into gear.

Sarah's laughter surprised Joss. "Don't worry, I'm used to icky old bastards like that. I actually had to slap one of my father's colleagues across the face once. He was drunk and audacious enough to proposition me in a roomful of people."

"Well, I'd kind of prefer if you didn't have to go that far with Sellers. Or at least, my bosses would prefer you didn't, since he bankrolls a lot of our research. He's a harmless but incredibly annoying, horny old prick."

"Well, thanks for coming to my rescue. Not that I needed it."

"I know you didn't. I was just trying to send him a subtle message."

"Oh? And what was that?"

"That…" Joss swallowed and could not cool the heat flushing her cheeks. "That I don't appreciate other people coming onto my, you know, girlfriend, if you will." The word *girlfriend* nearly stuck in her mouth, because she'd never formally called anyone her girlfriend before. But her excuse was only part of the truth. The rest of it was that she'd wanted to feel the warmth and suppleness of Sarah against her when she'd placed her arm around her waist. And she'd been rewarded when Sarah leaned into her with her soft pliancy and her scent of wildflowers. It'd felt nice, comfortable and very much like something she wanted to do again.

"Well, you were very convincing."

"Hey," Joss said to change the subject. "What was that about him wanting to use some of your paintings in his stores?"

"Oh my God, I know. I wasn't expecting that. And I'm sorry. I wasn't angling to use the occasion to try to sell my work."

"I know you weren't, and there's nothing to apologize for. I'd love to see you rewarded for putting up with the likes of him. I think you should go for it. And don't forget to ask an exorbitant price. He can afford it."

"You really think I should?"

"I do." Joss shuddered. "Just keep an eye on his roaming hands."

Sarah laughed. "All right, I will. Oh, and since we have an early day together tomorrow, what exactly are we doing?"

"Huh?"

"You told Sellers and the others that we had to leave because we have an early day ahead of us. I want to get our stories straight in case the horny old bugger ever asks me about the 'details,' as he called them."

"Eww," Joss said. "Did you get the feeling that the whole time he was talking to us he was picturing us in bed together?"

"Totally. As in every little thing he could possibly remember from every bad porn movie he's ever seen."

Joss grinned, ignoring the tiny pulse that had begun between her legs. "Who do you think he pictured on top?"

"You, of course."

"Me? Why me?" Joss had a sudden stark image of Sarah on top, straddling her, with that long red hair splayed out over her full breasts, like tassels that shimmered and swayed with every undulation. She had to squeeze her legs together, the throbbing between them intensifying into a second heartbeat. She'd need to do something about that when she got home.

"Easy. Because you have that air of authority about you. The kind that a man like him would expect to extend to the bedroom."

And would he be wrong? Joss wanted to ask. In her sexual liaisons, it was true she'd always been very much in charge, dictating the pace, the intensity, the positions, where and how often. And she'd always been the one to extricate herself in the middle of the night. But she had the distinct feeling that Sarah wouldn't put up with those things. Which might be a nice change, she thought, again picturing Sarah on top, riding her, needing her, taking charge. The image was beginning to cause serious discomfort—in more ways than one.

"Tomorrow," Sarah prompted as they pulled up in front of her apartment.

"Oh, right. Tomorrow."

"What do you usually do on a Saturday?"

"I usually spend the mornings in my office catching up on paperwork. And checking in on patients, if I have any in-house."

"How exciting," Sarah mumbled, rolling her eyes. "How about this? Why don't we have dinner together so we can get to know one another better? It might make it easier in our interactions at these shindigs. You know, like we actually have some history together."

"Okay, good idea."

"And before that, why don't I take you shopping for clothes?"

Joss looked down at her leather jacket, which she wore over a plain white button-down shirt and gray chinos. "I don't need to shop for clothes."

"Actually, Joss, you do."

"But I hate shopping for clothes." What did it matter how she looked? She had far more important things to do with her time and energy than to shop for clothes like she was a *girl*, for God's sake.

Sarah was having none of it. "We'll try to make it fun, I promise."

"The words *fun* and *clothes shopping* do not belong in the same sentence."

"Obviously you've never been shopping with me before."

Joss closed her eyes for an instant and pictured Sarah stripping down to her bra and underwear—Victoria's Secret, she hoped. With lots of satin and lace. Maybe red. Or blue to match her eyes. That kind of clothes shopping she'd be happy to do. *Oh, God, stop thinking about her that way! This is a professional hookup, a business arrangement and nothing more. You're being childish. And disrespectful.*

"Why don't you pick me up at two?" Sarah said, halfway out the door.

Joss sighed, the fight gone out of her. "Okay, fine, two o'clock."

She waited until Sarah was safely inside and wondered in astonishment at how easily and how intensely she came unglued around Sarah. Agreeing to shop for clothes? And what was with all the sex fantasies lately? *Jesus!* Obviously, her dry spell in the bedroom had gone on way too long.

Pulling away from the curb, she wondered with growing alarm at what the hell she was thinking, agreeing to an afternoon and evening with Sarah that was outside the parameters of their agreement. What did the fine print have to say about *that*? she wondered.

CHAPTER SIX

Sarah appraised Joss in the black Armani suit, cut femininely against her trim waist and flared a bit at the shoulders to emphasize the toned muscles there. It was perfect for her, not only because it was expensive and fit flawlessly, but because it matched the quiet confidence and power she naturally exuded. When Joss walked into a room, there was the sense that something important was about to happen, that *she* was important, in command and completely composed. When she spoke, people listened. It was easy to picture her in an operating room, cool, efficient, unflappable, absolutely in charge, entirely trusting in her team and not only prepared to handle anything, but eager for the challenge of whatever might transpire.

"Now take the jacket off," Sarah ordered and, with satisfaction, watched Joss obey. The white shirt was stark. Too sterile. "You need some color with that suit. Something that shows a bit of personality." She smiled at the saleswoman. "Can we get the same shirt in mint green? And deep red too. Oh, and a couple of accessories. Chunky necklaces perhaps? Or a scarf?

Something that makes a statement, but not too feminine. Thank you."

Joss chuckled softly. "Trying to turn me into a girl?"

"Just adding a few drops of estrogen to your wardrobe. It's actually more powerful this way. It makes the statement that you're a strong woman who doesn't apologize for being a woman." She lowered her voice an octave. "It's an extremely sexy combination."

Joss raised her eyebrows in apparent amusement. "You've just summed up my mother, except for the sexy part. She likes to dress well, but you'd never doubt she's in charge, even if she were wearing a tutu."

Sarah grinned. "I can see if they have any tutus here. Pink, perhaps?"

Joss tossed her jacket at Sarah, who scuttled out the door to allow her to change shirts but not before noticing Joss's strong shoulders and arms, the muscles that rippled along her back.

"Now that," Sarah said moments later on a soft whistle, "looks perfect on you. Brings out your eyes."

Joss looked embarrassed for a moment. Clearly, she wasn't used to compliments. At least, not compliments related to her looks. And yet she was a very handsome woman. Strong jawed, with lips that were just full enough for long, deep kisses, angular cheekbones that hinted at Eastern European blood and eyes that were direct and intense but held a measure of mystery. She was sexy. Sexy in a strong and authoritative way, but with a streak of underlying vulnerability too. For a moment, Sarah let herself imagine what it would take to melt that cool demeanor of Joss's. To make her forget she was in charge, to make her forget she had to be strong and so intensely private and so utterly perfect every single minute.

"I don't think this is fair," Joss challenged. "I'm the one doing all the modeling. I think it's time you gave me a break." To the saleswoman, Joss said she'd take the black Armani suit, an identical dove gray one and the red and green shirts with their matching necklaces and scarves. The woman nodded politely, draped the items over her arm and scurried away.

"You want me to try something on?"

"Yes. Something tight and slinky and classy. Next weekend is our annual LGBT MD dinner and dance."

"That's a lot of acronyms, but I'm guessing it's a bunch of gay doctors getting together?"

"You guessed right. It's for the gay medical staff and faculty at the hospital and the students and staff at the med school. I'm on the committee, so I have to give a little speech and sit at the head table and act all important."

"Nice." Sarah winked. "So why don't *you* wear the slinky dress?"

"Not a chance, now that I've got these new Armani suits. Besides, I've never brought anyone to one of these things before. Your presence will definitely elevate my reputation among that particular crowd. And set more than a few tongues wagging."

"I get it. You want someone to show off."

"It'll add to my mysterious charm having some eye candy on my arm for a change." Joss's grin collapsed as she stepped closer. "I hope you know it's not really like that. I mean, that I value only your beauty and all that superficial window-dressing crap. I'm only kidding around. I enjoy your company." Joss winced. "You actually make these events bearable."

A teasing grin came only after Sarah made Joss wait for it. "Eye candy, huh?" It'd been a long time since a woman had paid her this kind of attention. The fact that it was literally *paid attention* didn't seem to matter at this juncture. Joss made her feel beautiful and appreciated and that was something she didn't want to let go of just yet.

"You're a very beautiful woman, Sarah." Joss took another step closer. Her face was guarded but not her eyes. Her eyes told the truth, and they looked at Sarah as though she'd never said those words to another woman before and meant them the way she did now. Her lips were twitching in a rare show of nervousness, Sarah noticed. "In fact, I'm sure people look at us and wonder why the hell a woman like you is with someone like me."

Sarah swallowed, her throat suddenly dry as old driftwood. She had the fleeting urge to kiss Joss, to demonstrate that in fact she did belong at her side. And kissing her was exactly what she would do if Joss were her date and not her employer. Instead, she stepped back and forced a laugh that sounded hollow, at least to her ears. "Now that's the pot calling the kettle black. You're the one who's the successful surgeon, and I'm the very unsuccessful artist who's been living off her father, remember? Talk about out of my league!"

Joss stepped back too and closed herself up, the moment abruptly gone as if a door had slammed shut. "How about we call it a draw, and you try on a nice dress? I'd like to buy you one if you see something you like."

Ah, yes, Sarah thought with disappointment. A timely reminder that they were together because they had an agreement. Well, if Joss wanted to buy her a dress so she'd look especially good for a particular event, it was her prerogative to do so.

Sarah all but saluted. "Certainly. I'll be right back."

* * *

Joss had to sit down when Sarah emerged from the curtained part of the massive changing room. It was that or fall down. The dress was black and silver, and in the light it glimmered from tiny sequins everywhere like a million stars dotting an inky sky. It fit her perfectly—a sparkly, sleek glove snug over the length of her body—and the effect was dizzying. "Wow."

"You like it?" Sarah twirled around, and Joss sucked in a breath. She was so womanly with her soft curves—the dress revealing a round behind, strong and supple thighs that looked smooth as butter beneath the soft fabric. Creamy came to mind. And her breasts! They were so round and full, soft and tight at the same time—a place where Joss could lay her head and sleep and dream forever, a place of refuge where she could forget the exhaustion, the politics and sometimes the heartbreak of her job. Like that time she'd lost a five-year-old on her OR table. Talking about what had gone wrong was something she could—

and did—discuss with her colleagues. That night when she had gone home, however, there was no one there to whom she could unburden her emotions. Having someone like Sarah to listen without judgment or condemnation was something Joss hadn't really thought about before, but now she could think of little else.

She forced such neediness from her head. Forced too from her head thoughts about Sarah's breasts and luscious curves. It was damned inappropriate. And rude. She was sure Sarah was sick to death of one-dimensional and sexist attention from men and maybe from some women too. Joss had no use for those who considered women like Sarah to be no better than objects or accessories to be taken out and shown off like a piece of jewelry or a fancy car. Which, Joss assured herself, was *not* what she was doing. She appreciated Sarah for her mind and personality as much as for her physical attributes. For one brief and weak moment, she wished Sarah really was hers, that this wasn't all a paid circus act.

"I, ah…" Joss quickly gathered her wits. "It looks great. I'd love for you to have it. If you'll accept it, of course."

"It's too expensive, Joss. The tag says nineteen hundred dollars."

"No, we'll take it. It's perfect on you. Is there anything else you'd like to try on?"

"No, I think this is already too much." Sarah disappeared behind the curtain, and Joss could hear the soft swish of the dress sliding from her shoulders and down her body. "Besides, I thought you hated shopping for clothes."

"I do. I did. But today it's…it's not so bad after all."

The truth was, she could watch Sarah try on outfits all day if it meant she got a private showing like this. She had looked good in anything, but that dress! That dress was incredible on her. She couldn't wait for Sarah to wear it to their event, even if it meant every woman in the place wanted to be the one to take it off her. It wasn't lost on her that she wouldn't be taking it off Sarah either.

It had begun to concern her that for long, whimsical moments it was easy—too easy—to forget Sarah was not really her girlfriend, to mistake this make-believe world she'd created with her as real. It was a useless thought to waste time on, but part of her wondered if Sarah would ever actually go out with her for real. Not that she had any intention of exploring the idea further. The problem was that she had no time for dating nor the inclination. Being married to her work had cut off all avenues to a serious relationship a long time ago. Every woman she'd tried to date had terminated things very quickly, and she couldn't blame them. Sarah, she felt sure, would be no exception, because she, and rightly so, would expect much more. No, Joss reminded herself, their little arrangement was perfect the way it was.

"You ready for our next stop?" Sarah asked, the dress draped carefully over her arm.

"Dinner, you mean?"

"Nope. The stop before that."

They waited at the counter, Joss's platinum credit card in hand, as the saleswoman rang up their purchases. "I don't think I have much more shopping left in my tank."

"Good, because we're not shopping. We're going to a hair salon."

Joss drew a panicked breath. "Don't tell me you're going to color your hair? I love your natural color. That is your natural color, right?"

Sarah smiled appreciatively. "Yes. Thank you. And no, the appointment isn't for me. It's for you."

"What? *Me*? I had my hair cut last week. Any shorter and I'll be marching on parade with the marines."

Sarah's laughter was not the least bit deprecating. "I love the length of your hair." She reached up and ruffled it for effect. "But I think a lighter shade of blond highlights would look spectacular on you."

"Oh no. No highlights for me." Highlights were for vain people who wanted to look like sun worshippers. Or young, unemployed beach bums.

"Come on. Indulge me. I indulged you by trying on this dress, so it's only fair. And besides, it'll make you look like you just got back from an island vacation or something."

Visions of Sarah on a beach—in a skimpy bikini that left nothing to the imagination—danced in Joss's head. And the visions didn't end there. Long cool drinks, hot sweaty nights under the stars, the quiet lap of waves caressing the sand as the two of them walked hand in hand. Her legs trembled. *God, I need a vacation! And not with Sarah!* "All right, fine. But that's it for the makeover session. I'm not a dress-up doll, you know."

Sarah winked at her. "I was enjoying having my own little makeover doll. Although I don't remember my childhood dolls complaining so much."

Joss threw her a scowl, but it wasn't long before she was smiling. "Let me guess. You had twenty-nine kinds of Barbie dolls when you were a kid. I'd name some, but I haven't a clue what Barbies are out there."

"I still have a few of them if you'd like to come over and play some time. Ooh, and I had Doctor Barbie!"

Joss bit back a flirtatious retort—something about offering to be Sarah's real-life Doctor Barbie. "I tried to perform surgery on my best friend's doll once. She wasn't very pleased with the huge slit I made down its torso with my jackknife."

Sarah laughed. "I can totally picture that. What else did you play with? Tonka trucks? Cap guns?"

"Not quite. Tools. Lab kits. All my play pretty much mimicked being a doctor." Like her father. She'd dress in shirts and ties like he did, had a little black doctor bag identical to his, wore a toy stethoscope around her neck most of the time, even at the dinner table.

Sarah stopped, placed a hand tenderly on Joss's arm. "Did you ever once want to be anything else?"

Joss shook her head lightly. She'd never considered there were other options.

CHAPTER SEVEN

Sarah was inordinately pleased with herself for not only managing to convince Joss to buy herself new clothes, but to go through with the appointment at the hair salon. And she'd complied with only a few token complaints. The new suits were powerful and sexy on her, and the blond highlights were striking, instantly transforming her into someone more youthful, someone much more carefree and playful. If she threw on jeans and a pullover right now, Joss would look more like a medical student than an accomplished surgeon and professor and heir to the legacy of the great Dr. Joseph McNab.

A Google search before their first meeting had provided the goods on Joss. She was considered one of the top heart valve surgeons in the state, helping three years ago to pioneer something called a transcatheter aortic heart valve replacement procedure. It was minimally invasive, replacing a patient's main heart valve without having to open his or her chest, and the procedure was only being done at a few hospitals across the country. Impressive, to say the least. But Joss had barely discussed anything about her work with Sarah. When she did, it was only because Sarah pressed and never in a way that would suggest bragging. If anything, Joss was too modest, but unlike a struggling artist, she didn't need to sell herself, Sarah supposed. Nevertheless if they were going to be friends, business partners, whatever they decided to call themselves, Joss would have to let Sarah in. At least a little.

Between bites of the linguini in clam sauce, Sarah asked, "Was it as simple as following in your father's shoes that you decided to become a heart surgeon?"

"Basically," Joss said after swallowing a mouthful of chicken marsala.

"So you idolized him, obviously?"

Joss shrugged lightly. "I was good in science and math. And my father was an impressive man, an important man, in a child's eyes. Why wouldn't a kid want to emulate a parent like that?"

"Did you do it to please him?"

"My, aren't you full of questions."

Sarah casually sipped her wine, an expensive Barolo. She had insisted on going dutch, since this wasn't an official working event, but the sixteen dollars a glass price tag was giving her heart palpitations. "I thought we agreed it would be a good idea to get to know each other better."

"Right." Joss sighed impatiently, clearly not used to being grilled this way and not, it seemed, very happy to be talking about herself. "Well, my father was a legend in medical circles. And medicine seemed to come easy to me, so it made perfect sense to follow in his footsteps."

It wasn't lost on Sarah that Joss hadn't exactly answered her question about whether her career choice had been to please her father. She assumed it had, but given her relationship with her own father, she didn't assume much anymore where family was concerned. As Linda liked to say, you never knew what was boiling in someone else's pot.

"Do people compare you to your father?"

"I specialize in valves. His was almost exclusively coronary bypass surgery."

Sarah tried not to take offense at Joss's brevity, but she seemed to be barely trying. "But, in general, I mean, you must be compared to him. You're the cochair of the medical school department named after him. You do surgeries in the same operating rooms he must have worked in. You're both cardiac surgeons—although with different subspecialties. You were named after him—Joss, Joseph—right? Old photos show that you look a lot like him."

Joss's stare was hard, unyielding. Her shoulders had noticeably stiffened.

Sarah lowered her voice. "You didn't think I'd accept your offer without doing any research, did you?"

"Obviously. But it leaves me at a supreme disadvantage, don't you think?" A twinkle suddenly flashed in Joss's eyes, instantly replacing the guardedness that had been like tiny shields in her irises. "Fess up, Sarah Young. Time for you to tell me something extremely personal."

Stalling, Sarah twirled linguine around her fork. "I will, but not until you tell me how you deal with living in your father's shadow."

Joss sighed again. The mask was firmly back in place, and it made Sarah wonder how open she was with friends, girlfriends, colleagues, anybody. Not very, it seemed.

"I deal with it fine. He's been gone for almost five years, was retired for three before that. I chose a different subspecialty so the comparisons would only go so far. I don't expect to match his professional notoriety or accomplishments."

"Why not? You're well on your way, by the looks of it. And you're only thirty-eight. What was he doing at your age?"

"At my age, he was performing bypass surgery on the Vice President of the United States."

"Oh," Sarah said, momentarily at a loss for words. She sipped her wine. "Do you always put this much pressure on yourself?"

"Pressure, I can handle. Spilling my guts? Not so much."

"Well, thank you for being honest."

"Your turn," Joss said eagerly. "Girlfriends. Any serious ones lurking in your past? Or present?"

"A couple. Past tense."

"So I won't have a bunch of jealous girlfriends worried about our arrangement?"

Sarah hadn't missed the number of times Joss's gaze kept drifting to the cleavage exposed by her blouse, which she'd intentionally unbuttoned a little further than usual. She didn't want to think much about whether she was purposely testing Joss. Or how much she was enjoying the little game of cat and mouse. She wasn't normally a tease, but something about Joss made her want to push the boundaries a little. Maybe it was as simple as wanting to crack that icy shell she kept around herself. "No. And I'm not a dating machine, if that's what you're implying."

Joss had the decency to blush. "I didn't mean to imply that you were. Only that, you know…"

"What?"

"Well. You're so pretty. And fun to be with. I figured…"

Sarah was in no mood to accept flattery. "You forgot to throw in career-challenged. Not many women are attracted to a perpetually impoverished artist who may never make it. My last girlfriend told me there was no future in someone who spent so much time on something she would never make a living at."

Joss took her last bite and wiped her mouth with a linen napkin before setting it neatly back on the table. "So what's holding you back, Sarah? You've criticized your father for not believing in you and now your past girlfriends. But what about you? Do you doubt yourself as well? I mean, who cares what they think?"

Heat roared up Sarah's neck. How dare Joss cast such judgment about something she knew nothing about? Her snarling retort was preempted when the waiter came to remove their plates and ask about coffee and dessert. By the time they'd ordered two decaffeinated coffees, Sarah had cooled down enough to deliberately change the subject. She asked Joss about her romantic past, only to be told there hadn't been anything but a few superficial hookups. Oh, and a college sweetheart who wanted to travel the world after graduation and settle in Lebanon.

"Why Lebanon?"

"Because she heard the women there were hot."

Sarah gaped in surprise. "And that didn't bother you?"

Joss laughed quietly. "We weren't meant for the long haul, so no. I encouraged her. I was about to head off to Stanford anyway."

They used the car ride back to Sarah's to get their stories straight about how exactly they'd met and how long they'd been dating, should anyone ask.

"Would you like to come up for a drink?" Sarah asked in the awkward silence, not convinced it was a good idea, but it was the polite thing to do. "My roommate will still be at work."

"No thank you. Long day today, and I have my weekly Sunday breakfast date with my mother tomorrow morning."

"All right, another time," she said, reaching for the door handle. It was probably wise that Joss wasn't coming up for that drink because this wasn't a date, and she didn't want to confuse things. Still, the rebuff felt personal somehow. "Your new hair looks great on you, by the way."

"I'm not so sure, but thank you." Joss suddenly reached over and lightly tugged on her elbow before she could exit. "By the way, you never answered my question. The one about whether you doubt yourself. A loved one's criticism—or their indifference, for that matter—can wear a person down."

Needles of heat pricked Sarah's cheeks. "And you didn't answer when I asked if you went into medicine to please your father. Or maybe it was to get his attention?"

How dare she imply I don't believe in myself? Does she think I enjoy accepting handouts? Being Daddy's little princess? That I'm incapable of doing anything else? Doesn't she realize I'm only being her damned escort so I can support my art?

Sarah had had enough. She was about to bolt when Joss, still clutching her elbow, leaned toward her. Her mouth was only inches away, so close that she could simply…

Without another thought, Sarah placed her hands on either side of Joss's head and pressed into her mouth, wanting nothing more than to sear away the anger and indignation she felt for this stranger who intuitively knew exactly which of her buttons to push. The kiss held not a shred of tenderness. It was deep, hard, full of emotion that bordered on anger. Pushing, pulling, devouring, fitting perfectly together, their mouths fought the battle that had taken root in their minds, in their blood, in their words.

Damn if this woman isn't turning me on, Sarah realized as arousal flared deep in her belly. Her lungs fought for air and her body thrummed like an electrical current. Unable to stifle her desire any longer, she moaned, causing Joss to pull back with a sudden decisiveness that felt like the ripping away of a scab.

It was dark, but Sarah could see shock and fear—regret too, perhaps?—on Joss's face.

"Shit," Joss murmured. "I'm so sorry, Sarah."

Sarah stumbled out of the car. "I'm not," she threw over her shoulder, unsure—and not caring—if Joss heard her.

* * *

By the time she knocked and walked into her mother's house, Joss had given up hope that she'd be summoned to the hospital. The weekly brunch with her mother was not usually a chore, but today's she would have gladly skipped. Madeline would undoubtedly fire questions about Sarah at her with the speed of a machine gun. Worse than that was her expectation that Madeline would somehow guess that a slow fire had begun to burn between her and Sarah—a fire that was sometimes fueled by anger, other times by a powerful attraction that threatened to blow their little agreement into about a million pieces.

And oh, that kiss, Joss thought as she called out for her mother. She'd kicked herself in the ass about it all the way home last night and into the early morning hours too. What had she been thinking? Okay, she hadn't truly been the one to start it, had she? Sarah had started the damned kiss, but Joss had asked for it. In slow motion, she replayed it over and over in her mind, wondering why she hadn't stopped the kiss sooner, why she'd even set herself up for it in the first damned place. There was

5454 Tracey Richardson

no rational explanation. If anything, she and Sarah had been irritable with each other leading up to the kiss. Maybe their brutally honest accusations had sparked it, or maybe it was the residual heat from seeing Sarah change into that tight-fitting dress earlier in the day. There had been that luscious cleavage over dinner too that had made her forget her food. Made her forget her head too, it seemed.

Joss berated herself. Again. *You can't go kissing Sarah, any more than you can go kissing one of the nurses at the hospital or one of the other surgeons. This is a professional thing! Absolutely no mixing business with pleasure. It's unethical, uncalled for and extremely inappropriate.*

Joss knew better than to kiss Sarah, and yet, that forty-second act had nearly obliterated the carefully constructed control that was her hallmark around women. She'd been seconds and inches away from running her hands all over Sarah's body and sliding her mouth down to that lovely, silky throat. It was some consolation that she hadn't technically paid for the kiss, since yesterday wasn't part of their official arrangement. That, at least, let her off the hook a little.

Annoyance over some of the things Sarah had said at dinner continued to simmer. Like asking her why she put so much pressure on herself. Well, of course she put pressure on herself. If she didn't, she wouldn't be where she was today. Pressure was her motivation. And her reward. She did her best work in the pressure cooker that was the OR, and she was harder on herself than anyone else ever could be. For that reason alone, she had nothing to fear about her mother intuiting the underlying and unwanted attraction she felt for Sarah. Her mother couldn't caution her more seriously than she was already cautioning herself.

"Hello, dear," Madeline said, planting a kiss on Joss's cheek. "You're looking chipper this morning."

"I am?"

"A little color in your cheeks. It looks good on you. Come in for a spell and make yourself a cup of coffee. I've got a breakfast casserole in the oven." Madeline's hands flew to her open mouth. "Oh, your hair! You added highlights."

"Yes, Mama. Don't look so shocked."

"I *am* shocked. Completely!" She grinned. "It makes you look so youthful. I like it very much, Joss. It's very attractive on you."

"Thanks. I think."

The house smelled of sausage, potatoes and rosemary. And coffee. Joss's stomach growled. Her hour at the campus pool this morning had built up an appetite. So had all the emotional energy she'd expended thinking about Sarah.

Something on the way to the kitchen made her stop in her tracks. She'd never really paid much attention to the odd tapestry of small paintings on the foyer walls and along the hallway leading to the kitchen, because her mother was always adding to the busy collection. But now she wanted to examine them, perhaps because Sarah was a painter. She lingered over a watercolor of a forest, then a small oil painting of the Cumberland River at twilight, the cityscape in the background. She checked for the artist's signature and found it on the bottom right of the painting—SY.

"Mama, who did this painting?"

"Why, your Sarah."

"My what?"

Madeline's smile was smug and conspicuously triumphant. "Your companion friend, Sarah Young."

Joss tensed. "She's not a teddy bear or an old suitcase on my closet shelf. She's not *my* anything."

Her mother shot her a slow, teasing wink. "Would you rather I called her your 'wife'?"

Joss refused to rise to the bait, instead returning her eyes to the painting. "I never noticed this painting before. How long have you had it?"

"I bought it from Sarah's stepmother, Linda, a year or so ago. It's very good, isn't it?"

It was extremely good, Joss thought, her eyes riveted on the intricate shades of gray, blue, brown, gold. There was texture to every stroke, some bold, some nuanced. A tiny speck of color here, a wisp of a shadow there. The overall effect was instant, but it took several minutes of staring at it to realize the sophistication and complicatedness behind the piece. "I didn't realize she was so good."

"Not all struggling artists fail to make it because they aren't talented enough. You should know that by now, growing up in Nashville. Did you know that when Sarah was a teenager she was offered a three-month scholarship to paint in Paris at the Cite Internationale des Arts?"

"That sounds important. And like it would be a real career boost."

"It would have been if she'd gone. According to her stepmother, her father wouldn't let her go."

She'd never met the man, but Joss was really beginning to dislike Sarah's father. "Why not?" Her own parents would never have held her back from such an opportunity.

"Oh, that man," Madeline ground out between pursed lips. "He said he needed her at home and that she was too young to go so far away."

Joss finally pulled her attention away from the canvas. She was eager to see more of Sarah's work, but not with her mother hovering. More blown away than she'd expected to be, Joss wondered if she too had secretly doubted Sarah's abilities. She had. At least a little. Sarah was broke, mostly living off her father and some part-time teaching work. Joss could see that she too had fallen into the trap of defining Sarah's talent simply by how much money she earned—or in this case, didn't earn—from her art. She vowed to herself that she would never again be as foolishly judgmental as Sarah's father or her old girlfriends.

"I take it you've met Sarah's father?"

"Oh yes. Peter Young. Hearing him say something nice about anybody is as scarce as hen's teeth. That man is smug and pretentious." Madeline's headshake was full of condemnation. "New money," she hissed.

Joss quietly chuckled. *Now who's being pretentious.*

"But Linda says Sarah is nothing like him, and thank the good Lord for that."

Yes, Joss thought. *Thank God.* She popped a cup under the Keurig machine, peeking through the oven door as she waited for her mug to fill. She knew the inevitable was coming and decided to head her mother off at the pass. "All right, go ahead and ask me a million questions about how things are going with Sarah."

"What makes you think I have a million questions?"

"Because you look like you're going to burst."

"I don't really need to ask you anything. I can already see she's had a positive influence on you. Your hair, the color in your cheeks, the fact that you're noticing art now. I'm pleased, Joss. I'm also pleased you've finally accepted that my idea—and my finding Sarah—was genius."

Joss frowned more deeply than was justified. She didn't like to admit her mother was right. "Let's not go that far, Mama."

"Don't tell me she isn't doing a wonderful job escorting you to your functions. Two now, right? And the third later this week?" Madeline's voice, her smile, dripped with self-satisfaction.

All right, Joss thought, fine, she'd eat some crow, but only a little. "Okay, okay. You win. Sarah's been a hit so far. She's charming, pretty, bright, fun." And a great kisser, but she wasn't about to admit that to anyone, least of all her mother.

"When can I meet her?"

"No way, forget it. You've done enough already."

Madeline folded her arms across her chest and pouted. "If you won't bring her around, your old mother has a few tricks up her sleeve, you know."

Joss rolled her eyes. "I swear you're trying to kill me, Mama."

Madeline threw her head back and laughed. "Now why would I do that after going through all the trouble of giving birth to you, my dear? C'mon, let's eat."

CHAPTER EIGHT

Sarah expertly applied soft strokes of blue and pink eye shadow, the ritual of applying makeup briefly keeping her nervousness at bay. She hadn't been uptight about the other events she'd attended with Joss, but tonight she was. And she shouldn't be, she told herself. It was a reception for other gay doctors, nurses, medical students. If anything, she should be in her element. But no. That damned kiss continued to haunt her thoughts, giving her a little twinge in the pit of her stomach, keeping her off balance.

Joss had apologized immediately afterward, making it clear she thought the kiss was a mistake, but there were no regrets for Sarah. In the moment, at least, she'd wanted to kiss Joss. Wanted to gauge what she felt sure was mutual attraction, and there it was—all the simmering heat and raging fire of their anger, their flirting and the volatility of their sexual chemistry too—in that one passionate kiss. Their physical attraction to one another was undeniable. And completely off limits, which totally sucked, because Sarah genuinely liked Joss. They had fun together, they could talk to one another—even if they sometimes pushed the wrong buttons and ended up in a verbal duel. But more than all the physical reactions, Joss stirred something deep inside Sarah—the part of her that longed for someone with whom she could enjoy mutual support, loyalty and companionship. The part inside her that wanted the give and take, the rewards and sacrifices, of a life with someone else. She wanted, in short, all the things she never got at home while growing up. Joss was the first person in a long time who reminded her of exactly what she was missing in her life.

"Damn it," Sarah whispered to herself.

"You okay?" Lauren appeared at the open bathroom door.

"Yes, fine, thanks." *Other than feeling sorry for myself.*

Lauren whistled. "Wow, you look smashing. Hope your sugar mama appreciates it."

Sarah smoothed the dress along her sides; it was the dress Joss bought her a week ago. "Stop calling her that." Sarah turned, checked her reflection in the mirror. "She's my...Oh fuck, I don't know what she is."

"How about your hot doctor friend? Will that do?"

"Yes, that'll do, I suppose."

It was unsettling for Sarah to realize she was more comfortable in the company of Joss's colleagues, who believed they were lovers, than she was with Lauren, who knew the truth. The arrangement might be fooling Joss's friends and workmates, but it was a complete lie, and Lauren's constant teasing was like a slap in the face, reminding Sarah that without this special arrangement, she and Joss would never be together. The hard truth was that Joss *was* completely out of Sarah's league. She was at home in the insular world of medicine and medical professionals, science, higher education, antebellum mansions, BMWs and people dripping with money. She was independently wealthy, respected, had a father she idolized and a mother she was actually friends with. Joss didn't need Sarah in her life, save for the decoration Sarah provided on her arm, and the thought sent a rush of despair through her.

"It bothers you, doesn't it?" Lauren said.

"What?"

"When I call her your sugar mama. I'm only kidding around, you know. No harm intended, okay?"

Sarah couldn't admit to Lauren that there were moments like this when the charade she was leading with Joss made her feel pretty damned worthless. She didn't belong with Joss or her people. She was nothing but an actor in their presence. An imposter. "I know. It's fine, I just…I don't know what the hell to call her. Us. Or what we're doing."

"Sarah, promise me you're not second-guessing yourself about this. I totally get why you're doing it. And I don't think any less of you for doing it."

Sarah set her makeup down on the counter and was ridiculously grateful for the understanding of the friend she'd known since they were kids. College had separated them for a few years, but since they began rooming together back in Nashville three years ago, it was as though they were the same Sarah and Lauren who had once skipped classes together, double-dated, bitched to one another about family, borrowed money and clothes from one another, cried on each another's shoulders. She didn't have to pretend with Lauren, and that, she realized, was worth far more than the act she put on with a bunch of pretentious overachieving social climbers.

Her voice thick with emotion, Sarah said, "Thanks for saying that. But sometimes I burn up with the feeling that there's something cheap and dirty about all this." Not to mention completely disingenuous.

"It's not like you're a prostitute, if that's what you're getting at."

"High-priced call girl without the sex would be more accurate."

"Look, Sarah, remember that you're doing this so you can keep your dream alive. And it's not like Joss is a bitch or treats you badly, right?"

"No, she's great."

"And this is helping her too. Remember that."

Sarah sighed, leaned back against the bathroom counter. Joss's earlier accusation repeated in her mind—that perhaps she didn't truly believe in herself. She'd reacted with anger, had become supremely defensive and indignant, but now she wondered if there wasn't a kernel of truth to it. "I know, it's just…"

"Stop it." Lauren said. "Just go with this. It's not hurting anybody. And at least it's better than taking money from your father."

That part was true at least. She gave herself one last appraising look in the mirror and tried to raise a smile that looked believable.

* * *

When Sarah walked into the ballroom, Joss began to tingle all over, every sense on high alert. It was always this way around Sarah. First there was the hyperalertness, then a calming sensation that was both relief and a feeling of gladness, followed closely by an internal frenzy that showered a thousand thoughts through her mind and shot an overabundance of adrenaline through her veins. Her physical reaction to Sarah astonished and alarmed her. What lay behind it, she couldn't begin to guess, and frankly, she didn't want to examine it too closely.

"Hello, Joss," Sarah said, her smile radiating intimate familiarity. She kissed Joss's cheek and whispered, "Your new suit looks wonderful."

"Thanks." Joss breathed her in—faint jasmine, perhaps a hint of geranium—and let Sarah's scent fill her senses, her lungs, paralyzing her. Her voice came out muffled, as though she were a little high. "You look great, Sarah. That dress…"

"Thanks to you."

"No. You're the one that makes it look so good."

Sarah looked into her eyes for a long, questioning moment, and Joss wanted to whisk her to a quiet corner where they could talk. But others were suddenly upon them, an intrusion in Joss's mind, but she went with the flow of bodies and conversation even while thoughts of being alone with Sarah crowded out nearly everything else. They needed to talk about that damned kiss before it became so big they wouldn't be able to get out from under it.

"So the rumors are true." Nancy Connelly clinked champagne flutes with Joss, then raked an approving gaze over Sarah, who had moved to the next group over to mingle. "She's stunning, Joss. And I'm thrilled for you."

If any of this were real, Joss realized, she'd be beaming with pride and happiness. Instead she dipped her head in shame. She and Nancy, a pediatric cardiothoracic surgeon at the hospital, went back several years. Nancy had been patient and kind with Joss during her cocky resident years, and they'd become lasting friends. But Joss hadn't told her the truth about Sarah—or anything about Sarah—even though the hospital's rumor mill had already picked up on the relationship, something that was regarded as surprising—no, shocking—for the perpetually single and very guarded Joss McNab.

"Nancy, wait, there's—"

"Oh, Joss honey, is that your *girlfriend?*" Jayme Lopez, Nancy's partner of a decade, linked her arms through Joss's and Nancy's. She bounced up and down on her stilettos. "Let's go get acquainted. I'm dying to meet her."

Joss silently begged for a way out, but there was none. She hated lying to her two best friends—well, a lie of omission anyway—but now clearly wasn't the time to break it to them that Sarah was… What, exactly? How to categorize their relationship continued to puzzle her. Her mother's words surfaced in her mind: Your wife. *Except she's my paid wife*, Joss amended. And she knew how *that* would go over at the hospital. *Joss McNab is such a loser she has to pay someone to pretend to be her date.*

Nancy and Jayme showed no hesitation in barging right up to Sarah and introducing themselves, Joss tagging behind, her embarrassment making her wish the floor would swallow her up. Her friends peppered Sarah with questions that she either patiently answered or carefully deflected. Without missing a beat, they invited her and Joss over for dinner.

"We're free next Saturday," Jayme said in a voice pitched with excitement. "Please say yes. We'd love to get to know you better, Sarah."

Joss quietly panicked inside, wondering how she was going to extract them from that thorny situation. Or worse, how she and Sarah might endure it. But Jayme had just unknowingly offered Joss an out, and she jumped at it. "Sorry, we'll have to decline. I have to present on TAVR at a conference in Chicago next weekend."

"Oh, shoot," Jayme said. "I forgot about that dang conference." She turned laser-like brown eyes on Sarah, and Joss's relief was short-lived. "We'll just have to take Sarah on her own, then. What do you say, girl?"

"Um…" Sarah's eyes darted to Joss in a plea for help.

"She's coming with me," Joss said, reflexively placing her arm around Sarah's waist. The lies came like an avalanche now. "There's something at the Art Institute there she wants to see. Isn't that right, honey?"

"Ooh," Nancy chimed in. "A romantic getaway. All right, that trumps dinner at our place anytime."

Jesus, what the hell have I done! Minutes later, Joss picked at her food, but her appetite was lost in the knot that used to be her stomach. Her five-minute speech, something that normally gave her butterflies, didn't even rate a single flutter this time. Instead, she sailed through it like an automaton, all the time wondering how she might conceivably backtrack her way out of the massive hole she'd dug for herself and Sarah. It wasn't like her to be sloppy, to not have thought everything through to the finest detail, including how to break it to Nancy and Jayme that Sarah wasn't really her girlfriend. But every time she was with Sarah, she got lost in her perfume, got lost in those flirtatious little glances that had long ago blurred the line between what was real and what was for show, got lost in the little touches that were far more gravitas than innocent, and she was most definitely getting lost in the exhilaration of being part of something that made her feel good. Slowly, she'd begun losing her grip on what was part of their agreement and what had strayed beyond it, and worse, she'd begun hoping, wishing for things to go beyond their agreement.

A string quartet had couples jamming the dance floor, dancing to ballad after ballad. There were few times on campus where gays and lesbians could rule the dance floor in such a romantic fashion. Joss's first escape was to the washroom, her second to the bar. Sarah, however, wasn't easily dissuaded. She crooked her finger and beckoned Joss to the dance floor.

"People are going to talk if we don't dance," Sarah whispered, placing her right hand into Joss's left and stepping toward her.

She was probably right, Joss thought, but Sarah seemed to be enjoying the awkwardness of the situation a little too much. It took half the song before Joss relaxed her hold on Sarah enough to move in slow syncopation with her and to allow herself to yield to the softness of Sarah against her. She hadn't held a woman like this, not without sex being involved, in… She couldn't remember when, but it had been many years—back to a simpler, deluded time when she thought she could actually have both a girlfriend and a demanding career.

Sarah shifted slightly in her arms so she could catch her eyes. "That was some quick thinking earlier. About Chicago."

"Sorry, I didn't mean to draw you into my lie so easily. It was all I could think of to get you out of dinner plans with Nancy and Jayme. Don't get me wrong, I love them to death, but it would be an inquisition I'm not sure you'd enjoy."

"Actually." Sarah laughed softly, her breath a warm flutter against Joss's neck. It sent a pleasurable shiver up her spine. "I thought it was brilliant. And in fact there actually is an exhibit I want to see at the institute. When do we leave?"

"What?"

"Chicago. Which day do we leave, because I teach half days on Tuesdays and Wednesdays."

Joss stumbled, then strengthened her hold on Sarah so they wouldn't trip. It was incredible how easily Sarah could transform her into an uncoordinated, incoherent, blubbering fool, something that would surprise absolutely everyone but her mother. *Thank God my patients never get a glimpse of me like this.*

"Whoa," Sarah said. "Not having second thoughts, are you?"

"Second thoughts? I haven't even gotten to the first thought yet. I didn't mean for you to actually go to Chicago with me."

"I suppose your colleagues might think you're pretty serious about me if I go. On the other hand, if I don't go, the rumor mill will go roaring off into an entirely different direction."

Joss's head spun. "So if we go to Chicago together, people will think we're practically engaged. If we don't, they'll think we're breaking up. Jesus. This is more complicated than a soap opera. Is dating always this byzantine?"

Sarah laughed, her eyes twinkling with the kind of mischief and revelry that Joss envied. And adored. Risk averse by nature, she was not intimately familiar with these qualities. She thrived on routines and plans and preparation, which made her a very good surgeon but not an especially fun or spontaneous person.

"Yes and no. But know this. Sometimes planning is overrated, you know." She lowered her voice to a flirtatious octave. "Being spontaneous has its own rewards."

"Not in my world."

"No, you're probably right. In my world, however, there's a lot of instinct and feeling involved. I can start painting an object a certain way, then once I get into it, it can take on a whole different life of its own. One I hadn't considered. It becomes something I hadn't planned at all, but it can turn out spectacularly."

"I'm not so good at all that touchy-feely-artsy-spontaneous stuff. Spectacular endings or not."

Sarah shrugged lightly, her eyes full of the devil. "That's all right. I'm not so good at heart surgery. Spectacular results or not."

Joss laughed and twirled Sarah around. "You make me laugh, Sarah Young."

"Good. Take me to Chicago and I'll make you laugh some more."

Her comfort zone was about a thousand miles behind her, but Joss found herself agreeing to the idea. She had fun with Sarah. With her she saw the world differently than she did from the more familiar environs of hospitals and diseases. She imagined that being with Sarah was like being on the moon looking back at Earth, rather than being on Earth and gazing at the moon. Less grounded, maybe even a little scary, but far more interesting.

One thought refused to leave her mind. Could she spend three days with Sarah and not want to kiss her again?

CHAPTER NINE

Sarah had to hand it to Nathan Sellers—the man knew how to impress. The waiting area to his offices—there was an office for himself and two more for his assistants—was a showcase of taste and wealth. The sofas were Italian leather and chrome, the walls were a faint, earthy green that held several large frame-free canvas paintings by contemporary artists. Coffee tables made of glass and stainless steel were adorned with crystal vases of fresh white roses. There was a five-foot sculpture of petrified wood in one corner, an indoor lemon tree in another. A modern glass fireplace built into one wall danced with flames.

"Sarah Young?" A tall, slender woman who moved with elegant long strides approached and held out her hand. "I'm Raina Jenstone. Mr. Seller's vice president of furnishings. How do you do?"

The woman's handshake was softer and less formal than Sarah expected. "I'm well, thank you. It's nice to meet you."

"Come into my office and we'll talk. Is that some of your work?"

Sarah had brought a large leather portfolio case with prints of more than two dozen of her best paintings. "It is."

"Excellent. Follow me." Raina led the way down the hall, the soft fabric of her skirt quietly swishing around her legs. Her low heels made no noise on the plush carpet.

Raina's office was, Sarah guessed, not nearly as large as her boss's, but one could still play a game of tennis in here, she thought, even after it accommodated the large desk, conference table for eight, and a cozy seating area of two love seats separated by a sleek coffee table. Floor-to-ceiling windows looked out on the Cumberland River with the Titans stadium—LP Field— dominating the horizon.

"Nice view," Sarah said.

"I could say the same." Raina's smile was more appreciative than predatory, but her interest was clear.

She gestured for Sarah to sit in one of the love seats. To Sarah's relief, Raina took the one opposite. "I want to look at your work, but I also have to be upfront with you."

Sarah's heart sank. *Not again*, she thought. She'd been through this so many times before, the I-like-your-work-but-I-just-can't-help-you-right-now routine. She was clear-eyed about the competitive nature of her chosen field, which was every bit as cutthroat as Nashville's music scene, but it didn't make the hard lump of rejection any easier to swallow.

"I'm afraid Mr. Sellers can't use any of your work right now. And I apologize for his absence. He had to fly to New York this morning rather last minute."

"But you haven't even looked at my portfolio yet." Disappointed, petulant, however she sounded at the moment, Sarah didn't care. She was devastated.

"I know, and I will. But—and this information can't leave the room—Mr. Sellers is negotiating some very sensitive business right now with respect to his furniture chain, and it wouldn't be prudent to contract your work at this time."

Sarah stood, ready to make a hasty exit. There was no sense in wasting any more of her own time or Raina's. The only good thing about this little meeting was that she didn't have to put up with the lecherous man himself.

"Please. Stay." Raina began flipping through the portfolio, not even looking up to see if Sarah was still standing. "Wonderful. Oh, I like that one. And in this one, the leaves of the trees are so textured, so authentic looking. It almost looks like a photograph. Gorgeous."

Politeness inserted itself, and Sarah resumed her place on the love seat. "Thank you."

Raina went to her desk and returned with her smartphone. "Do you mind if I take a snapshot of some of these? Nathan may want to see these at some point, and besides, I'd love to think about purchasing something."

"Please. Be my guest."

Sarah knew better than to get her hopes up on either account. She'd been through this enough times before, and right now, she couldn't get out of town and to Chicago fast enough. Nashville was a place people came to dream, but the truth was, it was mostly a city of broken dreams. More artists and musicians had failed here than had ever made it, and Sarah was beginning to feel her own dream fraying at the edges. How long, she wondered bleakly, before she too gave up, the way so many other artists had? Before the mountain of rejections became too much? Money wasn't an issue anymore, thanks to her side job with Joss. Worse than being short of money, she was beginning to realize, was being short of motivation. There was only so much patience and perseverance one could expend before the dream itself began to die. Chicago, she could only hope, was the ticket out of her funk.

* * *

Joss had close to an hour to kill before the regular weekly cardiac surgery department meeting. Entirely too much time to be idle. Because idle time led to thoughts of Chicago and Sarah, and she didn't want to think about those two things right now, especially not together. She roamed the hall in the pediatric wing, looking for Nancy. If her friend was also free until the meeting, maybe they could grab a cup of coffee in the cafeteria.

"Ah, there you are," Joss said, glimpsing Nancy about to enter a patient's room.

"Come on in," Nancy said with a sweep of her arm, "and meet my favorite patient."

A rail-thin young black girl sat on the bed, her pajama'd legs dangling over the edge, and she looked up at Joss with dark eyes that nearly swallowed her face. She was gaunt, and her smile was like that of a plant too long without water.

"Roxi, this is Dr. McNab," Nancy said. "Dr. McNab, this is my best girl, Roxi Stanton."

Joss shook the girl's limp hand and smiled, willing some happiness into the poor kid, even if for a moment. A nasal cannula, which was attached to a mobile oxygen tank, was strapped to her head. It always broke Joss's heart to see kids suffering. It was the reason she had early on eliminated pediatrics as a specialty. Thank God people like Nancy were happy to do it.

"It's very nice to meet you, Roxi. How are you feeling?"

Bony shoulders shrugged. "Okay, I guess. Do you have to put needles in me too?"

"Absolutely not, sweetie." A sketch pad lay open on the bed beside the girl, a spray of colored pencils around it. "Are you an artist, Roxi?"

"She's an exceptional artist," Nancy answered. "And she's going to be famous one day, isn't that right, Roxi?"

Roxi gave another bony shrug, popped a finger in her mouth and stared glumly at her feet.

"May I see your work?" Joss asked.

The shrug was a little more enthusiastic this time. The kid was painfully shy.

Carefully, Joss flipped through the sketch pad. There were drawings of dogs, cats, a fairy with a magic wand, flowers, an angel. They were quite detailed and resembled the work of someone much older than what Joss guessed was an eight- or nine-year-old.

"Dr. Connelly is right, these are wonderful, Roxi. Do you take art lessons?"

The girl shook her head, her eyes darting up to Joss, then sliding back to her feet.

Immediately, Joss thought of Sarah and how she would love this girl's drawings and her obvious talent. "What would you say if I brought around a real artist to visit with you sometime?"

Roxi's eyes grew to twice their size, and Joss took it as a yes.

"Dr. Connelly, do you think it'd be okay if I brought my friend Sarah to visit Roxi sometime?"

Nancy smiled, patted Roxi's knee encouragingly. "If her mom says it's okay, I don't see why not."

"Well, it's a date then," Joss said to Roxi. "I'll check with my friend. She's going to be away for the next few days, but maybe after that, okay? As long as your mom agrees."

"Okay." A timid smile sprang to Roxi's lips, but it was genuine, and it lifted Joss's heart.

Nancy touched Joss's elbow and led her out of the room. "Spectacular idea, Joss. I think a visit from Sarah would really lift her spirits. Maybe Sarah could bring some of her own work to show Roxi."

"I'm sure she'll want to do it. Is Roxi the kid you were telling me about a while back? The one waiting for a new heart?"

"Yes, that's her. She was admitted yesterday. She's getting so weak, I don't know how much longer she can hold out. Not long, I suspect. Another month or two and she may not be strong enough for surgery, even if a new heart materializes."

"That sucks," Joss said.

"Sweet kid too. I'm getting close to hoping for a miracle at this point."

"Then I'll hope with you. Got time for a coffee downstairs before the department meeting?"

"Of course, let's go."

The cafeteria was packed, but they found a corner near a window that looked out on Highway 431, where the pavement and the gray sky blended together, the movement of the zipping cars the only thing defining the horizon. Nashville weather in November could be schizophrenic—sunny and seventy one day, gray and near freezing the next.

"So, Chicago tomorrow, huh?" Nancy's eyes gleamed. "Is it the first time you and Sarah are going away for a weekend together?"

The question made her blush. She hadn't wanted to discuss Sarah with Nancy, because she didn't want to keep perpetuating the lie.

"Nance—"

"You never did tell me the details, like how many dates you've been on, how you guys feel about each other. I mean to look at the two of you, it seems pretty clear to me—"

"Nance, wait—"

"—that you guys are madly in love, that you're perfect for each other. Although I must admit, I had you pegged as being single for life, but hey, I think it's great. Fantastic, as a matter of fact. And it's even more perfect that she's the artsy type, because God knows you've been surrounded enough all your life with the science geeks."

It was useless to try to stop Nancy once she got on a roll like this, so Joss let her go on about how happy she was that she had found someone, how perfect Sarah was for her. When she finally paused for breath, Joss bit her lip, then plunged ahead with the truth. She couldn't go off to Chicago with her best friend thinking she was on some kind of honeymoon. Besides, without the truth, she wouldn't put it past Nancy and her partner Jayme to have her wedding all planned by the time she returned.

It took an uncharacteristic minute or two for Nancy to find her voice, and once she did, it cracked in astonishment. "So, she's like, your *hired* girlfriend?"

"You look like you just downed a cup of cyanide. And yes, I guess you could say she's my hired girlfriend."

"So does that mean, like, a girlfriend in all respects, or…?"

"You mean, am I sleeping with her? Or more accurately, am I paying her to sleep with me?"

Nancy blinked. "It would be unabashedly rude for me to ask something like that, wouldn't it? But…well, are you? I mean, how does this work?"

All Joss's pent-up anxiety about her and Sarah exploded into a peal of nonstop laughter. Others looked at them, smiled, some even chuckled along with her, before turning back to their trays and their murmured conversations.

Nancy sat silent and stone-faced. "I wasn't trying to be funny."

"Fine, sorry." It took a few starts and stops for Joss to continue. "No, we're not sleeping together. And I'm not so pathetic that I need to pay someone for sex."

"But you'd like to sleep with her?"

Oh Christ, Joss thought, not wanting to answer the same question she'd been asking herself for a week now. Of course she wanted to sleep with Sarah, but that was only in her mind. Sleeping with her for real would lead to far too many complications and would make her no better than some creepy, patronizing, chauvinistic rich guy who figured he could buy love and loyalty and sex from women as effortlessly as walking into a department store and cleaning out the joint. Even if Sarah wanted to sleep with her for fun and not for money, it would still be creepy and inappropriate.

"Come on, you know I'm not the type to do that," Joss said tersely.

"Ha," Nancy said, making a face. "Since when? Don't you usually find a mindless, no-strings hookup at conferences?"

Her face burning again, Joss gave her friend an okay-you-got-me smile. "Sarah's not like that. And that's not what this is about."

"You mean Sarah's the type who would want a relationship, not just sex, and you're not up for a relationship. Humph. Now it's making more sense. I thought this whole girlfriend thing with you was too good to be true."

The edge of condemnation in Nancy's tone made Joss sit up a little straighter. "I wouldn't want to disappoint Sarah by being a shitty girlfriend. Because that's exactly what would happen. I'd be the preoccupied, absentee girlfriend who can't commit, and Sarah would wind up hurt and pissed off. And then she'd rightly dump my ass." Sarah, Joss felt sure, was the antithesis of her mother, who had been willing to take whatever cast-off attention she could get from her mate. And if Sarah *was* like Madeline, well, Joss wouldn't want her for a girlfriend.

"You know," Nancy said, gesturing at Joss with her empty coffee cup, "that kind of crap becomes self-perpetuating. If you think you'll never be a good partner to someone, you won't be."

"Thanks, Dr. Phil. It's all moot anyway because Sarah's too clever to ever choose me as a girlfriend." It was only because she was getting paid that Sarah put up with being the dutiful little wife at all these boring functions. *God*, she thought, *how did Mama ever do it? And more importantly, why?* She'd never thought to question her mother's role in her father's life until Sarah had entered the picture.

Nancy shook her head curtly. "That sounds like a handy excuse to keep her at arm's length."

Joss rose, signaling that it was time for them to go. "You missed your calling, Nance, but it's probably not too late to switch to psychiatry."

"With patients like you, I'd go nuts." Nancy smiled to show she was teasing, then bumped shoulders with Joss. "Try to relax in Chicago and stop being so pessimistic about women. And yourself. It could happen, you know."

"It won't happen, and I don't want it to."

It was easier for Joss to slip back into her single-for-life cocoon than to contemplate anything else. It was true that Sarah had made her poke her head out of that haven and dream for a brief moment of being half of something bigger, of being part of something that could make her feel whole in a way that medicine couldn't quite accomplish. But to the core, Joss was a practical-minded woman. She knew that anything with Sarah outside the parameters of their arrangement was ultimately doomed. And she wasn't one to embark on something that was destined to end in failure.

"You won't blab my dirty little secret around here, will you?"

Nancy laughed and shook her head. "It's more fun watching the gossipers think you've actually found the woman of your dreams. So yes, your secret is safe with me. But one day, I look forward to telling you 'I told you so.'"

"In your dreams, my friend. In your dreams."

"So," Nancy whispered as they walked arm in arm down the corridor. "Tell me how this little arrangement with Sarah works. How much do you pay her? How much notice do you have to give her? Does she meet you at these events or do you pick her up? Do you go your separate ways afterward?"

"I feel like I'm on the stand being grilled. Forget I said you should go into psychiatry. I'm thinking law is your calling."

Nancy laughed and squeezed Joss's elbow. It was a relief to finally confess her arrangement with Sarah to someone.

CHAPTER TEN

Sarah stared out the plane's porthole at the bar of clouds beneath them. It was a desert of snow if she let her mind believe it. Clouds should be simple to paint, but in truth, they were complex and one of the most difficult things to accurately capture with a brush. People were difficult to paint too, which was why Sarah had mostly stayed away from doing portraits. It wasn't that she was intimidated by things that were difficult to paint, but rather that she might not do the subject justice. People were supremely complex, and every expression was a tiny window into their multilayered world.

"You've been awfully quiet all afternoon," Joss said from beside her. "Everything all right?"

It was a simple question, one that people asked in casual conversation all the time, not really expecting an honest answer. Maybe it was because it came from Joss or maybe because it hadn't been a good week as far as her work was concerned, but the question brought Sarah to the edge of tears.

"Hey," Joss said softly. "What's wrong?"

"Nothing," Sarah said, retrieving a tissue from her purse and dabbing at her cheek. Nothing except very little in her life was worth a damn right now. Her career as an artist was going further and further into the toilet, no matter how hard she kept working at it. And her dating life was nothing more than a ruse. Her future looked like an endless loop of the same.

"It doesn't seem like nothing to me." Joss looked at her with eyes that were curiously cool and warm at the same time. They were like a blanket of grass on a hot summer's day, grass that could be soothingly cool or pleasurably warm, depending on the temperature of the soil beneath it and the air above it. Sarah wanted to remember the particular shade of green in Joss's eyes so she could use it in one of her paintings someday. If she ever bothered to paint again, that is.

"Thank you, Joss, but you don't have to do this. It's not part of the fine print." Sarah couldn't keep the shadow of bitterness from her voice.

"What are you talking about?"

"What I mean is, you don't have to be my friend. And you don't have to actually care about what I'm feeling or thinking."

Joss's jaw tightened and her eyes darkened, the cool/warm grass hardening to stone. "For your information, I would like to be your friend. And I'd like to help if I can. Anything wrong with that?"

Sarah shook her head, wiped the last of her tears. "No, I guess not."

"So tell me what's got you down?"

It was too easy to be drawn into the swirl of sharing confidences with Joss, to talk honestly and admit things that only her friend Lauren knew about her. Maybe her training as a doctor made Joss a good listener. Or maybe she really did care. Whatever it was, Sarah suddenly needed her as her salve. "I've been feeling a little hopeless about my career. My art."

She told Joss about the proposal with Nathan Sellers falling through. And the rejection letter from a gallery that had arrived in the mail that morning. "And if you lecture me about persistence and not giving up hope," Sarah said acidly, "I swear I'm going to scream."

Joss chuckled. "I wouldn't advise screaming on an airplane these days. People in uniform might meet you at the gate."

In spite of her bad mood and her reluctance to be yanked out of it, Sarah smiled. "I suppose you're right."

"Look, I won't pretend to know what an artist goes through to stay motivated and productive. The only thing I've ever known to do when I feel like I'm falling behind or when I've lost confidence in what I do is to work even harder. You probably don't want to hear that."

"You're right, I don't. Because right now I'm tempted to throw all my paints and brushes and canvases in the nearest industrial Dumpster. Soon as I get home."

"Well, if it means anything, I don't think you should. You're very talented, Sarah. You're extremely good at what you do, and it would be a real loss if you gave it up."

Sarah felt her eyes widening in response. "How do you know I'm any good?"

"My mother has one of your paintings. It's very good. I'd love to buy one myself sometime, if you'll let me."

"Thank you, but you'd have to buy a hell of a lot of my paintings to make up for all the time, energy and education I've put into them over the years." Sarah smiled a little to take the sting out of her words, but she'd spoken the truth.

"I don't want to buy one of your paintings out of charity, Sarah. If you were a stranger, I'd still pay top dollar for it, so please—stop discounting my interest in your work. You're determined to be upset and pissed off—for which I don't necessarily blame you—but I can't snap my fingers and make you a famous artist."

Anger bubbled up Sarah's chest until it formed a hard, choking knot at the base of her throat. Who the hell did Joss think she was, talking to her this way? As if she were a child? What did she know of how long and hard she'd worked to be recognized as an artist? She'd probably worked as hard at her career as Joss had hers, although she didn't have the bank account to prove it. "I'm not asking you to make me anything, Prince Charming."

"Hmmm." Joss smiled from one corner of her mouth. "Princess Charming, actually."

Sarah's anger dissipated as easily as it had come on. Joss had an uncanny and frustrating ability to fire her up until she wanted to throw something in anger. Then every bit as quickly, Joss would suck the wind from her sails and provide her a soft landing. "Did we just have another fight?"

Joss turned eyes on her that twinkled with relief. "I think so. And I remember how the last one ended."

Heat returned to Sarah's cheeks with a vengeance as she remembered the fiery kiss they'd shared in Joss's car. The kiss they hadn't brought up before now. "That's quite the method you have of resolving disagreements. Too bad we're on a plane, huh?"

"Ah, daring me now, are you?"

Sarah bit her lip to keep from laughing. And to keep the swell of excitement from deepening. "You were the one who talked about people in uniform waiting at the gate, not me."

"Good point."

Sarah looked through the window again as the plane began its descent over Lake Michigan. A freighter the size of a small pencil appeared below, looking as though it were standing still in the water, a miniature toy in a big blue bathtub. For the first time, the gloom that had been weighing her down all day felt much lighter and far less daunting. Her despair, she realized with surprise, had almost evaporated entirely.

"Thanks," Sarah said to Joss, meaning it. "For cheering me up."

"You're welcome. Did I?"

"Yes, you did. And I'm sorry about the woe-is-me act. Artists can be a temperamental bunch, you know."

"So I gather," Joss replied, more teasing than rebuking. "Actually, it's a nice change from the humorless, dour medical types who suddenly lose their ability to speak if you try to talk about anything other than medicine. Including myself."

That was an exaggeration, Sarah knew, because she'd had little trouble drawing Joss and her colleagues into conversation about numerous topics, none of them related to medicine.

"Well, you're certainly not dour or humorless."

"And you don't strike me as temperamental. Well…" Joss winked. "Not much, anyway."

"Touché," Sarah said, laughing. Lauren was the only other person in her life who could make her go from crying to laughing in about sixty seconds. She and Lauren had known each other since they were kids though. Joss was only a couple of notches above being a stranger, and yet there was a thread of familiarity between them that felt like it weaved back decades.

"Speaking of medical stuff," Joss continued, "there's someone I want you to meet when we get back to Nashville."

"Oh no," Sarah said, dreading the possibility that Joss was playing matchmaker. It would be so wrong, so objectionable, so…she didn't know what, but matchmaker was not the role she wanted Joss to play in her life.

"Oh no, what?"

"You're not going to try to set me up with someone, are you?"

Confusion deepened the lines around Joss's eyes. "Do you want me to?"

"No!" Sarah snapped.

"Good." Joss's smile was a mix of satisfaction and relief. "We're on the same page then."

And what page is that? Sarah wanted to ask but didn't. "So who is this mystery person?"

Joss went on to tell her about a young patient by the name of Roxi, a shy little girl who needed a new heart and whose artwork was surprisingly advanced for someone who, Joss had learned, was only nine years old. She might not have long to live, Joss warned, and art was the girl's saving grace, a place where she could escape what had become a harsh and fatalistic reality for her. Sarah's heart melted, not only for the little girl, but for Joss too. Joss hadn't said much about how patients affected doctors, how the losses and the difficult cases might weigh on them, but Sarah could see that she was very much affected by the little girl's plight.

"Of course I'll do it. I'd be happy to meet with her."

"Good. Thanks."

Joss reached for her hand. Sarah expected her to pat it, but instead, she held onto it as the plane approached the O'Hare runway. Sarah clasped her fingers tightly. "No. Thank *you*."

"For what?"

"For pulling my head out of my ass. I needed that."

Joss smiled smugly. "Well, since kissing you wasn't an option…"

* * *

Joss wished for more separation between the two bedrooms in their hotel suite. Like different floors, perhaps. But it was a nice suite at least, with a view of Lake Michigan, a full kitchen, two bathrooms and a fifty-inch flat screen television. It wouldn't be a bad place to hole up for a couple of days of vacation instead of a conference—except that led to thoughts of snuggling with Sarah on the sofa or cooking a meal together or enjoying a glass of wine together while taking in the view from the window. Other things began to crowd her mind as well, like kissing Sarah, like running her hands up and down the length of her silky thighs, like spanning her fingers across Sarah's stomach, just beneath the swell of her breasts. There were parts of Sarah she wanted to kiss too, like the soft skin of her belly and the tantalizing valley between her breasts.

It was imperative that she banish such dangerous thoughts in favor of something more mundane. And more real. Like the presentation she would give tomorrow as well as tonight's opening reception, which typically was a snore fest, although the buffets were usually good and the drinks were always on the house.

"Do I look okay?" Sarah said, adjusting an earring as she emerged from her bedroom.

Joss had known enough good-looking women over the years to know Sarah's question was rhetorical, but she had no trouble answering truthfully. "You look exceptional, Sarah." And she did, in a perfectly fitted jade green dress that didn't quite reach her knees and revealed one shoulder in a tasteful yet tantalizing way. Long dangling earrings matched the color of the dress, and so did her shoes, which lifted her to Joss's height.

"Thank you," Sarah replied, her soft pink glossed lips turning up in a smile. "You sure I'm not cramping your style by accompanying you to this thing tonight?"

"Absolutely not. You'll be a pleasant distraction from what will be a dry-as-dirt reception. Ready to go? I've already called a cab."

Twenty minutes later, a flute of bubbly in her hand, Joss busied herself scouting the buffet table. Bowls of salads, platters of four different styles of potatoes, a variety of hot vegetables and a small mountain of roast chicken, roast beef and pork tenderloin crammed every available space.

"Joss McNab, I thought that was you."

Joss turned toward the familiar French accent, feeling anything but thrilled. Especially with Sarah standing a few feet away.

"Rebecca Despres. Nice to see you again." Joss held out her hand, which Rebecca immediately ignored. She swept in and kissed Joss intimately on both cheeks.

"A handshake is no way to greet a former lover," Rebecca said in a provocative purr.

"I suppose not," Joss answered stiffly, shame heating her face. Although what she found shameful, she couldn't say. She and Rebecca, a cardiologist from Paris, had hooked up at a similar conference in D.C. fourteen months ago. Their liaison had been respectful, mutual, good but not especially memorable. They'd not kept in touch.

Remaining close enough for her breath to flutter Joss's hair, Rebecca whispered, "Hotel and room number?"

Joss took a step back. "I'm…" *What? Not single anymore?* That would be a lie, and yet she didn't want to hook up with Rebecca—or any woman—right now. There was no reason for her to remain chaste, and yet, doing otherwise somehow felt… maybe not wrong, but not quite right.

"Don't tell me you have a girlfriend?" Rebecca said in a voice thick with undisguised contempt. "We all have a girlfriend, darling."

From behind, a hand softly landed on the small of Joss's back. "Joss, honey. I would have figured you'd be all over that buffet table by now."

Sarah was beside her, her hand still on Joss's back—a possessive gesture that Joss found surprisingly satisfying, especially in Rebecca's presence. *Back off, we belong to each other*, Sarah's gesture implied. As did the territorial gleam in her eyes.

"Yup, guilty as charged, darling. Oh, Sarah, this is an old friend, Rebecca Despres. We were just catching up. Rebecca, may I introduce Sarah Young."

The two women shook hands stiffly, and it was clear Rebecca was sizing Sarah up, making calculations and deductions that momentarily appeared to leave her disappointed. Her deceptively sweet smile wavered before failing completely.

"A pleasure," the two women said simultaneously, though there was not a trace of enthusiasm in their voices or in their body language. They were two cats sharing a cage.

"I hope you're hungry," Joss said urgently to Sarah, steering her toward the lineup. "I'll join you in just a second."

She returned to Rebecca, who greeted her with a smile that belonged on someone who'd just won a Nobel in medicine.

"Just so you know," Joss whispered, anxious to deflate Rebecca's misguided expectations. "I don't know about *your* girlfriend, but *mine* is something special. I'll see you around, Rebecca. Oh, and happy hunting."

Rebecca turned on her heel like a practiced drill sergeant and marched away, and Joss was almost giddy with relief. A sure thing with Rebecca paled in comparison with what she anticipated with Sarah tonight. Oh, there'd be no sex. And that was fine, because, she realized with a start, being with Sarah was more than enough to extinguish the loneliness that was occupying her soul these days. Without even trying, Sarah was becoming her port, a place where she could rest and recharge, a woman with whom she could be herself. She liked being with Sarah, and it was disorienting to realize she could get so much satisfaction from a relationship that was devoid of sex.

From a few feet away, Joss took a moment to observe Sarah, who was engaged in conversation with a short, pudgy, but well-tailored man in line ahead of her. Sarah chuckled warmly at something he said, said something back that made him smile widely, and Joss felt her heart expanding, lifting, making room for another person. She was a soaring kite whose tether was about to snap, and it was all because of Sarah.

The image brought Joss back to earth with a thud. Joss had never had her heart broken, had never wanted to risk it. But Sarah…Sarah was exactly the woman who could, if she let her in, do exactly that. Instinct told her that having her heart broken by Sarah would be like dying a million deaths—something she could do without, thank you very much.

With that sobering thought, Joss straightened her spine and stiffened her resolve. They would be friends. Good friends. But they could never be anything more.

CHAPTER ELEVEN

A little bit of Tennessee in a glass helped smooth out the turbulence that marked Sarah's mood, but only a little. Joss had ordered a couple of mint juleps from the hotel lounge to bring back to their suite, and Sarah closed her eyes as she sipped the sweet and smoky concoction of mint and lemon and bourbon. Expensive bourbon too, her tongue told her. Clearly, Joss didn't do anything in half measures. But then, why would she? She was a woman who was used to getting what she wanted, including women.

"Sorry," Joss said, shedding her suit jacket and emitting a weary sigh as she took a seat on the sofa, leaving a respectable amount of space between them. "That reception was even more boring than I expected, which is not an easy thing to do."

The distance between them, physical and otherwise, was a gulf as big as an ocean in Sarah's mind. All evening long that French doctor had been sending bold glances their way, her big, imploring come-fuck-me eyes spearing Joss at every opportunity, her knowing smile seeming to brim with memories only the two of them were privy to. It was obvious they'd been lovers. Maybe still were. Or planned to be again. Joss had gone back and whispered something to Rebecca while Sarah was in line at the buffet. An invitation for later tonight perhaps or at some point over the next day and a half? The thought left a bitter taste in the back of her throat that the bourbon couldn't expunge.

"What?" Joss said, setting her glass down.

"What do you mean, what?" *Oh no*, Sarah thought, *I'm not going to act like the jealous sort-of-but-not-really girlfriend. We are so not going there!*

"You look like you want to say something. Like you're upset with me. What's going on?"

Why did Joss have to be so damned pushy in demanding what was on her mind? About getting her to express her emotions? It was annoying, disturbing, that the challenges thrown down by Joss were so difficult to resist. And whenever Sarah rose to the bait, a rocky exchange between the two of them usually ensued.

"No. If I tell you what's on my mind, we'll only end up fighting. Then you'll kiss me, and then where will we be?"

In one swift movement Joss eliminated the space between them. "You're right. Let's skip the fighting and head straight to the kissing."

Sarah's heart skipped a beat. She set her drink down. This was serious. Joss produced a smile, trying to disguise her comment as nothing but a flirtatious joke, but her eyes said she meant it, that she wanted to kiss Sarah more than she wanted to breathe.

"Joss—"

"Okay, I do want to kiss you, Sarah," Joss said, a slow, rising heat to her voice. "I know it's crazy, and I know I shouldn't— can't—want to, but I can't seem to help it." Her eyes had gone a bit wild, a bit reckless, almost pleading for Sarah to take the initiative, the way she had the one and only time they'd kissed.

Oh, God, Sarah thought, swallowing against her suddenly dry throat. It *was* crazy, but she wanted to kiss Joss every bit as badly. She wanted to get lost in that mouth, disappear in Joss's arms and never give another thought to her flagging career, her waning hopes, nor to the fact that she and Joss were only pretending to date. Losing herself in Joss, she knew, would be temporary insanity and would do nothing to solve any of the issues in her life. She didn't need the sweet but pointless diversion of kissing. And she sure as hell didn't need rescuing, didn't need Joss to be her savior. The realization dashed cold water on the nuclear reactor her body had become.

She pushed a hand lightly against Joss's rapidly rising and falling chest. "I'm not your damsel in distress. Your project. And I don't need you kissing me into next year so I can be your possession."

Joss stiffened, clenched her jaw once, twice. "Is that what you think you are to me?"

"Am I?"

"Absolutely not. I don't collect things and I don't take on 'projects,' as you call it. I have enough of a godlike complex in my work as a surgeon, thank you very much. I'm not looking for it in my private life too."

Sarah laughed. She didn't mean to, but it was funny, and she needed an outlet for her tangled emotions.

Joss's frown deepened, spreading across her face like an advancing storm front. And then a smile broke through, so radiant that Sarah immediately felt the tension snap. "I wasn't trying to be funny, but I do like making you laugh."

"You make me laugh a lot, Joss, and I adore that. And I want to kiss you, but not as your hired help and most definitely not because I'm a charity case."

Joss's face flushed with fresh anger. "I *never* kiss hired help and I only do charity that comes with a tax receipt. Look. I don't own the book on what the hell is going on between us, but can't we just be two single women who enjoy kissing one another?" Softly, her anger receding, she added, "I want to kiss you because you're beautiful. I want to kiss you because you've somehow managed to reach in and touch me in a place that hasn't been touched, ever. I want to kiss you for who you are and not for what you aren't or what you wish you were."

Sarah sucked in a breath, Joss's words coalescing into a hurricane-force wind that was quickly knocking down her walls.

It still came as a surprise that Joss seemed to have an instinct for knowing exactly the thing to say to get right to the nub of the issue. And not only that, but she seemed to know exactly how to melt Sarah's heart. "You do this…" She had to stop, gather herself again. "To me. Every. Time."

Joss edged closer until the length of their thighs touched, until her mouth was so close Sarah could almost taste it. "Do what?"

Pinching her eyes shut to hold back the tears that threatened, Sarah said, "Kiss me first and I'll tell you later."

Sarah was expecting a kiss, but instead Joss had lifted her hands to trace the shape of her face, her fingertips so light they barely registered. *Oh*, thought Sarah, *this is so dangerous.* Lips as soft as a southern breeze touched her own, and Sarah's heart took flight, slowly, like a heavy-winged bird. Her body began to tremble as the kiss intensified, unleashing an urgency of want in her that startled her, made her feel like her feet might never again touch the ground. She couldn't keep her hands from moving to Joss's head, and she ran her fingers through the soft, short strands there, because she needed more contact. Needed more than her mouth to convey how much she wanted this. How much she wanted Joss.

On the edge of a moan, she called Joss's name over and over again.

Breathing hard, Joss said against her lips, "Do you want me to stop?"

"Yes. No." *Why can't my answer be simple? Why can't anything with Joss be simple?*

The kiss was like nothing Sarah had experienced before. Certainly not with Margaret, her last girlfriend, whose kisses were dry and flat as paper and exactly twenty seconds long. Margaret was the kind of person who liked everything planned out into uncompromising rituals, who ate exactly the same thing every morning (dry toast and muesli), who liked sex every Friday and Saturday night, who never let her in-box overflow. No. This kiss had all the hallmarks of something that could easily rule them, control them and, finally, obliterate them.

Joss's mouth skimmed her jaw, moved to her throat in a wet, luscious trail of sucking, nibbling, licking. Their last kiss had been full of angry passion. But this, this was desire. This was an I-want-to-disappear-inside-you kiss. This was the kind of kissing that was one step away from making mad, crazy love, and Sarah knew they were reaching a point they wouldn't be able to turn back from. Simple was racing toward complicated in one hell of a hurry.

"Wait," Sarah commanded, pulling back with all the fortitude she could muster. Her breath came in hard, painful gulps.

Joss sat back, blinking and breathing rapidly through her nose. "You're right, Sarah. Jesus. It wouldn't be right if we went further. I'm sorry. I lose my mind around you sometimes."

Sarah angled herself to look at Joss. Her voice was still thick with residual desire. "We seem to get stuck in this place where the boundaries sometimes change. Where one minute we're just friends, practical companions, business partners, whatever you want to call it. And then…"

"And then we can't seem to help ourselves from taking more." Joss picked up her drink and took a long sip and then another. When she spoke again, her voice had lost its earlier heat. "It seems sometimes like…like we could be more. And I like you, Sarah, a lot. You're intelligent, charming, more down-to-earth than just about anybody else I know. You've got these layers that I haven't begun to discover yet. And you have to know I'm very attracted to you."

But…? Sarah thought. *There's always a fucking* but *when I get close to something good.*

"But I just can't do the girlfriend thing." Joss at least had the good manners to look a little tortured by her confession. "I'm a shitty girlfriend, Sarah. Between surgery and teaching and all these damned functions, I'm never home. I don't even know the first thing about putting someone else ahead of my career, my needs. Even if I wanted to have a girlfriend, I—"

"You don't have to explain," Sarah said, her voice as sharp as broken glass. "In fact, I'd rather you didn't, all right?" She strode to her bedroom, throwing a terse "Goodnight" over her shoulder, and clicked the door shut behind her.

Tears blinded her, exhaustion turning her limbs to rubber, and she lay down on the bed without undressing. She was tired. So tired of wanting things in her life she was never quite good enough to have.

* * *

No matter how many times Joss wished for and fantasized that she could take back the events of the previous night, the ending never changed. They'd each gone to bed without another word, and this morning Sarah was gone before Joss got up. She'd left a note saying she was spending the day at the Art Institute and having dinner with one of her old professors.

Might be just as well if they avoided each other until tomorrow's flight home, Joss consoled herself. She'd been a fool. And a damned coward. She was too scared to ask Sarah what she really wanted from their collaboration, which more and more seemed like a relationship rather than the efficient, one-dimensional label they kept trying to stick on it. She was too afraid to consider growing their relationship, of allowing it to become an actual, bona fide relationship. It terrified her to need Sarah, and it terrified her even more to think of shifting the primary focus in her life or at least splitting it. She was too much like her father, so completely absorbed in her own world, and yet she was unlike him in knowing that she couldn't subject another person to what he'd put her mother through. She was safe being single. Safe in her world of hospitals and operating rooms and teaching medical students. She'd begun to feel safe in her business arrangement with Sarah too. Except now, well, its rapidly fluctuating boundaries had begun to scare the shit out of her.

"Ah, Dr. McNab, my congratulations on your presentation this morning. Wonderful job."

Dr. Jeff Billings was the cochair of the conference and head of cardiac surgery at Northwestern Memorial Hospital. His enthusiasm was in direct contrast to her own analysis of her presentation. She had the material down cold, but, distracted by thoughts of Sarah, she felt as if she'd stammered her way through the talk, to the point that she wouldn't have blamed people if they'd concluded she knew little more about transcatheter aortic valve replacement than a fourth-year medical student.

"I'm afraid I wasn't exactly at my best."

His thick red eyebrows bunched together in confusion. "Nonsense, it was spectacular. Especially your comparison between the femoral approach versus the small incision in the neck. You know, we could use an exceptional, young TAVR surgeon at my hospital. Just say the word, and—"

"Thank you, Dr. Billings, but I'm happy where I am."

"Of course." His smile was polite but did little to hide his disappointment. "I understand. That's quite a legacy of your father's down there at Vandy. It'd be hard to leave that, I'm sure. His reputation is still legendary, even up here."

Joss mumbled her thanks, not wanting to talk about her father with a stranger. She was, she imagined, like the offspring of a fabled rock star whose loyal fans constantly talked about the famous parent. As if her accomplishments were nothing in comparison. As if she could never quite merit that same level of awe and respect.

He thrust an envelope into her hand. Tickets, he said, for a concert later tonight at the Chicago Theatre. He shook her hand again and said it was a small token of his gratitude for the sharing of her expertise at the conference.

When he'd gone, Joss pulled the tickets from the envelope. An intimate evening with Erika Alvarez and Dess Hampton, 8:30 p.m., main floor seating, the tickets said.

The two women's names sounded vaguely familiar. Last year they'd won a Grammy or an Oscar or something, and they were out as a couple, perhaps even married. But whether they sang country music or opera or something in between, Joss had no idea.

She scanned the room. Her first instinct was to pass the tickets along to somebody else, but then Sarah's voice insinuated itself in her mind, telling her, in an unmistakably reprimanding tone, that she didn't know how to have fun, that she never did anything spontaneous. She harrumphed to herself. Getting those blond highlights in her hair should have answered that criticism.

Fine. She could be fun. She pulled her phone from her pocket and texted Sarah an invitation to join her. It was a peace offering, as well as a means to see if Sarah was still talking to her. She didn't want to spend another night tossing and turning, worrying about badly she'd screwed things up between them. Again.

CHAPTER TWELVE

"Are you calling a truce?" Sarah asked Joss as she greeted her in the lobby of the Chicago Theatre. She'd almost declined the invitation, tempted to fib that her dinner with her former professor was running late. But Frank Redgrave had after-dinner plans of his own, and the idea of punishing Joss held waning appeal. They were both responsible for perpetually pushing the boundaries between them and running into a wall. A wall they couldn't seem to climb over or go around.

Joss's playful smile was clearly intended to raze Sarah's resistance. And it worked. "Absolutely. Am I forgiven?"

"Nothing to be forgiven for."

Silently, they made their way to their seats, which were in the second row from the stage. *Nice to have such connections*, Sarah thought. She was a big fan of Erika and Dess. "I'm…surprised you asked me here. But thank you."

"You were the first person I thought of. Who else would I have asked?"

Sarah's throat tightened. *Fine*, she thought. *I'll be honest, and if I sound like a jealous bitch, then so be it*. "You could have asked that French doctor. The one who was practically throwing herself at you last night."

Joss closed her eyes and faintly shook her head. She seemed to be biting back a smile, which only made Sarah angrier.

"I assume," Sarah said, biting off her words, "that you've slept with her."

For a long moment Joss didn't answer. Then she broke into a wide, self-satisfied grin that wasn't very sporting. "You're jealous. And yes, I slept with her once, over a year ago."

Blood pounded in Sarah's ears. How dare Joss make fun of her feelings, even if she was inappropriately jealous. And how dare she be so damned cocky about her sexual conquest. "I'm not jealous," she lied. "How could I be? We're business partners, not lovers. What you do with women is your business, not mine."

"Hmmm. Then why did you ask me if I slept with her?"

"It…it wasn't a question. I was making an observation."

"Then you're not jealous."

Sarah cast a sideways glance at Joss, expecting to see more of the same cocky attitude. What she saw startled her. Joss looked disappointed. Raising her chin and summoning all the bravado she could, Sarah said, "Fine. Would you like me to be jealous?"

"Yes."

The honesty behind Joss's answer shocked Sarah. And quickly put an end to the little game of cat and mouse. "All right," she said on a sigh. "I'm jealous. And I hate that I am."

On the armrest between them, Joss threaded her fingers into Sarah's. "Don't hate it. Trust it."

"What's that supposed to mean?" If Joss was trying to make her feel better, it wasn't working. She had no right to be jealous, and Joss had no right to want her to be jealous. *Christ, here we go again. Wanting each other but not permitting it. Getting into these little verbal jousts instead of ripping off each other's clothes.*

"It means," Joss said calmly, "that we have feelings for one another, even if we can't act on them. It makes me feel less alone in…in…whatever it is we're doing."

The auditorium had filled to its capacity of over three thousand people, and the lights dimmed.

"Tell me who these two women are," Joss whispered in a welcome change of subject.

Sarah filled her in, rattling off the duo's hit songs and a quick bio of each. "We're in for a real treat. They're incredible. I'm a huge fan."

Joss's hand was still in hers when Erika Alvarez and Dess Hampton strode onto the stage, holding hands, to loud cheers, a guitar slung over each woman's shoulder.

* * *

Joss, electrified by the show, suggested they stop somewhere for a glass of wine. Somewhere that wasn't their hotel suite. That territory was far too dangerous. Joss had been so close last night to begging Sarah to let her make love to her. Thoughts of touching her all over had filled her mind, clouded her senses and had driven her body until it was almost a quivering heap. She'd never before been pushed to the brink of losing her self-control like this, and she'd known instinctively that had she raised her hand and cupped a breast or lowered that same hand to the soft valley between Sarah's thighs, the night would have turned out much differently. They would, without a doubt, have made love all night long.

But Sarah wasn't a one-night woman, Joss reminded herself. Sex alone would never be enough with a woman like her, and it was a sobering thought that quickly brought Joss back to reality.

They ducked into a darkened restaurant that featured flickering candles on white tablecloths. They claimed a table for two in the corner and each ordered a glass of red wine.

"No mint julep?" Sarah teased.

"I think we know what the mint juleps lead to."

Color rose to Sarah's cheeks, and the effect made Joss want her all over again.

"Good point," she answered. "That show was incredible, wasn't it? What was your favorite part?"

"Besides Ms. Alvarez's cleavage?" Joss knew that would earn her a swat from Sarah and she wasn't disappointed. "I loved their version of 'Ain't No Sunshine When She's Gone.' It was so full of longing, it was almost painfully haunting, but in a beautiful way."

"I agree. They pulled off the same effect with 'If You Leave Me Now.' And I really liked that plucky song they wrote together, 'You Are The Song In My Heart.'"

"I enjoyed the part where they explained their rocky start as a couple."

"And how Erika gave up what she thought was a chance at fame and fortune to be with Dess."

Joss laughed. "Except the goddess decided there would indeed be fame and fortune if they stayed together and worked together."

"But they seem to have kept their heads through it all."

"And their love for each other."

"I guess that's the real challenge with a successful career. Finding and keeping love at the same time. Not that I would know."

"Me either," Joss said, taking a sip of her wine. It was a question that had only been an abstract one in her mind until Sarah had walked into her life and turned it upside down. Ridiculous as they were, thoughts of how one might juggle love and a career were coming up far too often of late. She hadn't a clue what she was supposed to do with it all.

Neither woman spoke for several moments until Sarah asked Joss if she felt her career in medicine was worth all the sacrifices.

"What sacrifices? I love medicine. I love heart surgery. I can't imagine doing anything else."

"What I mean," Sarah said, setting her glass down and looking earnestly at Joss, "is it worth it to the exclusion of everything else?"

"If you mean love, I'm doing fine without it, thank you. Like the old saying goes, you don't miss what you don't have."

Sarah absently tapped her fingers against the rim of her glass. The light from the candle danced in her eyes, fire and ice, and the effect was mesmerizing. "Why are you against love?"

"Is that what I am, against love? Like I'm against homophobia? Or racism?" Joss was in no mood for a sentimental discussion about love. And why did there have to be two camps? That you were either a romantic or an avowed loner? And why the hell did everyone think you couldn't be happy if you weren't in love? That was so damned unfair.

Sarah silently finished her wine. Joss signaled the waitress for another round. She rarely got to consume two consecutive drinks back home, between being on call at the hospital and being available to her students at almost any time of the day or night. The evening felt incredibly emancipating in an almost forbidden way, and she didn't want it to end yet.

"I'm not against love," Joss finally said. "It's just not for me. At least not at this point in my life."

"When you went into medicine, did it have to be an either or? I mean, your father had a career and a family."

"Ha." Joss took a healthy sip of her wine.

"What's that supposed to mean?"

"Nothing. You're right, he had a career and a wife and the whole nine yards. Men usually do."

"And you can't because you're a woman?"

The alcohol was loosening Joss's lips faster than she could process her thoughts. "Of course I can, if I want to treat my partner like crap. Never home, expecting her to be at my beck and call when I need something. Too tired or too occupied at the end of the day or at the end of the week to support her needs."

"Is that what it was like for your mother?"

"Not according to her. Life with Joseph McNab was all peaches and cream, sunshine on a cloudy day and all that."

"And you don't believe her?"

Joss swallowed the catch in her throat. She had long believed that her father, although not perfect, had been a good husband and father, if you conveniently didn't factor in his habitual absences and his perpetually distracted mind. Her mother seemed to want her to believe that it was acceptable for one person in a relationship to do most of the giving. Sarah was making her see, though, that having a wife jump every time you lifted a finger wasn't real love, wasn't a relationship, could not possibly be mutually satisfying. Long absences and superhuman dedication to a career as demanding as medicine were extremely unlikely to result in a strong marriage. A woman like Sarah deserved so much more. And so had Joss's mother.

"I'm not sure what I believe anymore," Joss said, unable to control the tremor in her voice.

"I'm sorry, Joss."

Joss finished her drink. "Don't be. We all make our choices. Are you ready to head back to the hotel?"

The tenderness in Sarah's eyes nearly undid Joss. She turned away and reached for their coats.

CHAPTER THIRTEEN

Sarah tightened her grip on the oversized portfolio case, which today contained half a dozen of her eleven-by-sixteen sketches, three smaller sketchbooks and an assortment of charcoal pencils. She'd also crammed into it an instruction manual for kids on how to draw. She was nervous, although not because she was meeting the budding artist whose young life hung in the balance, but because this was Joss's domain. The hospital was a world Sarah knew little about and in which she didn't belong.

When she rounded the corner leading to the room to which she'd been directed, she found Joss leaning against the wall, looking relaxed yet completely alert to everything around her. Her perfectly combed hair, her starched scrubs all seemed to brook no nonsense. She was a woman supremely confident in her abilities and in her authority. Not that anything about the working Joss surprised Sarah, but it threw her for a moment. A sudden smile from Joss let her know that she was the same old Joss Sarah had begun to know and care for.

"Hi," Joss said. "I'm so glad you could make it."

"Glad to be of help. If you think it will help, that is."

Joss winked. "Oh, I think it will help in more ways than one. Come on in and meet Roxi."

The little girl, stick thin, lay under a cotton sheet on her bed, reading a Wonder Woman comic book.

"Hi, Roxi," Joss said. "Wonder Woman. Excellent choice, she's my favorite too. How are you feeling today?"

"Okay. Is this the artist lady you told me about?"

"It sure is, sweetie. This is my friend Sarah."

Sarah stepped forward, set her case down and shook Roxi's delicate hand. Her veins ran through her translucent skin like tiny blue spiderwebs. "I'm so pleased to meet you, Roxi. Thank you for agreeing to spending some time with me."

Roxi's smile was tentative, but she tossed her comic book aside and sat up straighter. "Are you a real artist?"

"Yup. I hear you are too."

The little girl's frown was so deep, it was in danger of leaving permanent creases. "No. I'm just a kid."

"But you're going to be an artist one day, isn't that right?"

Roxi shrugged ambiguously, but her dark eyes gleamed with pride.

Joss pushed off from the wall and moved to the door. "I'll leave you two alone. Sarah, how about I come back for you in, say, forty-five minutes? You haven't lived until you've tried the coffee in this place."

"Really?" Sarah loved good coffee and was always on the lookout for new sources for her addiction.

Joss laughed. "No, far from it. But it was all I could think of to get you to say yes."

"You could have just asked."

"And you'd have said yes, even if the coffee tastes like old socks?"

Sarah grinned. "Well, let's not get carried away."

Joss winked and was gone.

"Is Dr. Joss your girlfriend?"

There was no judgment in Roxi's expression or tone, only intelligent curiosity.

"Hmm. Sort of but not really."

Roxi shrugged. "Okay."

If only adults would be satisfied with such a nonanswer, Sarah thought wistfully. She unzipped the portfolio case and handed a sketchbook and a charcoal pencil to Roxi. "Want to draw with me?"

Roxi beamed and eagerly accepted the sketchbook and pencil from Sarah.

"Show me what you can do, kiddo."

* * *

"So," Joss said, setting Sarah's coffee on the table in front of her. "What'd you think of Roxi?"

"Sweet kid. Bright too. And you're right, she's bursting with talent."

"Were you like that when you were her age?" Joss found herself picturing Sarah at nine, with her flaming red hair and big blue eyes, china doll skin and faint freckles. She imagined Sarah soaking in everything around her like a sponge, committing it all to memory and then retreating to a quiet place to draw or paint it.

"Pretty much, though not as shy." She sipped her coffee and made a face. "Okay, you weren't kidding when you compared this stuff to old socks. Yuck."

"Sorry. I'd invite you up to my office where I have a Keurig, but the walls around here have ears. And eyes."

Sarah leaned closer and narrowed her eyes. "And what would the walls of your office be hearing and seeing, exactly?"

Joss exhaled in relief. They were back to flirting, and it made her slightly dizzy. Chicago had been an emotional roller coaster. Kissing, fighting, making out, fighting, intense conversations. Spending time with Sarah was never boring, and while sometimes it drove her nuts, mostly it kindled a low, pleasurable flame in the pit of her stomach. The kind that made her want more, even though she knew such a thing was impossible.

Most days, she was okay with that. More precisely, the days she didn't kiss Sarah. On the days she did kiss Sarah, all hell broke loose inside her.

"I suppose they would be hearing and seeing that we were enjoying each other's company," Joss said innocently, refusing to share with Sarah the lusty fantasy taking shape in her mind of playing doctor with her.

To Joss's relief, Sarah didn't respond. They could only go so far before things heated up between them, and once that happened, they were limited to two directions—erupting into hurt feelings and frustration or taking their relationship to a deeper physical realm. Neither scenario was working so well for them. *Time to back off*, Joss reminded herself.

"About Roxi," Sarah said, her eyes moistening. "Is she going to die without a new heart soon?"

"I'm afraid so." Joss had never really learned how to paper over the losses that were inevitable in her line of work and the sadness that accompanied them. In her opinion, good doctors didn't. But the trick, she'd figured out early in her residency, was not to let the losses paralyze you with doubt or hopelessness. Sometimes there were things to learn from them and sometimes there weren't. Sometimes shit happened that was absolutely not fair and not right and were not your fault. You could drive yourself nuts trying to make order out of the randomness of the universe, and many times Joss had done exactly that, to no avail.

"I guess if a new heart arrives in time, it will be at the cost of someone else's loss. It's a tragic irony, isn't it?"

"It is," Joss agreed. "One family's devastation will be another family's gift. But it's better than two tragedies."

Sarah looked lost in thought, her mouth turned down in sadness. Joss wished she had something witty to say, something that would make her smile.

"So tell me how your art session went with her."

Sarah brightened, and Joss felt a corresponding lifting of her heart. She was so damned physically attuned to Sarah, it was crazy. And scary. Was this what it was like to want someone else's happiness more than your own? To care more about what they were feeling? Joss resisted analyzing her feelings any deeper than that because there was no point to it, she reminded herself.

"Roxi was like a sponge, so eager to learn from me. I gave her a sketchbook, and I'll bet it's filled by the time I come back to see her the day after tomorrow."

"I'm so glad you'll come back to visit her." Joss knew that Sarah wasn't feeling very optimistic or inspired about her own work lately. She hoped that her sessions with Roxi would be a two-way street in the reward department. "What will you guys do then, more sketches?"

Sarah thought for a moment. "I think I'd like to get her painting. Watercolors or acrylics. Do you think the hospital will object to me turning her room into a little art studio?"

"Not if I have anything to say about it. My friend Nancy is her doctor, and I know she'll be pleased."

"I wish Roxi were well enough to take to a gallery. She'd love that."

"I think that should be the first thing you do with her if she gets a new heart."

"That's a deal I would love to keep. But there is something that bothers me." Sarah had begun clasping and unclasping her hands in her lap. "I like this kid, Joss. I want to help her. But what if I grow attached to her and she…" Something crumpled in Sarah's eyes.

"Dies?"

Sarah swallowed. "Yes. How do you deal with that? I mean, what do you do at the end of the day when a patient you care about dies?"

There was no easy answer Joss could give that would make Sarah feel better. Death was something you worked hard to avoid in this business, that you fought against by using every ounce of your training, your experience and your best judgment. And sometimes it wasn't enough. "You go on and you help other patients you care about."

"That simple, huh?" Sarah looked unconvinced.

"Yes and no. It can be that simple—has to be—if you want to stay sane and keep doing what you're doing. But it isn't always easy."

They sipped their coffees, Joss contemplating whether to tell Sarah that her mother would be at next weekend's Christmas fundraiser. The event was the hospital's biggest annual fundraising event and one that Madeline hadn't attended since Joss's father had died. Now, however, her mother was on a mission and that mission was to meet Sarah and observe the two of them together. Madeline had acted boastful when she'd told Joss about her plans, almost as if daring her to try to keep her away. Joss, of course, didn't need *that* epic battle.

"Um, I have to confess something to you, Sarah."

"Am I going to need something stronger than this coffee first?"

"Maybe, but unfortunately they don't serve mint juleps here."

"Well, there is that sorry fact."

"The big Christmas fundraiser for the hospital next weekend?"

"Yes?"

"My mother insists on coming."

"Well, that makes sense, given your father's position here for so many years."

"Yes, but her motives aren't entirely altruistic. She wants to meet you. And spy on us together. And Lord knows what."

Sarah laughed. "What does she hope to see?"

"A wife for me and grandchildren someday for her," Joss mumbled so low that Sarah had to ask her to repeat herself. "Never mind. She's being a busybody, that's all."

"I look forward to meeting your mother. Why wouldn't I?"

"Some of her questions might be a little uncomfortable." The truth was, the questions probably would be uncomfortable for Joss, not Sarah.

"That's all right. I can handle a nosy mother. What I'm not looking forward to is having to put up with my father."

"Your father will be there?"

"Yes, Daddy and Linda are going. Linda helps the foundation occasionally with PR work, and Daddy likes to go so he can try to drum up business for his law firm."

Joss sighed. "So we'll be under two sets of microscopes, in other words."

"Looks like it, although I don't think Daddy knows a thing about you. I don't suppose we can wear disguises? Or opt out of going altogether?"

"Afraid not. On the other hand, it's an open bar for hospital staff and their escorts, if that helps."

"That may be the evening's only saving grace."

"Would you like a tour of where I work?"

Sarah perked up. "I'd love to see where you work."

"Deal. But only if you show me your studio sometime."

"It won't be nearly as exciting as your workplace, but I think I can handle that."

Joss smiled. "Good. Let's go take a walk. Oh, one more thing," she said as they pushed their chairs back and stood. "Speaking of my mother, she's in Knoxville for a few days. I have to be her stand-in at the city's annual community foundation announcement day after tomorrow. It's where they announce the recipients of about ten-million-dollars worth of grants."

"Let me guess, the McNab Foundation is a contributor to the fund?"

"Yes, a large contributor. It's late notice and you don't have to come. I just thought…" She wasn't at all interested in spending an hour or two of glad-handing and making idle chitchat with mostly strangers. Functions outside the medical sphere were the worst, and if Sarah came, she would at least make it tolerable.

"I can make it."

"You're sure? You don't need to be working in your studio or something?"

"I'm sure. And my work can wait."

There was something unreadable in Sarah's eyes at the mention of her work, but Joss let it go. "Ready for that tour?"

"Now?"

"Most of the ORs should be idle this late in the day. Come on."

CHAPTER FOURTEEN

Sarah knew something was wrong the minute she spotted Joss inside the city's massive, sparkling new convention center. There were bags under her eyes, which were glassy and red-rimmed, and she couldn't raise a smile when Sarah greeted her. She looked like shit.

"What's wrong?" Sarah whispered urgently. They were standing in one of the large ballrooms with its massive floor-to-ceiling glass walls. Waiters in tuxedos flitted among the crowd like butterflies zipping from flower to flower, carrying trays of tea, coffee, soft drinks and tiny bite-sized cakes of various flavors and brightly colored textures. The funding announcement, which comprised quite a long list of recipients, Sarah noticed in the program book, would begin momentarily.

Joss shook her head, and something in the simple gesture broke Sarah's heart.

Sarah's hand crept up to her mouth. "Oh, God, is your mother okay?"

"She's fine."

The mayor of Nashville, who was serving as emcee, took the podium and, once the room quieted, began his welcoming remarks.

"Do you have to give a speech?" Sarah whispered.

Joss shook her head.

"Then let's get out of here."

Joss protested, but only mildly, when Sarah took her hand and began leading her through the crowd and out of the packed room.

"Did you drive or take a cab?"

"Cab," Joss said, and Sarah wondered if she was ill.

Moments later, Sarah had hailed a cab and instructed the driver to take them back to her apartment. She didn't want to get to the bottom of things until they had privacy.

"What are you doing?" Joss said from beside her in the backseat. The traffic was light and the cab sailed through the downtown streets and onto the expressway.

"Taking you back to my place."

"Why?" Her eyes had gone blank, as if a curtain had been drawn across them, and it frightened Sarah.

"Humor me, Joss. You shouldn't be alone right now."

Joss turned away to look out the window. Whatever had happened to put her in this state, it might take some heavy lifting to get her out of it, it occurred to Sarah. But she was prepared to do whatever it took because she'd never seen Joss this vulnerable before, this shaken.

Lauren was at work, Sarah explained as they took the stairs to her second-floor apartment. Joss moved with the stiff gait of someone who'd been kicked in the ribs.

"Tea or coffee?" Sarah asked. "Or something stronger?"

"I don't need anything," Joss replied, sitting down heavily at the kitchen table for two. "I don't know why you brought me here. I'm terrible company. I'll walk home." She made no move to rise.

"You'll do nothing of the kind."

She poured them each a glass of bourbon—the cheap kind was all she could afford to keep in stock—and set a glass down in front of Joss.

She took the chair opposite. "Talk to me, Joss."

Joss closed her eyes tightly for a moment, exhaustion revealing itself in deep lines around her mouth, her eyes. The shake of her head was almost imperceptible.

"Tell me what's wrong."

Joss finally took a long sip of her drink. There was a tiny tremble in her fingers that was startling in its rarity. The accomplished surgeon didn't ever tremble, didn't lose control, didn't cry, Sarah had convinced herself.

"I don't need your sympathy. Or whatever it is you're offering."

Ouch, Sarah thought. It wasn't like Joss to verbally try to bruise her this way. "I want to help and I intend to help, whether you welcome it or not. And I'm not stopping this inquisition until you tell me what's happened."

"You sound exactly like my mother," Joss said. She finished off her drink in one long swallow.

"Good." Sarah's temper was beginning a slow burn.

"No," Joss said, reaching for the bottle of Jim Beam and topping up her glass. "I don't need a second mother, or a…a…"

"Wife? Is that what you were going to say? Well, too late."

Joss's laughter was full of derision. "It's not in your job description to try to take care of me. By design."

"Oh, I see. The great Joss McNab doesn't need anyone to lean on, is that it? Well, it looks to me like that's not working so well right now."

Joss took another long sip of her drink. "This is exactly what I didn't want."

"What?" Sarah fumed at Joss's stubbornness.

"You caring about me this way. And me needing…"

"Needing some emotional support once in a while? Jesus, Joss, what the hell is wrong with that?"

The alcohol had begun to infuse Joss's eyes with a dull sheen. "I live my life the way I want to, Sarah. I do what I want, go where I want, work as hard as I want, and I don't demand anything of anybody else. I can take care of myself. It's best this way. It's the way I want it."

Like a combination lock clicking into place, Sarah finally realized what Joss was so scared of. "I get it now. You don't want to be responsible for another person directing their emotional energy on you. Sacrificing for you. Making you the center of their world. You don't want to be your father at all, do you?"

Joss's face twisted into a mask of pain. Sarah leapt out of her chair, knelt beside Joss, and threw her arms around her. She tightened her hold as Joss began to cry softly against her shoulder.

* * *

All Joss could smell was the shampoo of rosemary and lemon in Sarah's hair and her faint perfume of wildflowers as she fell into her arms. She couldn't stop herself from seeking comfort in the soothing touch of her fingers, in the strength of her arms, and in her sympathetic murmurings. She hated this show of weakness, and yet she needed what Sarah was offering every bit as much as she needed air to breathe. Caving quickly, she admitted she'd lost a patient late yesterday and hadn't slept a wink all night.

"Tell me what happened," Sarah said with an unbearable tenderness.

There had been a routine surgery three days earlier, her patient a sixteen-year-old boy with a rapidly degrading bicuspid aortic valve that needed to be repaired, she explained. It was rare, but an infection—endocarditis—had set in. He didn't respond to the IV-drip antibiotics, she said, still full of disbelief. "He wanted to be a doctor someday. A cardiologist because of his own heart problems, he told me before he died."

"Oh, Joss, I'm so sorry." Sarah drew tiny circles on Joss's back with the softest of touches that couldn't have been more powerful. "It wasn't your fault, you have to know that."

"I know." Joss pulled away, retrieved a Kleenex from her pocket to wipe her eyes. "I've gone over and over it in my mind. I did everything right, but it shouldn't have happened. It just… it doesn't make any damned sense."

"A lot of things don't. You can't always force them to, and you can't control everything. You told me as much the other day when you talked about Roxi and how you handle it when patients die."

"I know. But it's my job to try," Joss ground out. She pushed her chair back and stood up. It had been much easier to be philosophical about losing a patient when she hadn't actually lost one in a couple of years. Now the stark pain of it was simply too raw to bear. "I need to go."

"Why? Stay here, I'll throw together something for us to eat."

Joss lifted her hand to Sarah's cheek, touched it softly. "Sarah, don't. Please."

"Don't what?"

"You were right," Joss said thickly, dropping her hand and stepping back. "I don't want to be like my father. And I don't want you to be like my mother." The words were strangled in her throat, but she pushed them out anyway. "I don't want you to take care of me."

CHAPTER FIFTEEN

With relief, Sarah watched the last of her students leave the classroom before slumping down at her desk. She hadn't given much of herself to them today, her thoughts dominated by Joss. She'd texted her that morning to ask if she was okay and gotten back only a terse response of "yes, thanks."

It dumbfounded her—no, frustrated her beyond measure—the way Joss had at first accepted and then quickly rebuffed her support yesterday. What she'd done for Joss—holding her, listening to her, comforting her—wasn't anything she hadn't done for others she cared about. Why couldn't Joss accept such a simple act of humanity? Why did she have to make letting Sarah in so hard?

Easy, she thought. *She's got me mixed up with her mother giving everything she had to her father. She's got herself convinced that she can't or shouldn't need anyone else, that it would be unfair to that person.* Well, Joss was misguided—because Sarah was not Madeline McNab. She was not about to sacrifice everything for Joss, would never give up her own dreams, her own career, so completely for someone else. She hadn't given up her dreams for her father and she wouldn't for a lover. But what she could do was be an equal partner to someone someday, and that was the part that Joss was being so ridiculous about. She knows nothing about equal partnerships, about give and take, because she never learned it at home, Sarah decided. Home hadn't taught Sarah many loving lessons either, but she'd learned enough through her friendship with Lauren and her two failed relationships.

Sarah retrieved her phone from her bag and texted Joss: "We should talk. Can we meet?"

"See you tomorrow night at the Christmas gala. Talk then," came the reply.

Sarah sighed and jammed the phone back into her bag. *Joss McNab, you are way more high maintenance than you could possibly imagine!* The thought amused Sarah, only because she knew how appalling Joss would find her observation.

* * *

Joss downed a bracing glass of champagne as the string quartet played a slow waltz. She felt in need of a little shoring up tonight, and so did Sarah, judging by the enthusiasm with which she too was consuming her first glass of bubbly. With luck, the wine would also cool Joss's libido, which had been in a state of Code Red since she'd picked up Sarah. That dress was giving her all kinds of heart palpitations. And not only the dress. Sarah had all the right accessories to accentuate her sexiness too—black stilettos, long sapphire earrings and a matching necklace so delicate that it made Joss want to twine it lightly between her fingers. It took great effort to force the thoughts from her mind. They hadn't kissed since Chicago, hadn't touched intimately since then either, if you didn't count her tearful collapse into Sarah's arms two days ago. *That* she didn't want to think about either.

Nancy sidled up to her and Sarah. "Have you ladies bid on anything for the silent auction yet?"

The silent auction was a treasure trove of pricey items: a year's rental on a Mercedes, a nine-hundred-dollar bottle of scotch, a private box for a Titans game, seasons tickets to the symphony, gift certificates for spas and restaurants and clothing stores. To be polite, Joss had bid on a diamond bracelet, which she would give to Sarah if she were lucky enough to win it. Although Sarah probably wouldn't accept it, meaning her mother was next on her recipient list.

"I think Joss should bid on the trip to Disney World," Sarah teased.

"Yes, because spending the day with a bunch of screaming kids is right up my alley." Joss grimaced. Quiet, well-behaved kids were one thing. But overstimulated, oversugared, overexhausted little brats were quite another.

"Actually," Sarah supplied, "Disney would be the perfect place to take Roxi if she gets a new heart. Don't y'all think so?"

"Ooh, I bet she'd love that," Nancy enthused.

"All right, all right. I'll bid on it," Joss said. Nancy and Jayme could take Roxi if her bid was successful or Sarah by herself could take Roxi. She'd even drive them to the airport.

Nancy nodded toward her partner, chatting animatedly in the distance with a couple of hospital foundation members. "My lovely wife has ordered me to win the trip for two to Sanibel Island. Now *that* I could handle, especially the week before Christmas." Nancy heaved a cinematic sigh. "A private cottage on the beach for a week. Piña coladas at sunset, mimosas for breakfast. Does it get any better than that?"

"Your vacation plan sounds like an alcoholic's dream," Joss teased.

"Oh, shush, you. I'll drink plenty if I get a whole week of not being on call and having no surgeries."

"Hear, hear. I wonder what that would be like?"

Nancy gave Joss a playful shove. "Don't even pretend you want a vacation. You couldn't pull yourself away from here for all the tea in China. I, on the other hand, would have no problem saying sayonara to the place for a week."

Madeline rushed toward them like a house on fire, and Joss drained the rest of her second drink. *Oh, great.* "And here comes Mama."

"My cue to go rescue my wife," Nancy said. "Not that I don't love your mother, but she looks like she's on a mission."

"You can say that again," Joss said under her breath as Nancy scurried away.

"Darling!" Madeline planted a smeary kiss on Joss's cheek and produced a canyon deep smile that nearly cracked all her layers of makeup. "You look very handsome in your tux. And *you*." She took Sarah's hands in hers and enveloped her in a scrutinizing gaze that would have surpassed that of a beauty pageant judge. "You, my dear, are even more gorgeous in person than I've been led to believe by your stepmother. I'll have to scold Linda later for not extolling your virtues enough." She winked to show she was kidding. "And let me just say—"

"Mama, you could try letting Sarah get a word in edgewise."

"Oh, Joss dear, don't be rude."

Joss rolled her eyes discreetly. Fortunately, Sarah seemed not to notice Madeline's smothering behavior.

"As I was about to say, Sarah dear, I've been *so* looking forward to meeting you. Linda has been telling me how wonderful you are, and of course, I'm well aware of your talent as an artist. Your work is absolutely marvelous."

"Thank you, Mrs. Mc—"

"Oh, honey, I insist you call me Madeline." Finally, she let go of Sarah's hands. "And I hope my daughter has been treating you well."

"Your daughter," Sarah said with a brilliant smile, "has been incredibly generous and the perfect gentlewoman."

Or not, Joss thought, recalling the make-out session in Chicago that had nearly ended in the two of them getting very naked. And very sweaty.

"Well, will wonders never cease," Madeline muttered, then laughed. "You two look so beautiful together. Perfect, as a matter of fact." She took each of their hands and squeezed tightly. "I'm so proud, Joss. So proud."

Joss's eye rolling was less discreet this time. "Mama, really, there's no need—"

"Oh yes, there is. You don't know how long I've waited for this."

Joss's heart thumped in annoyance. *Waited for what? For your daughter to hire herself an escort?*

Madeline retrieved a thick linen hankie from her clutch purse and dabbed at her eye, further embarrassing Joss with her Southern theatrics. "Let your mother fantasize for a moment about you finding such a lovely woman, would you, darling?"

"I think I need another drink," Joss mumbled to herself. She was in no mood for further histrionics from her mother, which, while embarrassing, were also a reminder that she was a disappointment to her mother in some important ways. "How was Knoxville?"

"Fine, dear. Cousin Anabelle says hello. Oh, and Sarah," Madeline said pointedly, stepping closer to Sarah if that were possible.

So much for the change in subject, Joss thought. Her mother was a missile locked onto its target.

"I'd love to get to know you better later. Without my daughter present," she added in a stage whisper. "Lunch perhaps? Right now, however, I need to make some bids on the silent auction before it closes. Adios, children."

"Sorry about that," Joss said to Sarah. "She's not normally that irritating."

"She's lovely. And I can tell she loves you very much."

"Yes, well, that she does, but she's over the top tonight."

"Oh shit."

"What?" Joss quickly scanned the room.

"It's my father, and he's headed this way."

CHAPTER SIXTEEN

Peter Young was a master at making an entrance. His short red hair, flashing blue eyes and a trim body that shaved ten years off his age were usually enough to attract an audience, especially of the female variety. And then there was the efficient, slightly urgent way he moved that naturally generated a path, as though he were an icebreaker charging through a frozen lake. Sarah's father was magnetic, a man people immediately wanted to impress, and she sometimes still found herself under his spell. And she hated it. She'd wanted to grow up and leave Daddy years ago, but yearning for his approval and needing his money kept drawing her back too many times.

She wasn't proud of those times, but it was going to be different now, she vowed. She didn't have his approval and probably never would, but at least she no longer needed his money. She was making and would continue to make her own way through life now.

"Hello, Daddy," she said calmly, accepting a brisk peck on the cheek.

"Sarah, a pleasure."

So formal, so devoid of emotion, Sarah thought with frustration. *So typical.* "Where's Linda?"

"Oh, she'll be along. Probably got hold of somebody's ear. Good evening," he said to Joss, extending his hand. "Excuse my daughter's poor manners. I'm her father, Peter Young."

"Nice to make your acquaintance, Mr. Young. And I would have pegged you as Sarah's father from a hundred yards away."

"Daddy," Sarah interrupted. "This is Dr. Joss McNab." She would not, she decided, offer any further explanation.

"Ah, yes, of the esteemed McNab medical dynasty, how wonderful." His eyes had come alive at the McNab name, and Sarah guessed he was calculating how he might impress someone as important as Joss. "I'm *very* pleased to meet you."

He glanced sidelong at Sarah, and she didn't miss the flicker of surprise in his eyes as he took in the close proximity with which she and Joss stood together, the way they leaned slightly into one another the way couples do when they're presenting a united front. He smiled and shook his head a little, making it clear he didn't think she'd had it in her to bag someone like Joss—someone with more money and social credentials than he had. It was a stretch to call the look on his face prideful or boastful, but he'd never looked at Sarah like that—like she'd accomplished something good—because of one of her paintings or because of her graduations and degrees. Bile collected in her throat, and she wanted to get the hell away from him as fast as she could.

"Likewise," Joss muttered, and Sarah could tell something had gone cold in her too, that her politeness took effort.

"Well, well, this is good news." Her father turned to her, and Sarah froze at the chill in his eyes. "Guess this means the Bank of Dad is officially closed, hmm?" His smile was granite hard, like it'd been chiseled there. He was mocking her. "Well done, my angel. Well done." He leaned closer and lowered his voice. "Now if only you can get her to sell your paintings for you too, you'll be all set."

"Daddy, please." She was past the age where the pompous jerk could make her cry, thank God. But if she could have turned on her heel and stalked away without making a scene, she would have. Slapping him would be a better idea, but that too wasn't an option.

Joss stiffened beside her. "Mr. Young, your daughter is an absolute delight, and I'm honored to have her in my life. You've raised a good woman. And a very talented one. You must be very proud."

Her father looked momentarily chastened, which made Sarah far happier than it should have. She should have stopped giving a shit what he thought years ago.

"W-well," he muttered before lifting his square chin and aiming it defiantly at Joss. "I do hope you're going to make an honest woman of her."

"Honest woman?" Madeline swept in. She laughed like he'd said the funniest thing she'd heard all day. "Oh, Peter, you make it sound like we're in the 1950s. But if you're in the mood to spring for a wedding, I vote for a reception for at least five hundred with a complimentary bar and no less than a small orchestra. Of course, you'd need to fly in fresh lobster from Maine. Oh and champagne from France. Caviar from Russia too." She clapped her hands together in delight.

Sarah nearly giggled at her father's crimson face. "Daddy, you might want to take one of your blood pressure pills," she whispered, not bothering to disguise the jubilation in her voice.

"Wedding?" Linda strolled up to her husband, setting a placating hand on his arm. "Somebody getting married? Do tell!"

"I'm not exactly sure yet," Peter answered dryly. "Our Sarah perhaps."

"Oh God," Sarah whispered, louder than she intended. This was getting out of control. Was it too much to ask for a tornado to swoop down and scatter them all into the next county?

"Nobody's getting married," Joss answered smoothly. She swung her gaze to her mother. "Unless, Mama, there's something you'd like to tell me?"

Madeline laughed. "Oh Joss, you're such a card, bless your heart." She turned to Linda and struck up a conversation with her just as Nancy and Jayme arrived with perfect timing. Sarah nearly swooned with relief.

Joss's friends pressed fresh drinks into their hands and led them to one of the round tables for eight, where guests were beginning to collect.

"Thank you for that," Sarah said to them. "Your timing was perfect. One more minute in Daddy's presence and I would have been arrested for assault. He can be such a horse's ass."

"I'm used to in-laws from hell," Nancy supplied, then closed her mouth abruptly as Jayme cuffed her on the shoulder. "Sorry, honey, just trying to make Sarah feel better."

Sarah flashed an apologetic glance at Joss, who merely shrugged and gave her a what-can-you-do smile. If ever she decided to get married one day, her father was definitely not going to be on the guest list. Madeline's jab about him paying for an elaborate wedding had had the intended effect, however. One about as pleasant as a root canal, Sarah hoped.

The microphone at the front of the room squealed. The emcee, an elderly woman in an elegant pantsuit, asked for everyone's attention so that she could announce the auction winners. It was a long and mostly boring list interspersed with polite applause. Sarah paid little attention until Nancy and Jayme whispered with excitement that the Sanibel Island winner was next up.

Joss held up a hand to display crossed fingers. "I hope you guys get it."

"And the winner of the Sanibel Island retreat for a week is…" The announcer tried to draw out the suspense, which earned a sigh from Nancy loud enough to be heard across the room. "Dr. Joss McNab!"

The women sat stunned, even as Joss's face began to cloud with embarrassment. Within seconds Nancy and Jayme began shooting accusatory looks at her, as though she had stolen something from them.

"What?" Joss blurted. "I had nothing to do with this. There was either some mistake or—" Her eyes cut across the room and settled on her mother, who was sporting a broad smile. "I think I know the culprit behind this, and I promise I'll get to the bottom of it."

She started to rise, but Nancy held her back. "She means well, Joss. Probably just wants you to take a much-needed vacation. Come on. When's the last time you've been away?"

"Chicago, remember?"

"No, no. I mean for a vacation, not a conference."

Joss's shoulders sagged in defeat. "I don't know. It's been a while."

"Good," Nancy said triumphantly. There was no longer any trace of disappointment in her voice. "Then you're going to Sanibel Island. And I know for a fact you already have that week blocked off, so it's perfect."

"You have a week blocked off?" asked Sarah, surprised to hear Joss had planned some time off work. Workaholics rarely did.

Nancy was quick to supply the answer. "She always arranges a week off before Christmas to recharge. Exams are done, and she works on the curriculum for the next semester. And most of our nonemergency surgeries are on hiatus that time of year."

"And what you didn't mention," Jayme said to her wife, "is that Joss then works on call right through the holidays."

"But what about you guys?" Joss asked. "You two should take this trip, since you wanted so badly to win it. Seriously. Take it."

Jayme shook her head in regret. "Thank you for that, sweetie, but we probably couldn't go anyway. My aunt in Lexington is in the hospital right now, and we're not sure she's going to make it. I think the idea of a week away was wishful thinking on Nancy's part."

"True," Nancy said. "Besides, I want to stick around for Roxi."

"I'm sorry," Joss said.

"Don't be," Jayme said. "In fact, nothing would make Nance and me happier than to have you take a week of sun and rest down there." She bumped shoulders with Joss. "You need it, sweetie."

Joss started to rise from her chair again. "I'm still going give my mother a whoopin'—yet again—and then I'm going to see what I can do about getting out of this trip."

"Or," Sarah said, lightly clamping her hand around Joss's arm, "you could accept your mother's gift. Maybe if you let her help you more often, she'd stop trying so hard." What seemed so apparent to Sarah was that Madeline wanted her daughter to have a life. Wanted her to take a break from the almost physically impossible standards her father had set for her.

Joss sighed in resignation and sat back down. "Y'all are ganging up on me, aren't you? All right, fine. I'll try your strategy, Sarah. If it doesn't work, I'm back to drawing up plans for her imminent demise."

Sarah grinned at Joss. "I'm not buying the big meanie act."

"Hmm. Guess I need work in that department. And since I'm a big softie in your eyes, why don't we get out of here so you can show me your studio?"

"You're not implying that we artists are softies, are you?"

There was a twinkle in Joss's eyes and an unmistakable huskiness in her voice as she replied, "Only in the places that matter."

Sarah's heart pumped wildly, as it often did upon a certain look or phrase from Joss. They could have all the binding and nonbinding agreements in the world—verbal, written, notarized—but her body reacted to Joss with a mind all its own. There was something primal, something chemical, in the way they reacted to one another, and Sarah didn't know how much longer she'd be able to resist what felt, with every fiber, inevitable.

"Have fun you two," Nancy and Jayme called out in unison.

* * *

A bright overhead light flooded Sarah's small, windowless basement studio on the edge of campus, momentarily blinding Joss. When she could see again, she noticed there was a radio-CD player on a shelf, a large easel and two smaller ones, a stool on wheels, a chair with a straight back and canvases—some blank, some painted—stacked against the walls. Tubes of paint were laid out on a tray, orderly and neat and ready to use. Brushes sat in a large coffee tin of Varsol, its odor faint. Nothing suggested Sarah had been working in here recently. The smells of paint and paint thinner were so faint as to be almost nonexistent.

"It's starker than I imagined," Joss said, "considering your genius with a brush."

Without smiling, Sarah said, "It's a place of work, that's why I keep it workmanlike."

"You haven't been here in a while."

Sarah shrugged, her cocktail dress and heels at odds with the austere character of the place. "I've been taking a little breather."

"Why?"

Sarah's face closed up, her lips pinching together in a hard line before she spoke. "I haven't been feeling very inspired lately, I guess."

Joss thought for a moment, then decided she would not let Sarah off the hook. Fireworks be damned. "Sometimes you have to rely on your knowledge, your technique, your work ethic, to push you through those times. I don't always feel inspired operating on peoples' hearts, you know. My patients don't like to wait around for the mood to strike me. You can do this, Sarah. It's what you do, who you are." Joss saw the tiny pulse in Sarah's throat throb harder with what she imagined was a rising temper.

"It's not the same thing as with you. Lives don't depend on my work."

"What if they did? Don't you think you have enough talent and skill to grind through those tough times and get the job done?"

"Joss, please don't."

"Don't what?" Joss took a step toward her. "Don't believe in you, even when you don't believe in yourself? Don't push you when you refuse to push yourself? Don't tell you how incredibly talented you are? Look what you did for me the other day. You told me what I needed to hear, even if I seemed ungrateful." She took another step, close enough now to see the tiny, heartbreaking pools of tears beginning to collect in Sarah's eyes. "What, exactly, do you not want me to do? Don't tell you that your dad's an asshole and to forget him and his petty, belittling criticism?"

The tears sloshed over, and Joss crushed Sarah against her. She held her tightly, stroked her back with the tips of her fingers, turned her nose into Sarah's hair and inhaled the floral scent there. The urge to hold Sarah like this for hours, days, overwhelmed her. "He doesn't matter, Sarah. Why can't you believe that? Why can't you believe you're good enough?"

"Oh, Joss." Sarah sniffled, and Joss could feel the wetness of her tears dampening her tuxedo shirt. "It's not that simple. I try, but I keep hearing his voice in my head. I keep believing his crap. When I was away, in school, I felt like I could do anything. But here…"

"I know. I don't always believe in myself either, as you now know." Joss's emotional outburst still embarrassed her. She hadn't meant to expose that place in herself to Sarah, but she had, and she couldn't take it back. Funny thing was, it had felt kind of good afterward. Like pressure had been released through a valve.

Joss slipped a palm under Sarah's chin and tilted her face up. The anguish in Sarah's eyes, in her trembling chin, brought a lump to her throat. "Come away with me," she whispered before she had time to think about what she was suggesting.

"What? Where?"

"To Sanibel Island in two weeks. Just…come with me."

"But, our agreement? Our…we…It might mean…"

Joss thumbed a tear from Sarah's cheek. "Yes. It might." And it probably would. They would go away together and if they were meant to make love, they would make love. All night long, if need be. On the beach, under the moonlight, in the pool, under the palm trees, in the cool satiny sheets of a bed that would already smell of sex and suntan lotion. The tingling flared between Joss's thighs, sizzled its way into her belly, her spine, and she knew with certainty she would not be able to keep her hands off Sarah. Her words came out in a rush. "If you can take a break from painting and I can take a break from surgery and teaching, we—we can take a little break from our agreement. We can have one week, Sarah. One week to be the people we want to be with each other. To give each other whatever we want to give, even if it doesn't fit the parameters of our agreement."

There was nothing, at this moment, that Joss wanted more than a week of having Sarah all to herself. Of waking up next to her and having the whole day and evening stretch out ahead of them like a blank canvas. And then, like paint that wasn't permanent, they'd be able to wipe it away afterward.

Sarah's eyes were wide, questioning, and then they were suddenly full of comprehension and quiet acquiescence. "Yes."

CHAPTER SEVENTEEN

Sarah noticed immediately the decline in Roxi. In a matter of days, the child had grown thinner, if that was possible, and her skin was flaccid, scaley, as if it might fall off at the slightest contact.

"Oh, Roxi, honey," Sarah said, enveloping her in a gentle hug but not wanting to alarm her. "How are you feeling today?"

With a brave face, Roxi said, "Okay."

"Are you sure you're up to this?"

The girl nodded, and Sarah began to set up the small folding easel she'd brought. *I'll talk to Joss and Nancy*, she resolved, *and beg them to find Roxi a new heart before it's too late*. But she knew begging would do no good. Joss and Nancy wanted Roxi to be well as much as Sarah did. It was simply out of their control, and that was the frustrating part. Sarah didn't know if she believed in God, but she believed in justice and felt sure that eventually, somehow, there was justice in this world for those who deserved it. And Roxi surely deserved a new heart.

"Have you been drawing some sunsets?" Sarah asked. "Because today we're going to paint one. Would you like that?"

"Sure," Roxi answered, pulling her sketchbook from the night table drawer and showing Sarah.

"That's wonderful," Sarah said. "Good job. I like the way you've got the sun sinking into the water. Now, how much do you know about primary and secondary colors?"

"Um, red, yellow and blue?"

"Yes, that's right. Those are the primary colors." Sarah clapped her hands together in excitement. "And if we mix combinations of those colors together, we get secondary colors like green, orange and purple. Watch, I'll show you."

From a large canvas bag, Sarah pulled out tubes of acrylic paints in the three primary colors. She placed blobs of each on a plastic palette that she could later wash, then took a brush and began mixing the colors, demonstrating how yellow and blue made green and how red and blue made purple and how red and yellow created orange. She then handed the brush to Roxi and let her experiment with different quantities of the paints to make different shades of the secondary colors.

While Roxi worked on manipulating colors, Sarah showed her a chart demonstrating warm colors (those along the red, orange, yellow spectrum, she explained) versus cold colors (the blues and purples). She could see the understanding take root in Roxi. Sarah remembered learning all about colors at that same age and how it made her begin to see things differently. Where she once saw things mostly for their shape, she suddenly began to notice their colors and all the intricate shades within. Learning about textures came after that, and from then on, Sarah's world had irrevocably changed.

By the time Joss dropped by to say hi, Roxi had begun painting a new sunset—not over water this time, but behind a mountain.

"That's awesome, Roxi," Joss enthused, peering closer. "Your colors are fantastic. Look at that, they look so real. This shade of tangerine you've created looks good enough to eat!"

Roxi beamed with pride. "I learned all about them today from Miss Sarah."

"I can see that. You've done a great job." Joss turned to Sarah. "And so have you."

Sarah's heart began to race at the hint of desire she saw in Joss's eyes and at the steadiness in her voice, which was like a deep but fast-moving river. Knowing that they were going away together in less than a week's time was only intensifying her physical reaction to Joss. It was as though every nerve ending was exposed now, waiting in a state of high anxiety for the consummation of their physical and emotional connection. Although Joss had made it clear it was only to be one week of satisfying their physical needs and nothing deeper. When the week was over, the agreement would be reinstated. *The damned thing was like one of Moses's precious stone tablets*, thought Sarah. At moments like these, she wanted to throw the stupid thing out the window and start over. With no rules and definitely no damned celibacy clause.

"Can we talk for a minute?" Joss whispered.

When Sarah joined her out in the hallway, she looked every bit the doctor in full control, ramrod straight and perfectly still—except for her eyes, which were jumpy.

"Are you all right?" Sarah asked, immediately worried. Was Joss about to cancel their trip? *So help me, Joss McNab, if you've gotten cold feet I'm going to drag you into the nearest empty room and have my way with you. I can't last much longer, dammit. Not in this state of heightened arousal.*

"Yes, I'm fine. I wanted to check and see if you're all right."

Relief swamped Sarah. "You mean about Sanibel Island?"

Joss nodded, tension in her jaw.

Sarah drew out her smile, and it was like the air slowly leaving a tire. "I can't wait."

"Good. Me either." Joss relaxed into a smile of her own.

"But I'm worried about Roxi. She can't last much longer, can she?"

Joss's face tightened. "No. If it goes past Christmas, it's going to be tough. But Nance has pulled out all the stops. There's nothing more we can do now."

"We can hope," Sarah said quietly.

"Yes. There is always that. Come here."

Joss wrapped Sarah in a hug. It was warm, tender, reassuring—everything that was Joss when she let all her barriers down. Sarah could have stayed there forever.

* * *

Madeline's arrival at the cardiac wing of the medical school was announced in the usual way—a quiet rustling that grew into a dull roar within minutes. She knew all the staff, most of whom dated back to Joseph McNab's days at the school, and the newer staff had become acquainted with her via various functions or visits. She moved through the building like a yacht creating a massive wake, her energy and notoriety swamping everything smaller in its path.

"Ah, there you are, my darling daughter," Madeline said, standing at the open door to Joss's office. "Not working too hard, I hope."

Joss closed her laptop to put it to sleep. It was exam time, which meant the school was pretty much empty of students.

"Nope, just goofing around with curriculum. I get a reprieve for a few weeks now." It wasn't her job to grade exams, thankfully.

"I'm glad to hear that. Do you have time for lunch?"

"Is this a peace offering for your dirty little manipulations at the foundation auction last week?"

"Maybe." Madeline didn't look sorry at all.

Joss gathered her coat and briefcase. "In that case, I'd be happy to accompany you to the deli around the corner. As long as you're buying, of course."

"I wouldn't dream of you paying," Madeline said, raising one finely shaped eyebrow.

The place smelled of fresh brewed coffee, baked bread, sautéing onions and hot beef. Joss ordered the corned beef sandwich—the place was renowned for its mounds of corned beef and cabbage—while Madeline ordered minestrone soup and a slice of homemade bread. They both ordered a cup of coffee.

"And yes," Joss said, "before you ask, I'm still angry as a snake at you for bidding on that trip in my name."

"Hmm. Still not going to admit I did you a favor?"

"That's not the point. You shouldn't have gone behind my back."

"You're right, I probably shouldn't have."

Madeline's tiny smirk did not look contrite at all, and Joss gave her a castigating look until she amended her apology.

"All right, I shouldn't have done it behind your back, but it was the only way I could get you two to stop this…this arrangement you've got and, and to…"

"And to what?" Joss was pretty sure her mother was never going to say "have sex." But it might be fun if she did.

Her face as red and shiny as a ripe apple, Madeline sputtered again, then set her coffee mug down with a clank. "You and Sarah need time away together. To explore what might be there, outside of this business arrangement you have together."

"That so-called business arrangement, I might remind you, was your idea, Mama."

"Yes, and a fine one it was. But…"

The waitress appeared with their tray of food, and Joss's mouth began to water at the thick sandwich—rye bread crammed with corned beef and cooked cabbage.

"I'll admit," Joss said around a mouthful of her sandwich, "you did good setting me and Sarah up in our little business arrangement. But as for something more, it's not going to happen."

Madeline shot her a look that could have stripped wallpaper. "I beg to differ."

"Why?" Joss's patience gave way to irritation. It was none of her mother's business whether she and Sarah—or she and any woman for that matter—developed a romantic relationship.

"Because I see what she does to you." Madeline averted her eyes and took a bird-like sip of her soup. "She makes you happy. Don't deny it. And don't you dare deny the chemistry between the two of you. I saw it myself the other night. I saw the way you looked at one another. Like you wished everybody else would disappear."

No, Joss couldn't deny it. Sarah did make her happy. Even when they were disagreeing about something, she wanted nothing more than to make things right with her. And yes, there was chemistry, and it was so much more than just the physical variety. Sarah made her think about why she was alone, about why she poured so much into her career, about why she was afraid to share her deepest thoughts and feelings with someone else. Sarah made her think more clearly and honestly about her father and about her parents' marriage and about her own future than she ever had before. It was unpleasant at times, all that thinking and analyzing. Yet it felt like they were slowly working their way to something good, something honest and sustainable. Something that mattered. Something they could build upon. It was her instinct to fight it, but something told her she'd one day be on the losing end.

"So what?" Joss replied, raising her chin. She wasn't about to raise the white flag yet.

"So, I want you to be happy, darling. That's all I've wanted for you."

Happy like you were with Daddy? Joss wouldn't say it, because she was afraid her sarcasm would bleed into her tone and put her mother on the defensive. But she really did want to know if her parents had been happy together. Or at least, if her mother had been happy. Until recently she'd assumed their marriage, while not perfect, had been satisfactory. But thanks to Sarah, Joss was beginning to learn what a relationship might look like. And it sure didn't look like one partner sacrificing everything for the other. A relationship took work, compromise, patience, time, selflessness by both parties. All the things for which Joss had little natural aptitude or inclination, and neither, she assumed, had her father. Social mores of the time dictated that a man of his stature needed an attentive wife, but did he truly enjoy being part of a couple? Did he ever feel like one half of a whole? Did he ever truly respect his wife?

Swallowing her curiosity, she ate in silence for a few moments, digesting her mother's motives for interfering before processing her much more complicated feelings for Sarah. While Sarah had gotten closer to her heart than any woman ever had, that didn't mean there was room for her there. Not right now. And maybe not ever. She'd worked far too hard at her career to start slacking off now, and really, in the world of heart surgery, she was still just beginning to make a name for herself. She aspired to be one of the country's leading heart valve surgeons, but she was not quite yet in that exalted echelon. There was still a lot of work ahead of her, and if she were honest, a relationship would only drag her down. *I won't do it to myself and I won't do it to Sarah.*

"Mama, I know you want me to be happy. And I am happy. My work makes me happy."

"I know it does, dear. But is it enough?"

Ah, the million-dollar question. It had always been enough before, Joss thought. But now? She didn't want to begin to question the state of her happiness—or unhappiness. Sarah had rocked her world enough as it was. She wasn't about to completely throw it all in the trash bin.

"Look," Joss said, using her hand to mop up the crumbs she'd spilled on the Formica tabletop. "Sarah and I will take that little trip to Sanibel Island, but only because we both need a vacation. After that…"

Madeline's eyes twinkled. "After that, what?"

"After that, nothing." Joss rose, glancing at her watch. "Thank you for lunch, Mama, but I need to go."

"I expect a postcard next week."

Joss laughed. "Go ahead and keep expecting."

"Hopefully," Madeline said with a smile in her voice, "you'll be a little too busy for writing postcards."

The shock of her mother's words nearly made Joss drop her jacket on the floor. "You're not suggesting premarital sex, are you?" she teased.

Madeline laughed into the back of her hand. "I'll leave that decision up to you, my dear. Just be safe about it."

"Wow. I never thought the day would come when my own mother would encourage me to go out and have sex."

"Hush now, you don't have to advertise it, you know."

"Hell, I'm going to take out a full-page ad in *The Tennessean*."

CHAPTER EIGHTEEN

Sarah's attention wandered throughout the flight to Fort Myers. She'd spent five minutes on the same page of Helen Humphreys' new novel, and she was envious of Joss's remarkable concentration. You could set a clock to the regularity with which she turned pages of *The New England Journal of Medicine* in her lap, her brow furrowed in concentration as she read. Clearly, Joss was not nearly as anxious about the trip as Sarah.

Sarah's heart leapt to her throat every time she thought about what might happen between them tonight. Or if not tonight, then one of the six nights they'd be spending in the cozy, two-bedroom, beachside cottage. She was ready to give in to the fathomless physical need to be close to Joss—to touch her, taste her, kiss her. To be touched and tasted and kissed by her. To be held in her arms. To be swallowed whole by those green eyes that looked at her with a desire that seemed greater each time they were together. Sarah felt the connection between them growing in her body too. An innocent touch by Joss was now enough to ignite a spark that could nearly destroy her. She couldn't imagine how a romantic, sexually charged touch might unravel her.

By the time their hired car pulled into the driveway of crushed seashells outside the white clapboard cottage, Sarah began to doubt all her preconceived conclusions about the trip. What if she'd gotten the signals all mixed up? What if Joss simply wanted some innocent companionship? Or worse, what if she dove into that thick briefcase of work she'd brought with her and hardly bothered with her at all? Sarah had brought only a sketchbook and a couple of novels to read. Would she have to amuse herself most of the week? Do her own thing and only be at Joss's beck and call when she felt like a distraction? That would mean their trip was merely an extension of their little arrangement back home, and that was not at all what Sarah had in mind when she'd agreed to come here.

The truth was, she was growing weary of their arrangement and all its constrictions. It'd been fun at the start and provided her a much-needed financial boost. They'd pulled the whole stunt off remarkably well, she thought, and they'd grown to be good friends in the process. But she liked Joss as more than simply a friend. She was attracted to her. So attracted that she was nearly ready to throw herself naked in front of her. But the attraction was not limited to physical. She wanted, needed, to cross the boundaries and explore the forbidden emotional territory between them. She ached to find out if her gut instinct was right—that there was a very special bond between them, that they'd begun to need one another. Whenever she looked inside her heart these days, there was Joss, staking out a bigger and bigger claim. With a little more time together, she could, she realized, very easily fall in love with her.

"It's cute," Joss announced as they set their suitcases inside the small foyer. "I like it. Small but cozy."

How cozy did you have in mind? Sarah was dying to ask, but she feared the answer.

The floors were ceramic tile, the walls a pale moss green. The kitchen was small but updated and functional—a full fridge, gas stove, double sinks, granite counter. It opened to a small eating area with a table for four and, beyond that, a living area with massive floor-to-ceiling windows that offered an unobstructed view to the beach. A small gas fireplace was nestled into the wall.

"I'm going to check out the bedrooms."

Sarah hoped Joss wouldn't follow, but she did. The first bedroom—the master—was large and bright. There was a skylight above the king bed, and sliding glass doors that appeared to lead to a private patio and the swimming pool. An en suite bathroom contained a two-person shower and soaker tub, double sinks.

"You take this room," Sarah said, assuming Joss should have it, since her bid had won the trip. She bit her bottom lip, wishing Joss would suggest they share it, but at the same time, praying she didn't.

"Not a chance," Joss said. "You take it. I'll take the other."

The second bedroom was smaller and much less bright, with room only for a double bed and a small dresser. Joss threw one of her suitcases on the bed by way of claiming the room. They were (God, please!) going to make love on this trip. Joss had pretty much promised (hadn't she?), and now Sarah found herself wondering when and in which bed. This one or the larger one? The thought sent a streak of excitement through her, and for a split second, she considered suggesting they just get it over with now so that it wasn't sweet torture hanging over them. Maybe, she thought wickedly, she should strip off her clothes and throw herself on the bed. See if Joss could resist *that*! But as tempting as the idea sounded, she knew she'd never be so bold.

Back in the kitchen, Joss discovered a bottle of expensive champagne and a cheese plate in the refrigerator along with a welcome note.

"Shall we toast ourselves?" Joss asked, removing the foil from the bottle.

Sarah laughed, glad to have the champagne as a distraction from thoughts of sex. "It's well past noon. We're safe." *Except I don't want to be safe with you. I want us to drink that bottle and then I want you to ravage me.*

Standing in the small kitchen, they clinked glasses and sipped the champagne. Joss had set the cheese plate on the breakfast bar, and she snatched a piece of Swiss.

"The apple cinnamon cheese looks delicious. Aren't you going to try something?" Joss asked between bites.

Sarah shook her head, not trusting her voice. She couldn't stand being this close to Joss while talking about something as mundane as food. She was deeply curious about Joss's thoughts, about whether they were on the same page or not. And about what came next. This was worse than high school, worse than a first date, and the anticipation and confusion were driving her nuts. She'd thought she knew what Joss wanted, but now? Now she had no clue.

Joss set her glass down and stepped toward Sarah. "Are you okay, Sarah?"

Sarah nodded, setting her own glass down. She tried to play it cool, to let Joss make the first move. Or any move. Joss had invited her here, Joss had always set the rules, dictated the pace and nature of their relationship. *No*, Sarah thought, *I won't make the first move.*

"You don't really look okay," Joss said, stepping closer, putting her hands lightly on Sarah's shoulders. "Tell me what's going on."

Sarah stared at Joss's mouth, her lips, wanting to reach up and touch them with the tip of her finger, now that they were so close. She breathed in Joss's scent, tried to decipher the jumble of emotions in Joss's eyes, and couldn't speak for a long moment. Roughly, she said, "I don't know what you want."

"What do *you* want, Sarah?"

Sarah drew a nervous breath. Someone had to do something, dammit. "I want to kiss you. And then I want you to make love to me." Like we'd agreed, Sarah wanted to say. *Or kind of agreed. Unless I got it all wrong.*

"Oh, Sarah." Joss pressed her to her, held her tightly, buried her face in her hair, her neck. Sarah could feel her inhale deeply and felt the heat of her hands on her back.

Worried suddenly, Sarah said, "Don't you want to?"

Joss began to kiss her—slowly, tenderly, carefully, as though she were afraid to turn up the heat too much. The tingling began at the base of Sarah's spine and spread to the pit of her belly, a pleasure-pain that only Joss could create. And relieve.

"Yes," Joss muttered around the kiss. "I do want to. So much."

Sarah pressed herself harder against Joss, licked the sweet champagne from her lips and kissed her again. "Why do I detect a *but* in there?"

Joss pulled back to look at Sarah, and Sarah was pleased to see the high color in Joss's cheeks, as if she'd stepped in from the cold. "I need to go slower, that's all. I need a little time."

Abruptly, she moved away. She was all business suddenly, picking up the champagne flutes and handing Sarah hers. "I read about a great seafood place we can walk to from here. And I'm starving. How about it?"

Sarah raised an accusatory eyebrow at Joss. "Nice change in subject."

Joss paused, then broke into a slow grin. "Did it work?"

"Maybe. But when we get back, I want us to take a stroll on the beach." It was not a very original tactic, but she hoped a moonlit walk might move things back in the right direction.

* * *

Moments ago, Joss had been starving, but now that the huge plate of shrimp pasta was in front of her, her stomach seemed to shrink. She couldn't help thinking about what Sarah had in mind later. Sure, the walk on the beach sounded innocent enough and like something she could handle. But what about after that? When it was dark and they were inside that little cottage together? Sarah had made it obvious what was on her mind. Hell, the same thoughts had been tantalizing her for days, the way a fire begins with a few sparks before gradually consuming every ounce of air in its path. And now that Sarah was seated in front of her, wearing a bright yellow sundress, Joss only wanted to slide the straps down her creamy shoulders and kiss the soft, faintly freckled skin there.

"You're awfully quiet," Sarah ventured, her eyebrow posing that little challenge again.

I can't stand much more, Joss thought a little desperately. Not moonlight, not more champagne and most certainly not another kiss. She was beginning to buckle under the pressure, but she was a coward, and she changed the subject to Roxi. She told Sarah how she'd made Nancy promise to text her if anything changed in the girl's condition.

Once dinner was behind them, there was no possibility of Joss evading the walk along the beach outside their cottage. The stretch of white sand was deserted, the soft lap of the rhythmic waves hypnotic in their tranquility. The hazy moon cast a soft glow, like light being filtered through muslin. Palm leaves waved languidly in the light breeze, and Joss turned her face into the warm caress of the humid, salty air. It'd been years since she'd enjoyed tropical weather in the winter.

"I love a beach at night," Sarah proclaimed, closing her eyes and inhaling deeply. "It's so peaceful. So soothing. So nourishing."

And romantic, Joss thought. Although she did not consider herself a romantic, she felt sure Sarah had wanted to use that word, because Sarah was most definitely a romantic. She probably liked flowers too and little love notes on her pillow and unexpected kisses in the middle of the day. *Jesus*, Joss thought with sudden alarm. *Why am I thinking of flowers and love notes and kisses?*

As they walked, they were so close their shoulders almost brushed. Holding hands would have made it perfect, but then, that would be romantic, Joss thought derisively. *And I don't do romance, especially not with a woman who could easily wrap me around that little finger of hers and make me lose myself. No. I cannot and will not lose myself in Sarah. Or in any woman.*

Sarah announced, "You're still being awfully quiet. Are you having second thoughts about…all this?"

"No," Joss lied. She was long past second thoughts and was onto third and fourth thoughts.

"You said earlier you need more time. I'd like to know what's on your mind, Joss. Because this…this distance you're putting between us is killing me. It's almost like we're strangers again."

They stopped and faced one another, their bare toes sinking into the soft, fine sand.

"I…" Words escaped Joss. There was no question she wanted to make love with Sarah. And there was no question that Sarah wanted her to. They both knew, going into this trip, that sex was pretty much a foregone conclusion. But Joss's feet had been growing steadily colder, and she was panicking a little. She'd never been this hesitant about making love to a woman. Had never had the question roll around in her mind like a spinning top that never came to rest.

Sarah reached out and ran a finger along Joss's forearm, and the touch nearly undid Joss. "Please," Sarah whispered. "Talk to me. Tell me what's worrying you."

Joss halted the traveling fingertips of Sarah's right hand. With her other hand, she brushed the fine strands of Sarah's hair from her face. God, she was so beautiful in this moment. The way the moonlight was golden on her hair, the way it shadowed her eyes but not her lips, which were full and naturally pink and *so* in need of kissing.

"You," Joss said in a voice thick with desire, "frighten the hell out of me."

Sarah stepped closer, her breasts faintly brushing against Joss's chest. "I don't mean to. Will you tell me why?"

Joss couldn't move. "If we make love," she finally said in a trembling voice, "I'm not sure I'll recognize myself anymore."

"You say that like it's a bad thing." Sarah's cheek nuzzled against Joss's palm. Her skin felt warm, flushed, and Joss's breath left her in a rush.

"It could be a very bad thing. For you. For me," Joss said.

"Let me worry about me." Sarah began kissing the palm of Joss's hand.

Her legs quivering, Joss fought the urge to run. So what if she was a coward. So what if she turned down this gorgeous woman who was offering herself up on a silver platter. So what if she added another layer to the concrete wall she had built around her heart. It was *her* heart, *her* life, and if she didn't want to fall in love, didn't want to give herself up to this woman, then so be it, dammit.

Sarah's lips were now at the corner of her mouth, planting soft little kisses that were not much stronger than the sultry breeze.

"Sarah," Joss whispered, dizzy suddenly. She closed her eyes and let her chest swell as Sarah kissed her full on. It was a slow, tender kiss that shook Joss to her toes. It was the kind of kiss that made you forget where you were, who you were, and that made you think you were borrowing trouble kissing a woman on a deserted moonlit beach like this, with a bed only a few dozen yards away.

Sarah's arms moved around her neck, stroking the back of her head as their mouths continued to explore and claim one another. Joss's hands had their own ideas and began to move, sliding lower and lower down Sarah's back until they brushed the soft fabric of the light sundress covering her backside. Her hands lingered, caressed, and finally cupped the solid mounds of flesh.

"Ohh," Sarah moaned against her mouth, pressing her body harder into Joss, rising onto her toes so that Joss's hands could travel lower.

One little flick of her wrist, Joss knew, and her hand would be under that dress and up that satiny thigh. Maybe even guided to the warm, moist apex between those thighs by Sarah's own impatient hand. Would her underwear be satin? Cotton? Lacy? *Oh God*, Joss thought. *I can't do this. I cannot do this without losing my mind. Without losing everything I am, everything I've built, everything I want in the future.* When she'd asked Sarah to join her on the trip, she wanted hot crazy sex with her. Ten times a day and another ten at night, truth be known. But now that they were here, she feared that sex would only be the beginning of things. Things that were too dangerous to contemplate.

She pulled away quickly, midkiss, and held Sarah by the arms to keep her at a distance. Breathless, still questioning what the hell she was doing *not* going down on her knees right now and pleasuring Sarah with her mouth, Joss said, "Sarah, if we make love…"

"What?" Sarah looked hurt, confused, her mouth turned down in anger. "What's the worst that could happen? We're both single, consenting adults. We both want each other."

"You don't understand."

"Then tell me."

Joss's mouth was impossibly dry and already regretting the loss of Sarah's moist lips and slick, skilled tongue. "I'm afraid… if we make love…that we won't be able to go back to the way things were before. And I need to. I need for us not to…not to…"

"Become a real couple?"

Joss nodded, the rest of her words caught up in her throat.

"You have my word." Sarah's voice had a chill to it, like a cool fog rolling in off the sea. "What happens here stays here, Joss. I promise you."

Except, Joss thought, *I don't know if I am capable of promising that. I don't know if I can make love to you and not want all of you. Forever.*

"There's one more thing." Sarah shrugged free of Joss's grip and took another step back. "I do plan to seduce you before the week is out, so consider yourself warned."

CHAPTER NINETEEN

A good night's sleep had a calming effect on Sarah. Maybe it was the rhythmic sound of the endless tiny lapping waves or the salty air breezing through the open window all night long. Whatever it was, by morning Sarah had come to some conclusions. The only possible conclusions, really. She didn't see how they could stay celibate all week. There was no question that the heat between them was going to explode into full-on, sweaty, blow-the-roof-off-the-house lovemaking. They were close, so close, to giving into their desires. Sarah had even briefly considered slipping into Joss's bed in the night, naked, to cut the final thread holding them back. But no, she had other ideas on how to push Joss closer to what they both wanted and needed.

Sarah understood that Joss was scared, that she needed her emotional space and that in fact she might never be able to overcome her insecurities about relationships if left to her own devices. No. It was time to push, time to make a decision for both of them. They would have sex because they needed to satiate the raging desire that both could barely contain anymore. But what happened on Sanibel Island would stay on Sanibel Island, exactly as she had promised Joss. There would be nothing more. Sarah was no fool. She knew Joss would never commit to her emotionally. This would strictly be a one-off, a brief interlude, a timeout. She wasn't a lawyer like her father, but perhaps they could call it a temporary amendment to their agreement. A codicil that would become null and void as soon as they left the island. There would be no pressure that way, no expectations, no disappointments, no one getting her hopes crushed and no one getting hurt. She could handle it, she decided, and she was pretty sure Joss could too if only she had the guts to try. It was the only way forward for them—sex with no strings.

Cycling halfway across the island ate up the morning. They stopped for a light lunch of chicken salad and sweet tea before heading back on the bike path that wended its way along the ocean. It was a warm clear day without a cloud in the sky. Perfect, Sarah thought, for an afternoon swim in the cottage's pool. And perfect for the bikini she'd brought with her—fire engine red and not much bigger than postage stamps in all the important places. It was not something she'd ever wear publicly, but for this? This was war, and it was time to bring out the big guns. The suit was lethal and something, she felt sure, that Joss would not be able to resist. She grinned to herself as they stashed the bicycles in the shed next to the house.

"What's so funny?" Joss asked. "You've been looking all morning like you're holding on to a state secret."

"No secret, but a surprise maybe."

Joss narrowed her eyes, but her grin matched Sarah's. "What've you got up your sleeve, young lady?"

Sarah laughed wickedly. "Trust me, there are no sleeves involved."

"Hmm, do I need to be scared?"

"Oh yes, you definitely need to be scared, but I promise it won't hurt." Sarah thought again of that tiny red bikini, how it left nothing to the imagination. She only hoped Joss would be anxious to rip it off her. On second thought, it wouldn't even need to come off since it almost wasn't even there. *Oh no*, Sarah thought, enjoying the tickle of anticipation that was beginning to control her body. A mouth or a hand could easily get around those little pieces of obstruction.

"Good, because I'm not really into pain. Care to share your plans?"

"A swim, that's all." *Yeah, right, an innocent little swim. With me as the shark.* "In the pool. I thought it might be a good way to cool off."

Joss shrugged, her eyes far too trusting and her smile way too innocent. She was unknowingly setting herself up to be the perfect prey. "Okay. Sounds good."

Poor little lamb about to be led to slaughter, Sarah thought wickedly. If Joss could in fact resist seduction that red hot and blatant, she was hopeless. Or turning straight. "I'll meet you out back in about ten minutes."

* * *

The pool was small, Joss noted, but pretty with its bordering garden of bamboo, aloe, hibiscus, jasmine, some wild grasses she didn't recognize and, of course, the ubiquitous palm trees. It was a veritable jungle offering maximum privacy, which appealed to her, since she didn't like parading around publicly in her one-piece bathing suit. Not that the suit was racy in any way. The opposite was true. It was light blue and its cut was practical, meaning that one could actually swim in it. In Joss's opinion, swimming was the only reason for wearing a bathing suit anyway. But it didn't mean she liked people seeing her wear one. She probably should have thrown on her swim trunks and a workout top, but it was too late now.

For shade, there was a cabana rigged out of bamboo poles and canvas, walled on three sides with its open side facing the pool. It was a pleasing little oasis, complete with the unseen, soft sounds of the surf a couple of dozen yards away. A narrow stone path led from the private yard to the beach. If they got tired of the pool and the confines of the small yard, Joss supposed, they could always drag their chairs down to the ocean.

She perched her sunglasses on her nose and spread her towel on one of the canvas chaise lounges in the cabana. Sitting down, she stretched her legs out in front of her and contemplated the paperback in her hand. She hadn't wanted to bring a novel, but Nancy had thrust Jodi Piccoult's *Sing You Home* in her hand and practically commanded her to leave her medical journals and texts behind. Advice which Joss had somewhat ignored. "I bet you don't even recall the last novel you read," Nancy had teased her, and Joss conceded the point. She didn't have time to read for pleasure and hadn't, really, since high school. She thumbed now to the first chapter, wishing the book was a little thinner. Or that her vacation was longer.

"Nice setup back here," Sarah announced as she entered the cabana. "It's beautiful."

Joss, engrossed in the third page by then, mumbled her agreement without looking up. A flash of bright red in her periphery demanded her attention, but it was another minute before she glanced at Sarah, who by now had stretched out beside her on the matching chaise lounge. "Oh. My. God."

Her book fell from her hand. Her sunglasses suddenly felt too small for her eyes. If her heart didn't start beating again— and soon—Sarah was going to need to do CPR on her, because she damned well might not survive the vision before her.

"I…uh…do you…um…" *Lord have mercy*! Her mouth would not work. With more effort, she finally rasped, "Do you have any idea…" Her mouth quit on her again.

Sarah smiled nonchalantly, her eyes dancing with a playful challenge. She was a kid putting her best toys on display, knowing full well her playmate wanted to touch them all. "What? See something you like?"

"Okay, this is so not fair."

"What? Oh, are you talking about my bikini, by chance?"

It was red. And skimpy. And made of some kind of material that was shiny and looked wet already. But it was everything else that thoroughly riveted Joss and left her a blithering, dopamine-addled fool. Sarah's skin was creamy and soft and perfect, her legs were strong and sculpted, she had a tummy that looked in need of caressing and her breasts were perfectly round and more than a handful and so inadequately covered by those tantalizing triangles of cloth that barely covered her hard nipples. Goddammit, her hands needed to be all over Sarah.

"Oh, no," Joss answered. "Not just your bikini. It's what your bikini is showing off to maximum advantage. That's what I call hitting below the belt."

Sarah held all the cards, and she laughed like she knew it. "I did warn you, remember?"

"Oh no, you didn't. I would have remembered if you'd warned me about that…that…thing you call a bikini. If that's what they're calling those little scraps of cloth these days." *Jesus, what must her ass look like in that thing? Probably like two naked orbs with the narrowest strip of cloth between them.* The thought made Joss's heart, which had mercifully started beating again, do a little stutter step. She might not, she realized, actually survive this trip.

"No, I didn't warn you about the bikini, but I did warn you I was going to try to seduce you."

"Hmph. We'll see about that." Joss didn't want Sarah thinking she was an easy target. No sir-ee. She picked her book up from the floor and opened it, pretending to read again. Christ, she'd never be able to get through a sentence, never mind a paragraph, with a near-naked Sarah beside her. And not just quietly sitting beside her, but with a promise to seduce her. *Well*, Joss thought, *I'm tough, I can handle this*.

"Good book," Sarah said. "I read it a couple of years ago. And since you have such amazing powers of concentration, I might as well leave you to it and take a dip."

She stood up, tossed her towel aside and stretched her arms above her head, languid as a cat in no hurry to move on. And not a whisper of shyness over displaying all her goods.

Holy mother of God, Joss thought with an inward whimper, sliding her sunglasses down her nose and sneaking a peek. Yup, that ass was perfect and needed her hands on it. She watched Sarah finally saunter to the pool, wiggling that backside to full effect. She slid in, sinking to her neck, then stood up in the shallow end, facing Joss. Rivulets of water rolled down her neck, her arms, and into the crevice between her breasts. *Oh God.* Joss's mouth watered. *If I keep looking…No, I can't keep looking, especially at those nipples perfectly outlined and standing at attention.* She told herself she was not struck by the way the wet ends of Sarah's hair, made a darker shade of red by the water, curled at the edges. Nor by the way the sunlight reflected from the water's surface illuminated her eyes. She tried to concentrate on her book again. Really tried. And failed miserably.

"The water's lovely. Care to join me?"

Tentatively, Joss stood. Carefully she set her book and towel down, wanting to give the impression she was in no hurry. She was fully aware of the old adage, if you can't beat 'em, join 'em. And, well, she *was* working up a sweat in this Florida heat. "You won't, like, do something silly if I come in there, will you?"

Sarah tilted her head. "Depends how you define silly."

Hmm, Joss thought. *Like jump on me? Like peel your top off and flash your breasts at me?* If Sarah did either of those things, Joss knew her resistance would go up in smoke. It pretty much had anyway. This was playing with fire, and yet she couldn't resist the desire to touch her fingers to the flame.

Joss slid into the water. It was warm, like bathwater. She tossed her sunglasses onto the pool deck, dipped her head under water, slowly paddled around. She kept her distance from Sarah, who was still in the shallow end, her back to the pool wall. She was watching Joss with the eyes of a shark sizing up its prey. *Oh fuck*, Joss thought, *there's no escape. She's going to want to kiss me and I won't be able to say no.*

It wasn't long before Sarah crooked her finger at Joss.

"What's the matter?" Joss replied. "Your water wings not working?"

Sarah grinned, kept motioning with that damned finger. "Why don't you come and see for yourself?"

Joss wanted so badly to remain rooted in place, to have the strength of ten women when it came to resisting Sarah. *But this…this is way more than a mortal human being should have to handle*, she thought with a new flutter in her chest. She inched her way to Sarah as though she were being pulled along on a rope. Of course she could say no, could leave the pool, go inside, go to the beach, hop on her bicycle and flee. But Sarah, in all her wet, near-naked loveliness, could no more be resisted than a warm fire on a frigid day. Joss knew she was at Sarah's mercy.

She stood in front of her, the water at her waist, and tried to play it cool in order to maintain some semblance of control. "You rang?" Inside she was a trembling, weakened mess. The trick, she decided hopefully, was to maintain eye contact. *Whatever you do, do* not *look down!*

"I did. There's something I need."

Joss swallowed. "What would that be?"

Sarah threw her arms around Joss's neck and pulled her closer. "This."

Instantly, they were kissing. Not gentle, not polite, not timid kissing. This was full-fledged, I-want-to-swallow-you-whole kissing. Sarah's mouth was hard and demanding against Joss's. Her tongue hurriedly demanded entry, and once inside, it teased and danced and plundered until a soft moan escaped Joss's mouth. Joss could think of little else but the fact that she was standing in a swimming pool, having the absolute hell kissed out of her by Sarah and wanting it never to end. How, she wondered, had she not spent every waking moment thinking and conspiring to kiss Sarah like this? How had she been satisfied these last number of weeks with the few kisses they'd shared? And how the *hell* was she going to be able to concentrate on anything else ever again? Plainly and simply, she'd become undone in about thirty seconds.

Sarah's hand dropped away from around her neck, reached for her hand, placed it on her waist and then, guiding it up past her stomach, her rib cage, settled it against the underside of her breast.

Joss moaned again, the soft yet firm heft of Sarah's breast now filling her hand. More than filling her hand. She cupped it, squeezed it as if it were something fragile, something to be worshipped. God, it felt good.

"Oh, yes," Sarah murmured, pulling her mouth away from Joss's and arching her neck to present her throat to Joss.

Joss slid her mouth to Sarah's neck, to her throat. She sucked and nibbled softly, eliciting a sharp intake of breath from Sarah, a moan of encouragement. She cupped both of Sarah's breasts in her hands now, marveled at the feel of them, and dared finally to look at them.

"God, Sarah, you're so beautiful." That chest that was rising and falling rapidly, that was swelling and pushing into her hands, abolished any further thoughts from Joss's mind. She squeezed harder, thumbed Sarah's rigid nipples until she felt Sarah tremble against her.

Urgently, Sarah whispered, "Joss, please."

Yes, Joss thought, bending and dipping her head to Sarah's chest. Her mouth locked onto a nipple, hard as a pebble, the cloth covering it wet against her teeth. She sucked it, flicked her tongue against it, felt Sarah push greedily into her mouth. A bolt of electricity shot through her and with it came a stark moment of clarity. She stopped, kept her thumbs caressing where her mouth had been, and looked at Sarah. Her eyes were half-lidded; she was already gone.

"Sarah," she whispered, unable to give voice to anything further. What she was thinking was how impossible, yet how right it felt to be on the cusp of making love to this woman. Her hands, her mouth, seemed already to know Sarah intimately. And yet, as much as her body wanted to share the highest form of pleasure there was with her, she couldn't help but wonder what it would cost her. Cost them. Could they really do this and then pretend next week that it had never happened? Could she possibly give only her body to Sarah? It was her last thought before her mind went completely blank, so absorbed was she in Sarah's body and with all she wanted to do to it.

"Wait." She tried one last time, but her heart wasn't in it.

"No," Sarah said in voice that left no room for compromise.

Decisively, she took Joss's hand, removed it from her breast and slid it down to the small triangle of cloth between her legs. Joss's knees buckled.

CHAPTER TWENTY

As Joss's fingers lightly traced the cleft between her legs, then skittered in random, frenzied patterns, Sarah grew so dizzy with desire that she lost track of space and time. The weight of her body became light and liquid, like the pool water that eddied about her thighs. Her legs seemed no longer able to function.

Even as she pressed Joss's hand harder against her crotch, Sarah said, "I…can't…do this…here. Oh God, Joss." She bit her bottom lip to keep from screaming out.

"The cabana," Joss whispered urgently, every bit as breathless as Sarah.

"Yes." Sarah let Joss precede her out of the pool, then help her up and onto the pool deck, before tugging her the short distance to the cabana.

The reticence that had seemingly paralyzed Joss mere seconds ago had vanished. With hurried efficiency, she spread their towels onto the canvas floor, pulled Sarah down and wasted no time in moving on top of her. She kissed her with surprising fervor, insinuating a rock-hard thigh between her legs. *Please*, Sarah thought, *do not stop, do not pull away from me with talk of agreements and rules and cautions against becoming too emotionally entangled.* Right now all Sarah wanted—needed—was to come. For Joss to make her come in the most exquisite, most wrecked way possible. *Yes*, she thought, *wreck me, destroy me, ruin me for anybody else, I don't care, just take me.* She could think of nothing but sweet release. Blood pulsed wildly through her veins as Joss's lips left hers and began exploring her throat, trailing down to her chest, her breasts. Sarah wanted no barriers between them. Frantically she pulled the fabric of her bikini top over her head. When Joss's mouth found first one nipple, then the other, Sarah pushed her entire body more intensely into her, wanting friction, wanting the persistent throbbing between her legs answered.

"Oh, Joss, I want you so badly," she squeezed out between heaving intakes of breath.

That mouth, Sarah realized, was talented beyond expectation. Joss's tongue on her nipples was driving her wild, driving her nearly to orgasm. But she didn't want to be cheated of…other things, she thought desperately, pushing herself against Joss's hand, which continued to cup her, to stroke her lightly.

She was going to come fast, hard, and found herself hoping this wouldn't be their only time. If it was, she thought dismally, it would never be enough, because she needed, wanted, to experience everything Joss had in her lovemaking arsenal. Joss's hand had found her beneath the wet cloth of her bikini bottoms, and she shuddered pleasurably at the touch. The friction was good. *So good!* But as her orgasm began to rush toward her, Sarah needed Joss inside her. She told her as much—ordered her, more like—and arched into Joss as two fingers slipped inside. The pace of Joss's thrusts was fast, deep, as the waves of pleasure ripped right through her core and took her higher and higher until she felt as though she were floating above them. She rode it until they began to crest and coalesce into one spectacular wave that crashed over her, consuming her with a power she had rarely felt before. She cried out, bucked hard against Joss. The intense pleasure finally released her, leaving her quivering, blinking, clinging tightly to Joss.

Joss continued to softly kiss her breasts, the touch of her lips so tenderly contrary to the violence with which Sarah had just come.

"That," Sarah said, still breathless, "was amazing."

"No," Joss replied, trailing tiny kisses back up Sarah's throat. "That was only an appetizer."

Sarah smiled, not sure how much pleasure she could take all at once, but more than willing to give it a try. "You have more in your bag of tricks?"

"Way more. I'm just getting started."

"Ohh, I do like the sound of that."

Joss moved against her, sliding her body back and forth over her. She was solid and strong without being overpowering. Sarah moved with her, effortlessly matching her rhythm.

Joss nuzzled her neck, her breath warm puffs against her skin. "This feels so good. Like this. With you. The way I always knew it would. But there's one thing."

Sarah raised questioning eyebrows at her lover. *Yes*, she thought with a small gasp of wonder. *Joss is my lover. For now.*

"These." Joss fingered her bikini bottoms. "Need to go. I need to feel all of you."

Her hand was like silk as it slid her bottoms down her thighs and off. The motion, slick, patient, sensual, left Sarah's breath trapped in her throat. Much as her desire swelled and propelled her to wanting more and wanting it now, she would let Joss do with her as she wished, even if it was a slow, unyielding torture of the sweetest kind.

Joss caressed Sarah's inner thighs, drawing lazy circles on her skin before she slid lower and kissed Sarah's belly. Hard and wet, Sarah had to command herself to wait, to enjoy, to see what pleasures Joss brought next. The anticipation left her quivering and breathless, but she casually ruffled the soft hair at the back of Joss's head. Its texture was silky, light, like golden wheat blowing in a summer breeze, and she sifted it through her fingers.

Lower and lower Joss slid down her body, and although Sarah knew what was coming next, she squeezed her eyes shut at the first exquisite contact of Joss's mouth on her. She let herself be carried on the tide of pleasure it brought, growing wetter and harder yet as Joss's tongue began stroking her slow, then fast, soft, then hard and harder still. A light show exploded behind her eyelids, and her moaning sounded almost as though it were coming from someone else. She was apart from her body and yet every nerve ending was on fire and intensely attuned to each one of Joss's magnificent touches.

"Oh, Joss," she murmured, thrashing her head back and forth. "Your mouth…"

Joss's tongue circled her clit, stroked it. Her lips sucked it lightly. A finger slipped inside her, its thrusts matching perfectly the strokes she'd begun again with her tongue. Sarah was a goner. She rose off the towel, almost levitating, pushing herself harder and faster into Joss's eager mouth, as the first strands of another orgasm swept up her legs and shattered her into about a thousand pieces of throbbing ecstasy. She felt herself gushing into Joss's mouth, felt Joss thirstily swallow every last drop. *Yes*, she concluded after a moment, and not unhappily, *I'm ruined forever.*

* * *

Joss held Sarah firmly in her arms as her orgasm spent itself in tiny, full-bodied spasms. Sarah was so beautiful when she came. So beautiful naked. So beautiful in each raucous and delicate way she responded to Joss's touch. Bringing this woman such joy, such physical pleasure, warmed Joss from the inside out. She could almost come herself simply by pleasuring Sarah. Except, well, she wanted to come from Sarah touching her, from Sarah doing the same things she'd done to her.

Remembering each response her tongue, her fingers had elicited from Sarah, she was at first unaware of Sarah sliding her bathing suit down her shoulders.

"Not fair," Sarah said huskily, "that I'm naked and you're not."

Joss laughed, placed her hands over Sarah's and helped her ease off the one-piece bathing suit. She watched Sarah's eyes, the way they lit up, as she took in all of Joss, then she lightly caressed her shoulders.

"You're strong," Sarah said, a hint of awe in her voice. "Muscular."

She let Sarah ease her onto her back. "My morning swims."

"Mmm," Sarah moaned. "I'd like you to skip the swimming part this week and use your muscles for...other things."

"Well, they do say you should mix up your workout routine."

Sarah rolled on top of her. Her eyes were busy scanning every inch of Joss. And apparently liking what they saw. "Good, because I can help you with that."

"I'll bet you can."

Joss's breath left her in a rush as Sarah's breasts brushed firmly against her own. God, they were full, so soft and so fucking sensual. *Oh, baby, I need you,* Joss thought, unsure if she'd given voice to her words. Sarah began grinding into her, firmly, rhythmically, murmuring against her throat, kissing her collarbone, her chest, nipping at her breasts, sucking her nipples. She wanted to soar with this woman, reach new heights of pleasure together for...*God, I don't know, the rest of my life maybe.* She was high with desire, so high, that she didn't want to analyze that last thought. It was the sex, the thrill and anticipation of orgasm that was making her needy and sentimental and a bit crazy. *Yes, that's it.*

She could have stayed this way forever, enjoying each new sensation pulsing through her. But Sarah had moved down, and now her mouth had found her sensitive, wet flesh. Sarah kissed and suckled Joss, licked her in long languid strokes that took her higher and higher. *Oh, God, I can't hold on.* She wanted to come this way, with Sarah's mouth on her. It was exactly what she had dreamed about, fantasized about, for weeks now. And yet it was so much better too. She whispered Sarah's name over and over. Her body tightened, to the point where she thought it might snap, and then she was quaking uncontrollably. Her body turned to liquid as her orgasm tore through her, possessed her with a violence she was unfamiliar with, and then slowly released her.

She moaned softly, momentarily sleepy and sated and spent, but also ridiculously happy. Making love with Sarah was everything and nothing like she'd imagined. "Jesus, that was spectacular, Sarah."

She kept her eyes closed, even as Sarah settled into the crook of her arm and rested her cheek against her chest. She couldn't look at her this minute, afraid of the weakness, the need, her eyes might reveal.

"I suppose," Sarah said after a quiet moment, "we should find somewhere more comfortable before we fall asleep."

"Hmm, yes, a bed would be nice." Joss rolled over until she was facing Sarah. "But not until I have shower sex with you."

Sarah laughed, her voice sweet and soporific. "Yes. Shower and a bed. Although, we have to get ourselves there first."

Joss pushed herself onto her elbows, then, with effort, to her knees. She felt boneless, but her desire for Sarah was far from exhausted. She helped Sarah up. "Come on. You can lean on me."

"Good. But I might need you to carry me."

CHAPTER TWENTY-ONE

The smell of coffee stirred Sarah from her slumber. She sat up in bed as Joss carried in two steaming cups and handed one to her.

"You know exactly the way to my heart," Sarah groaned, taking a gulp and nearly burning her tongue. She was limp with exhaustion. Every one of her muscles screamed at her, but not out of pain. Or if it was, it was the good kind of pain, the kind that said you'd used your muscles for a rewarding purpose. And oh, she had! They'd made love as the sun set outside, paused long enough to raid the fridge of what was left of the cheese and fruit plates that were part of yesterday's welcome gift, then retreated once again to bed for another round of magnificent sex that went late into the night. If she closed her eyes, she could still feel Joss's fingers on her flesh and the moist imprints of her lips from their insistent explorations.

Joss, in an oversized T-shirt and nothing else, climbed into bed beside Sarah, her mug held securely in her hands. "Are you as tired as I am this morning?"

"If it wasn't for that damned sunlight peeking through the blinds, I'd try to convince myself it's still night."

"The only thing that's telling me it's daytime is my stomach. We're going to have to get some food in today. Or go out."

Sarah slumped back against the headboard. "Mmm, I don't want to leave this bed."

Joss leaned over and kissed her. "Me either, but we have to keep our strength up."

"Good point." Sarah sipped her coffee and thought about the bulging briefcase of work Joss had brought on the trip. A lot of it, Joss had told her, had to do with curriculum for next semester at the medical school. It was highly unlikely, especially now, that much of it would get done. "About the plans you had for this to be a working vacation…"

"Ha, work? Christ, I can't keep my hands off you." Joss ran a finger down Sarah's naked thigh. "But since you're so disciplined, what about that thick sketchbook you brought? You going to do some sketching?"

"I only brought it out of habit. I haven't felt much like sketching lately. Or painting." It'd been weeks since she'd done any real work, not counting her classes and tutoring Roxi.

"I know. But you'll get it back."

Sarah wasn't so sure. Roxi had renewed her spirits a little, but not enough for the amount of work and focus she needed to put into her art if she were to have any chance of making a living at it. Her discipline, her joy for painting, had lost its luster. It was probably something like what writers called writers block, she supposed. It was all new to her, this inertia, and she didn't have the first clue how to get out of it. "Have you heard anything about Roxi?"

"No, but I'll text Nancy right now if you'd like."

"Okay, but don't take too long."

"Oh yeah? Got plans for me?"

Sarah leaned into Joss, kissed her firmly on the mouth, then, with her tongue, traced the outline of her lips. "Does that answer your question?"

"Yup." Joss retrieved her phone from her nightstand and quickly typed a few words. Within a minute, an incoming text chimed. "Nope, nothing new with Roxi." Another chime. Joss grinned.

"What?"

"Nancy. She's being a smartass. She says she figured I was busy working on my new medicine specialty with you this week."

"What's that supposed to mean?"

A wider grin from Joss. "That you're helping me with my gynecology skills." Joss typed a few characters. "I told her I'm learning plenty."

"Actually," Sarah said, rapidly growing wet as visions of Joss making love to her began to overload her circuits. "I think Nancy raises a very good point."

"You do, do you?" Joss set her phone down, rolled on top of Sarah and pinned her arms above her head. "I think it's a very good point too, and the practical exam is about to start."

"Ooh, I love the idea of you playing doctor with me."

Joss licked a trail down Sarah's throat, down to the valley between her breasts. Her thigh began pulsing long, slow strokes against her center. "Since I have you in this weakened state, there is one more thing."

"Oh, God, I'll do anything at this point as long as you don't stop."

Joss stilled herself and looked into Sarah's eyes. "I want you to sketch me. This afternoon. On the beach."

A lump settled in her throat. "Why?"

"Because I want to see you work. I want to see what you'd do with a portrait of me."

Sarah's palms began to itch. She didn't want to sketch anybody, didn't want to do any work this week at all, and if she did, it would be a crap job. "I don't really do portraits."

"Please? For me? I'll pay you."

Joss looked so earnest, so serious about it. She'd done so much for Sarah these last couple of months, it wouldn't be right to say no. Besides, a sketch was nowhere near as demanding as a painting. "All right, but as long as you don't expect much. And you insult me by offering me money."

"All right, thank you. I was thinking I could give it to my mother for Christmas. She'll be thrilled. And besides, if it's not great, I'll blame your subject."

Sarah grinned and kissed the tip of her nose. "If you don't soon get busy with me, it's going to *be* Christmas."

Joss laughed. "Your wish is always my command." She dipped her head and delicately took a nipple into her mouth, tracing its contours with her tongue, sucking lightly.

Sarah arched at the tendrils of pleasure that were soon vining their way around her body.

* * *

They managed to make it out of the cottage for a deli lunch and loaded the baskets on their bicycles with bread, milk, cheese, tomatoes, eggs, bacon, sausage and salad fixings. Their restocking was followed by a dip in the ocean—the plan being that they'd have to behave on a public beach versus their backyard pool—then an hour or so of Joss pretending to read while she studied Sarah through her sunglasses beneath a palm tree.

Sarah was a classic beauty. A straight, strong but feminine nose, a firm jawline, dimples that made her look youthful and slightly mischievous so that, while smiling, she seemed secretly to be planning something naughty. Her eyes were sky blue when she was happy, but deep and cold like the north Atlantic when she was upset or intense about something. Her smile was warm, intelligent, curious. And that hair, streaked to new hues of gold and red from their time in the sun, was a thick, wavy mane that made you want to run your hands through it.

When it came to her own looks, Joss knew there was no comparison with Sarah's. All her life she had been told that she was "handsome," something she'd come to appreciate. But Sarah—she was the kind of woman who turned heads when she walked into a room. People wanted to know who she was.

Wanted to *know* her, as if they couldn't wait to see if there was the payoff of a personality beneath all that beauty (there was). What was extraordinary was how Sarah paid so little mind to the endless compliments, to the outright salivating (mostly by men, but by plenty of women too) in her direction. She was a woman with far more substance, far more layers beneath the looks. She could make a miserable old man like Jack Pritchard downright jolly. She could entice the most hard-core introvert into talking. Alternately, she could also make the most self-absorbed, pretentious idiot shut up long enough to sit back and listen to her talk. Sarah was a woman with many gifts. Gifts Joss did not come close to possessing herself.

"You're looking very intense," Sarah said. "Enjoying that book?"

"Enjoying the view, more like."

"Speaking of views, are you ready for our portrait session? If you were serious about it, that is."

"I'm deadly serious about it. And yes, I'm ready."

While Joss did need a Christmas present for her mother, she had asked for the portrait because she wanted to do something, anything, to get Sarah working again. It was the only thing she could think of that wasn't begging or nagging or bribing.

Moments later, Joss had thrown on a button-down shirt over her bathing suit, finger combed her hair, then watched as Sarah placed her sketchbook in her lap and arranged her pencils and charcoal on a towel beside her.

"Should I look out over the water?"

"No. I want you looking at me."

"That won't be hard to do. Should I smile? Or should I look serious?" Joss had never sat for a portrait before and hadn't any idea how she was supposed to act. It was nearly as intimidating as performing one of her first surgeries, being watched and appraised by her superiors.

"You don't have to do anything. Just be natural, be yourself."

That was easy to do in Sarah's presence. Easier, she was finding more and more, than in anyone else's presence, which included her mother and her longtime friend Nancy. With

Sarah, she didn't need the walls to be so high anymore. The ease with which she'd cried on Sarah's shoulder about losing her patient a couple of weeks ago had shocked her. And yet she'd not been able to help herself. There was something about Sarah that made her want to confess her deepest feelings, mostly because she sensed they'd be safe with Sarah, that she would be comforted and not judged by her. Even when they had a disagreement, when words and disclosures between them became heated or painful, it brought them to a new level of mutual understanding, of closeness. All of which had kept Joss up a few nights, pondering how the hell she was supposed to deal with this kind of intimacy with not only another person, but a lover. Joss rolled the word around in her head, trying to get used to it. Sarah was her lover now. What, in God's name, was supposed to come next?

Joss breathed out, breathed in again, slow and steady to try to quiet her galloping heart. Now that they'd made love, there was no more physical distance between them and even less emotional distance. How, she wondered with a sliver of panic, would they be able to go back to being platonic friends? Would she be strong enough to do it? She knew it would take all her willpower, all her powers of concentration and discipline, to be able to dial things back at the end of the week. Sarah was not a woman in whom you deeply invested yourself and then, with the flick of a switch, divested yourself. She was far too unforgettable, too complicated for that. Sarah was, Joss feared, forever tattooed on her heart and body now. *Fuck, I wished I'd figured that out a few days ago.* And yet, no. She would not have changed anything.

She shifted her attention to watching Sarah work—the little furrows of concentration in her forehead and at the bridge of her nose, eyes that were clinical, like a doctor's, as they scanned Joss's face, then flicked back to her sketch pad. Her hand moved expertly, sometimes in short strokes, sometimes in longer, more fluid strokes. She'd stop to brush at the image with a finger, then go back to her pencil. The charcoal came later, after, Joss supposed, she had the image down first in pencil. She liked watching Sarah work, found herself appreciating the knowledge and expertise and efficiency with which she went about it. It was probably the way she herself looked when she performed surgery, she supposed. It was the look of knowledge, skill and experience coalescing into efficient, confident action.

God, Sarah was so freaking hot! If this was a test for Joss, a challenge, she considered that for the first time in her life she might not be strong enough to get through to the other side. She just might not get out of this unscathed.

CHAPTER TWENTY-TWO

After a thrown-together dinner of grilled cheese sandwiches and a Caesar salad, as the sun met the horizon beyond their little patio at the back of the cottage, Sarah sipped her glass of cool, crisp Chablis and deflected Joss's halfhearted pleas to let her see her work in progress.

"I'm not happy with it yet," Sarah said. "But I'll have it done for your mother for Christmas, I promise."

"What if it, like, shows me naked or something?"

"Nice try. You'll have to trust me. And no snooping. I've packed it away for now."

"Oh, you're no fun, you know that?"

Sarah gave her a suggestive look that quickly had Joss recanting. They'd had more fun in two days—most of it in bed—than seemed humanly possible. Sarah's body had so quickly become accustomed to Joss—the way Joss touched her, the way she pleasured her—it felt as though they'd made love a million times before. She could get used to this, she knew, and yet she couldn't. The comfort and familiarity they'd effortlessly slid into would come to a halt in four days. Joss would go back to being a workaholic with little time for anyone, and Sarah would go back to…to what, she wasn't sure, other than her part-time teaching once the holidays were over. Returning to the grind of trying to sell her paintings and of creating more paintings held little appeal these days. She'd need to make some decisions soon. Life-altering decisions. And as she snuck a look at Joss gazing at the setting sun, she wondered how and if Joss would fit into any of those new plans, whatever they might be. She wished she could be as committed, as dedicated, as chained to her career as Joss. Then she'd be able to relegate everything and everyone else in her life, with an iron will, to a distant back burner. The way Joss seemed to be able to do so effortlessly.

"There's something I asked you about a while back that you never really answered," Sarah said. She wanted to *understand* Joss, and one of the keys to that, she felt sure, was knowing more about her relationship with her father. "You never answered me when I asked if you went into medicine to please your father, or to get his attention."

"Why is that important to you? It was a long time ago."

"I think it *is* important," Sarah pressed.

Joss sipped her wine, her face revealing nothing of her thoughts, but her eyes had drifted to the window. "Like I said, I was good at math and science," she finally answered. "It was easy for me."

"Then why not engineering? Or rocket science?"

"I knew what a surgeon's life was like. I didn't know anything about those other things."

"So you chose a profession where you would never be home? Where you would never have time for a family or a spouse? For other interests? Because that's the lifestyle you knew based on his, right?"

Joss's eyes shone with something. Unshed tears, or perhaps anger. "People respected him. They looked up to him."

"But did you? Did your mother?"

"Of course!" Joss's voice split the air like an ax splitting a log.

The desire to provoke Joss, to burrow into why she emulated

and worshipped a man who, as far as Sarah could tell, gave very little of himself to his family, was tempting. Instead she softened her voice as she thought of a young Joss, who probably had to perform cartwheels to get her father to notice her. "But did he love you, Joss? Did he respect you?"

"Why wouldn't he? I was his daughter. His only child."

Now we're getting somewhere, Sarah thought. "Could it be, that becoming a doctor, just like him, was the surest way of earning his love and respect?"

Joss waved a hand and sipped her wine without looking at Sarah. "That's silly."

"Is it?"

"Yes." Joss's voice and eyes left no room for doubt. "And while we're on the subject of fathers, what about yours? Why haven't you cut your father loose for not respecting who you are? Why do you still keep him dangling? For financial security?"

The accusation felt like a slap. "You make it sound like I'm using him."

"Aren't you?"

No more than you and I are using each other, Sarah thought with a sense of detachment. "It's complicated, him and me."

"It seems to me rather simple. You fulfill a role for him, he fulfills one for you. And neither of you respects the other."

Sarah bristled with anger. It was so easy for Joss, who'd grown up with two parents, to sit in judgment. "After my mother left us, he was all I had. We were all we had."

"Then maybe you should get back to that. Back to that place where the two of you lost everything but one another. Tell him you won't be somebody he's trying to make you into, that you are who you are. But it also means you can't ever accept another penny from him."

Tears gathered in Sarah's eyes. Joss moved next to her, the quiet fury between them morphing into an alliance of understanding. They were more alike than not in their father-daughter dynamics.

"You'll be okay, you know. If he can't accept you."

Sarah shook her head, not at all sure she was ready to go it alone. As uncompromising as her father could be sometimes, it scared her to think she had no one she could go to in a pinch. No blood family outside of him. She'd be alone.

"I won't," Joss whispered, "ever let you be destitute."

The heat of her outrage propelled Sarah off the love seat. "So now you're suggesting that you take my father's place? That I replace one despot with another?"

Her voice razor sharp but calm, Joss said, "I'm going to pretend you didn't just call me that. And I'm saying that as your friend, as someone who cares about you, I won't let anything bad happen to you, all right? I will be here for you. I promise you that."

"I don't need to be anybody's kept woman, you know." Tears, hot and insistent, flowed down her cheeks. Is that really what Joss, what her father, thought of her? That she was a little girl who needed to be taken care of? That she would ultimately fail and needed some kind of security blanket? "You know what, Joss? Fuck you. And fuck my father too."

Sarah stalked to her bedroom and slammed the door.

* * *

Sleep eluded Joss for much of the night. Three times she reached across her small double bed, feeling for Sarah. Amazing, she thought, how quickly she'd adapted to having someone share her bed. Her banishment last night was well deserved. She hadn't meant to push her so far, but it upset her how much crap Sarah put up with from her father. It was no wonder she often doubted herself and her ability, given her father's low expectations of her.

Shortly after dawn, Joss padded to the kitchen and, as quietly as she could, pulled a frying pan from the cupboard. Sarah's relationship with her father was none of her business. Just as Joss's feelings about her own father were none of Sarah's business, even though Sarah had ventured into some uncomfortable territory last night. Her questions, her accusations, continued to reverberate in Joss's mind. Why shouldn't a kid emulate a man who saved lives for a living? A man who was among the best at what he did and was revered for it? Of course Joseph McNab had his shortcomings as a husband and father. What man didn't? Medicine was a noble profession, and Joseph McNab had been a master at it. He wasn't superhuman, wasn't perfect, and so something had to give, which was his home life. Joss was simply smart enough not to make the same mistakes.

She cracked three eggs in a bowl, added butter and milk and whisked the contents. He had been a good man, her father, if absent much of the time. And her mother had made up for it as best she could. Like the time they were all set to drive to the Gulf coast in Texas for a week's holiday when Joss was eleven. Her father had canceled an hour before they were to leave, but Madeline and Joss went on anyway, determined not to miss their vacation. There were too many missed school plays and concerts and the state track meet where Joss won a gold medal when she was twelve that her father couldn't make because of work. She got over it because she had to. Because, as her mother pointed out from her earliest memories, other people were counting on Daddy more than they were. Her needs, and her mother's needs, were less important in the grand scheme of things. And Joss went along with it because she'd had no other choice.

She poured the egg mixture into the hot frying pan, spatters leaping up. She knew all too well the obligations, the distractions that defined a doctor's life. But it sure beat the hell out of a boring nine-to-five job, and it beat the hell out of boring relationships with their obligations, expectations, rituals and roles, resentments and unfulfilled dreams. Her life was fine the way it was, thank you very much.

Moments later, she carried two plates to Sarah's closed door and tapped lightly on it with her elbow. She hadn't been wrong in the things she'd said last night, but she owed Sarah an apology for the blunt, insensitive way she'd gone about it.

"Come in."

It took a juggling act and a contortionist's skills to get the door open. Joss brought the plates to Sarah's bed, handing one to her. She pulled a wooden chair up to the bedside and settled her plate on her lap.

"I'm not sure I deserve this but thank you," Sarah said, rubbing the sleep from her eyes. "It's very thoughtful of you."

Joss dug her fork into her eggs and took a bite. "I pushed you too far last night. I'm sorry. I was an ass."

Sarah had been so angry last night, so full of red-faced fury. Now her voice was soft as the breaking sun and full of contrition. "No," she said, her cheeks pinking. "I overreacted. And I'm so sorry."

"I guess we shouldn't have gone to bed angry, huh? At least, that's what couples seem to say in the movies." Okay, that sounded stupid, but she didn't know anything about this making up business. Or about being part of a couple.

"At least we're not waking up angry." Sarah smiled, and Joss's worry dissolved. "And I'm starving by the way." She dug into the eggs like she hadn't eaten in days and took a big bite of her toast.

"There's coffee too, but I only had so many hands."

"What, the multitalented Joss McNab couldn't carry two plates and two cups of coffee?"

"I guess my résumé is deficient in the waitressing department."

"Mine's not. Maybe *I* should have brought the food in."

"You waitressed?"

"My first couple of years of college."

Joss knew it would earn her a slap if she told her, but her fantasy of Sarah in a tight-fitting, low-cut, high-thighed waitress's outfit was turning her on. "I bet you were the sexiest waitress there was at…Where did you waitress?"

Sarah blushed again. "Chili's."

Joss laughed. "A Tex-Mex place? With your red hair and light skin, I would have pegged you for working at an Irish pub."

Sarah's voice dropped an octave. "I know what your dirty little mind is picturing."

Joss raised an eyebrow. "Oh you do, do you?"

"A green bustier and fishnet stockings, aren't you?"

It was Joss's turn to blush. "You think you have me all figured out, don't you?"

"When it comes to some things, yes. Now put these plates aside and let me prove it to you."

Joss didn't need to be told twice. She set the half-finished plates on the dresser and scooted onto the bed beside Sarah. Her breath caught as she peeked under the sheet. Sarah was naked. Talking was overrated, she decided. Sex was not.

"Did you miss me last night?" Sarah whispered.

Joss leaned over her and kissed her long and slow and deep. "Does that answer your question?"

"Sort of."

"Need more evidence?"

Sarah's eyes danced. "Absolutely."

Joss reached under the sheet, cupped a breast, squeezed it lightly. With her thumb she caressed the already rigid nipple. "Oh, that so needs my mouth on it."

"Oh, it certainly does," Sarah said, desire straining her voice, her breath becoming more shallow.

Joss moved on top of her, began sucking and licking the breast Sarah practically pushed into her waiting mouth. Sarah had the most beautiful breasts Joss had ever seen, and she'd seen plenty if you factored in what she did for a living. Sarah's were full and round, as smooth and white as the richest custard. Her nipples were a soft shade of pink that became dark red when she was aroused. She could spend hours loving these breasts with her hands, her mouth, but already Sarah was fidgeting. Her hands were in Joss's hair, her body had begun moving beneath her, signaling its need for more.

Sarah moaned as Joss moved lower to suckle and lick her way south, fully aware of how badly Sarah wanted her, how she craved Joss to pleasure her. She could easily stretch out the torture, but she didn't want to. She wanted to taste Sarah, wanted to make her come every bit as badly as Sarah wanted her to.

"You're so wet," she said to Sarah as she touched the tip of her tongue to her.

"Oh, God." Sarah's head thrashed from side to side. Her chest heaved. "Joss, you have no idea what you do to me."

"Oh, I think I do, darling."

What she didn't want to think about was what Sarah was doing to her.

CHAPTER TWENTY-THREE

The thirty-two-foot catamaran sliced through the water as easily as a knife bisecting a block of butter, kicking up a fine mist of spray that, thankfully, stayed out of Sarah's champagne flute. The sun was setting, weaving streaks the color of orange and cranberry through the sea. Three other couples were enjoying the cruise, which came with complimentary champagne and trays of cheese and fruit. It was romantic, loose, intimate. And maybe, Sarah realized belatedly, not the best setting for a couple that wasn't really a couple and certainly wouldn't be in two more days when they returned to Nashville.

Beside her at the railing, Joss sipped from her glass, her eyes fixed on the horizon. There was nothing about her posture or her expression that indicated she had a care in the world. And maybe she didn't, but before their trip home, they'd need to talk about where they stood, to make sure they were both on the same page. Sarah dreaded having that talk. Dreaded having to pretend she was tough and stoic and able to handle returning home where everything would go back to the way it was—two people in a mutually beneficial business arrangement. The closer that time got, the more Sarah feared she wouldn't be able to do it. But she would have to do it, she told herself, because the only other choice was a heart full of pain she might not recover from.

She cleared her throat nervously. "When we get back, I'm going to talk to my father."

Surprise registered in Joss's face. It was another moment before she spoke in a voice that was softly encouraging. "I'm glad. Will you be okay?"

"Yes. Eventually." Sarah didn't know if it would bring to an end her relationship with her father, but it was a gamble she needed to take. "You were right. I can't reach my potential until I stop feeling…I don't know, almost like I'm embarrassed around him for being an artist. I need to fully commit to being an artist and that means telling anybody who doesn't believe in me to go to hell. And be prepared to not have them in my life."

Joss reached for her hand and gave it a squeeze. "If there's anything I can do…"

"No. Thanks. You've done enough."

Joss's cell phone chimed, its intrusion momentarily exasperating Sarah. They'd had almost no interruptions all week. Friends, family, workplaces had all mercifully left them alone.

"Sorry," Joss said, retrieving her phone from her pocket to read the text. Her expression stilled, then worry lines deepened around her mouth and between her eyes. "It's Nancy. She has news on Roxi."

Sarah's breath stalled somewhere in her chest. "Yes?"

"They found her a heart."

"Oh, thank God." Relief brought tears to the surface. "When?"

"They'll do the surgery in about six or seven hours."

The middle of the night, Sarah calculated. The thought occurred to her that Joss might want to scrub in on the surgery. Or that maybe they should both be at the hospital for support. "We should get back there, shouldn't we?"

An aggregate of emotions rose and fell in Joss's eyes, so quickly they were hard to read. She nodded once, revealing no sense of disappointment that their trip would be cut short by a couple of days, nor a sense of excitement that the young girl they'd come to adore was about to get a new lease on life. Clearly, Joss was in professional mode, nothing but ice in her veins.

"I'll call the airline as soon as we get back to shore," Joss said.

At the cottage an hour later, Joss put her phone down and announced that they wouldn't be able to return home until the next morning because the only flight to Nashville that night was booked solid.

"We have tonight then," Sarah whispered, a lump rising in her throat. Things come to an end eventually, good things, bad things, all things. She knew that, yet a finger of panic touched her spine. *I don't want this time to end. And yet it must. It will.*

"We have tonight," Joss echoed, then she turned and disappeared inside the bedroom.

They made love slowly, intensely, as if savoring every moment. For Sarah it was like deeply inhaling the perfume of a rose, softly caressing its satiny petals between patient fingers. She touched Joss's skin with her lips. Lingered there, then traced slow, circular patterns with her tongue. The smoothness, the unique scent of Joss's skin filled her, left her aching for more. This woman made her want to give so much—everything—of herself. And yet she couldn't, because it wasn't part of the deal. It wasn't, as Joss had made clear numerous times, something she wanted. She didn't want Sarah's heart. Well, tonight, dammit, Sarah was going to make love to this woman with every ounce of everything she had inside herself. She would make *love* to Joss and hold nothing back.

She stroked the inside of Joss's thigh, felt the shifting and trembling of her muscles in response. Up, down, then back up her fingers glided and skittered, until she moaned and began to shift her body in anticipation. Fingers tangled gently in Sarah's hair, not demanding, but not entirely patient either. With the

By Mutual Consent   173

lightness of a feather, Sarah moved her fingers over Joss's center and watched with breathless pleasure as she moaned again, arched her neck. She was wet. So wet that it gave Sarah a sense of pride that she'd made her that way. Made her that way and would soon undo her.

Gently her fingers explored—caressing, tiptoeing, dancing. She slipped one inside, just to the first knuckle, and Joss gasped and shifted her hips to deepen Sarah's entry. She slid further in, began to pump rhythmically, and at Joss's urging, slipped a second finger inside. Joss gasped hard for breath, rocked to the pace with her hips. But Sarah didn't want her to come this way. Not until her mouth was on her.

"Oh," Joss groaned as Sarah's lips grazed her labia, her clit, before planting soft kisses. "Yes. Please, baby."

Sarah felt her own quiet spasms build as her tongue began to caress Joss. Fast, then slow. Hard, then soft. Then all over again, deliciously driving Joss mad. Her hips pushed against Sarah's mouth, hotly in pursuit of maximum pleasure. Sarah held nothing back with her fingers and her tongue, stroking, giving, taking, stroking some more, pushing her to the precipice, then pulling her back again. More ambrosial torture, and moments later, Joss's body began to quake and shudder, her orgasm tearing through her body with terrific force. Her chest heaved, her mouth gulped for air as she continued to rock against Sarah's mouth until, finally, her orgasm tapered and disappeared.

"Oh, God, Sarah," she rasped. "That was incredible. *You're* incredible."

Her chest was still heaving as Sarah slid up her body, stopping to kiss her neck, her throat, the underside of her chin, her jaw. When Joss opened her eyes, they were moist and dark, and full of...something that Sarah didn't want to think about. *Probably the sex*, she reminded herself and lay down beside Joss.

* * *

Sarah's nose remained firmly planted in her book on the plane ride back, but the pages rarely changed. She was worried,

Joss supposed, about Roxi, even though Nancy had texted her just before they took off that Roxi was out of surgery and doing fine.

It wasn't until they'd retrieved their bags and were following other travelers to the taxi stand outside that Sarah announced that they needed to talk. Her mouth was set in a grim line, and Joss's heart sank.

"Can't it wait? Maybe we can have lunch later or meet for dinner? Or talk at the hospital after we check on Roxi?" Anything to delay the inevitable.

A large overhang kept the rain off them, but Joss almost wished the icy needles were soaking her, along with the spray being kicked up by the taxis speeding away. Being cold and wet would at least explain the shaking that had begun in her knees and was working its way up.

"I don't think it should wait, Joss."

Her gut told her what Sarah was going to say—that their little honeymoon was over. Well, that was no news flash. Of course it was over. They couldn't carry on playing house now that they were home, now that they had other priorities. They'd go back to their little arrangement. It had been working well for them before this after all, though that didn't mean it couldn't be improved. Maybe they could tweak it to include spending some time together in the sack every now and again. That part of their week had certainly been a smashing success. Adding a little sex to their arrangement from time to time didn't have to be a big deal, didn't have to mean anything.

"Look," Joss said in a tone that sounded much breezier than she felt. "I understand. We're both going to be busy with work and things. We might only see each other once or twice a week. I'm good with that, okay?"

Sarah shook her head, her eyes as dull as the December sky. "No, Joss."

"No what?"

"I can't…" She dropped her gaze, bit her bottom lip. The look would have been adorable on her were it not so heartbreaking. "We can't do this anymore."

Joss swallowed. "Do what?"

"This. Any of this. Us. I don't want to see you, Joss."

She tried to wait Sarah out, because maybe in the seconds it took to outline what she meant, she'd change her mind. "What do you mean, you don't want to see me? You mean we can't sleep together like we have been this week, right?"

"No. I mean all of it."

All of it? Seriously? No, she can't mean it, not like that. "You mean…you m-mean…" Jesus Christ, she needed to get hold of herself. She hadn't stuttered since the third grade. "You don't mean our agreement too?"

"Yes, I do. I don't think we should see each other anymore. At all."

Forming words was difficult when Joss's mouth felt like it was filled with poured cement that was beginning to harden. "Why not?" was all she could manage to get out, even though she knew asking why—or trying to convince Sarah to change her mind—was pointless.

"Because I can't do it anymore. It…" Sarah shook her head faintly. "It hurts too much. And I need to save myself."

"Save yourself from what? From me?" *What the hell have I done wrong?*

"From me," Sarah said quietly. "I care too much for you, Joss. I care enough that all this pretending makes me realize…" She took a deep steadying breath, never taking her eyes off Joss. "Makes me realize what I'm really missing."

So, Joss thought. *There it is. Sarah is a braver woman than I am.* She was making it clear she would no longer fool herself that they could keep playing their little game—appearing at functions as a couple, then going their separate ways afterward with a few stolen kisses, a few forbidden touches, maybe sex a couple of times a month if she really wanted to hope for more. A lot had happened this week. Too much for Sarah, obviously. And she couldn't blame it all on the sex. It wasn't the sex complicating things. It was their deepening intimacy. Their hearts understood that what was happening between them was far more than physical. They had begun to need each other and to enjoy one another far more than they should have. She'd rolled the dice in thinking they could have a week to enjoy themselves without promises, without rules, without expectations. And now she'd lost.

"All right," she answered. What else could she say? It wasn't all right, but she had to trust that putting some distance between them was what Sarah needed. For a while, at least, because she refused to believe Sarah was suggesting a permanent separation.

For a long moment Sarah looked at her as if she was waiting for something else, something more. Then she pivoted toward a waiting cab. "I'll be checking on Roxi today. I'll probably see you there."

Sarah didn't look at Joss as the cab pulled away from the stand, didn't see her still standing on the curb, too numb to move.

CHAPTER TWENTY-FOUR

Sarah didn't want to see Joss again today, but the overriding need to check on Roxi, to at least *be* there, even if she wasn't allowed in to see the kid, had her at the hospital a few hours later.

She sat in the pediatric ICU waiting room, drinking the stale coffee, waiting for someone, anyone, to give her an update. The nursing staff had been reluctant to say much given that Sarah wasn't family. It gave her unwelcome time to stew about Joss, to relive their "breakup" and the wisdom of her decision to end things. Already, being without her made her feel like she was missing a limb. They'd spent every minute together for four nights and five days, talking, reading, walking, riding bicycles around the island, swimming and, of course, making love. With an ache she couldn't soothe, she remembered how easy it had been being with Joss, how complete she made her feel. They answered things in one another, matched things too so that there was a natural balance most times. Sure, they sometimes pushed each other into painful emotional territory, but only because they wanted to reach a deeper level of understanding. And they innately wanted to press one another to be better, to be happier, to be fuller human beings.

Sarah would have been willing to give things a try, to see where they could go as a real couple. But Joss… Joss had made it clear that was a dead end, and Sarah simply didn't want to waste any more time on an avenue that held no hope. What she wanted, she realized now more strongly than ever before, was a mate in every sense of the word. Joss had, unknowingly, implanted that desire in her by making it so easy, so comfortable, to be with her. Joss had given her a glimpse of what a life together could be like, and now that she'd had a taste of it, she couldn't go back.

"Sarah." It was Nancy, wearing a crisp white lab coat and a friendly smile. She plopped down in the seat next to Sarah's. "How are you? I'm sorry your vacation was cut short."

"I'm okay, thanks, and don't be sorry. Roxi's new heart is the best reason ever to cut short a vacation. How is she?"

"She's doing very well. Would you like to see her?"

Sarah grinned. "You'll sneak me in?"

"Of course. Come on. You can meet her mom too." Nancy rose, straightened her lab coat. "Father's not in the picture, just mom and Roxi."

"God, that must be so hard on them both, especially right now."

Nancy nodded and pushed open the door.

Roxi looked so tiny in the adult-sized bed. Tubes ran in and out of her like the ramps leading to an expressway. Beeps and hisses indicated she was breathing normally, although she was asleep. Already, her color looked better and her skin healthier than it'd looked before the new heart.

"Hi," Sarah said, extending a hand to the slender, close-cropped woman sitting in a corner chair. "I'm Sarah Young."

The woman rose and shook Sarah's hand. "Oh, yes, her art teacher. Roxi can't stop talking about you. I'm Vanessa Stanton. I'm real glad to meet you."

"The pleasure's mine. How is she doing?"

"She's doing great." The woman's chin trembled, and she wiped a tear from the corner of her eye. "It's a miracle, what's happened. Very much longer and it would have been too late for my little girl."

Sarah squeezed her hand. "It was meant to be. I'm so happy it's worked out."

"Thank you. And thank you so much for all you've done for Roxi. You sure brightened her days. And I know she will be anxious to get back to her art lessons with you as soon as she's feeling better."

"I would love that and I look forward to it."

A faint rustling at the door attracted their attention. It was Joss, dressed in scrubs and an uncharacteristically rumpled lab coat. The collar stuck up at an odd angle, as did her hair, making her look shockingly untidy. She shouldn't even be working today, since she was still technically on holiday. But then again, thinking Joss would actually take a full week's vacation was probably crazy.

"Dr. McNab," Vanessa said. "It's nice to see you again."

"I hear our patient is doing well."

"She's doing real well." Vanessa smiled through her tears. "Thanks to all of you and the wonderful staff here."

Joss barely looked at Sarah, but the same couldn't be said of Nancy. Nancy studied the two of them like they were part of a science exhibit. A wave of heat overtook Sarah suddenly, making her feel almost claustrophobic. Her breathing turned shallow, and it occurred to her that she might be having a mild anxiety attack, something she'd experienced a couple of times in college before big art exhibits.

"If you'll excuse me," Sarah said, turning to Vanessa. Spots were beginning to appear in her field of vision. "I'll stop in again real soon if that's okay."

"It's more than okay. Please visit often."

"I will."

She rushed out the door. She felt grief at the death of what they'd become together on Sanibel, pain at Joss's acceptance of that death and anger at her for not wanting what she wanted. She hated that Joss would barely look at her. Hated that they had nothing to say to one another. Putting an end to their arrangement was the right thing to do, but it left a bigger hole in her heart than she'd expected.

* * *

"What are you doing in scrubs? You're still on vacation for a couple more days," Nancy scolded Joss. She was very familiar with the rarity of her friend taking time off. And while, like most young surgeons, Nancy didn't take a lot of holidays herself, she took more than Joss. Her wife Jayme saw to that.

"I spilled coffee on my shirt when I came in and had to change."

Nancy steered her down the hall toward the cardiac surgeons' lounge on the fifth floor. "Well, you look like crap when you should be looking relaxed and..." She lowered her voice, "oversexed. Let's grab a cup of coffee."

Moments later, warm mugs in their hands, the women claimed two La-Z-Boy chairs in an unoccupied corner where tall glass windows overlooked the hospital grounds and the campus beyond. Joss had fallen asleep in these same chairs on more than one occasion after a long day—or night—in the OR.

"Crap, I forgot to ask you how Jayme's aunt is doing," Joss said.

Nancy chuckled. "Miraculous recovery. On death's door a few days ago, now she's talking about busting out of long-term care and moving back to her house."

"Glad to hear it, although I'm sorry it kept you two from going on vacation."

"Never mind that, plus I'm glad I was here for Roxi. It was more important that *you* go away. Except I'm getting the distinct impression that things suddenly aren't turning out so well in the Sarah department." Nancy's eyebrows shot up over the rim of her cup. "So, what happened, champ?"

"What makes you think something happened? And I don't look like crap, by the way. Well, all right, maybe a little."

Joss knew she had only precious seconds before Nancy got her to confess all. When it came down to it, her mother and Nancy were the only people—well, besides Sarah—that could get Joss to confide in them. The fact that intimacy had come so quickly and so easily with Sarah continued to be a source of astonishment. One look from Sarah seemed enough to cut through years, layers, of walls she'd built up around herself.

"To be perfectly honest, you look like you've just lost a patient. Which I know is impossible since you've just come back. So what gives with you and Sarah? I thought you two were having a fabulous time down there?"

"We were."

"And then you weren't?"

"Something like that." Joss gazed out at the cold rain falling in tiny droplets. It was more like a drizzle and matched her mood perfectly. "It was good, Nance. Better than good." She thought about the long walks on the beach that were sometimes full of chatter, other times comfortably quiet. There'd been snuggling on the couch, laughter over glasses of wine, make-out sessions in the pool and then of course the lovemaking sessions that had left Joss desperately wanting more. When she closed her eyes, she could still feel Sarah's fingers, Sarah's mouth, on her. She wished she could slow things down, time-travel enough to revisit their time together, to make it somehow last a little longer.

"What happened? Was it my interrupting you with news of Roxi's surgery?"

Joss shook her head. "I wish it were that simple. She dumped me, Nance."

"What? When?"

"This morning. Soon as we flew in."

"Why?"

Joss twirled the ceramic cup in her hands. "I'm not really sure, except, I think maybe she's had enough. I mean, considering that I'd made it clear from the start there was no chance of a relationship between us. Guess she thought it was time to bail."

"You mean to say she didn't offer you an explanation?"

"She said it hurt too much to continue. Something like that. And that she had to save herself, whatever the hell that meant."

"I see." Nancy was quiet for a long moment, joining Joss in staring at the gloomy vista below. "And what about you? How do you feel about it?"

Joss shrugged, trying to convince herself that it was okay, because it *had* to be okay. She'd had no say in Sarah's actions, and really, it was all her fault anyway. "I don't have any choice. That's the way she wants it."

"Wait a minute. Are you saying this doesn't bother you?"

"Look, we had an agreement. A business arrangement. And yes, this past week was more than that. It was fun, it was exciting, but it was meant to be temporary. All of it was meant to be temporary."

The muscles in Nancy's jaws clenched, then unclenched. Her dark eyes turned to granite. "You are so full of shit, Joss McNab. This is killing you. Admit it."

"It's not killing me. I'm a big girl and so is Sarah. I'm fine, okay? I don't need a girlfriend. Never have, never will."

Nancy shook her head. "Good one, Joss. Still trying to convince yourself of that old load of crap?"

Now Joss was getting pissed. She was in no mood to have her relationship—or lack of—psychoanalyzed by her best friend. Things with Sarah were done, over, end of story. It had to end sometime, after all, and while she would have loved to have it last longer, well, it hadn't. "Leave it alone, all right? It's best this way."

"You know what, Joss? Sometimes you are such an egotistical idiot!"

"What the fuck, Nance? I don't deserve that!"

Nancy took a deep breath, expelled slowly. "All right, I'm sorry. But you are sometimes. You think you're such an expert on yourself. That you don't need anybody. That you're happy going it alone. You've convinced yourself that you'd be a shitty girlfriend, which means you deliberately sabotage any relationship before it gets off the ground."

"You're wrong." There should have been more to say in her defense, but Joss couldn't think straight anymore. Not when it came to Sarah. It was easier to fall back on her old tried and true arguments.

"I'm not wrong. *You're* wrong. Honey, listen to me." Nancy paused, then took Joss's hand and squeezed it—a rare show of affection between the two friends. It was her wife Jayme who was the more effusive, affectionate one. "Everyone needs somebody sometime in their life. We're humans. Most of us aren't meant to be alone. Hell, without Jayme, I'd…Well, I don't know what, except I'd be miserable most of the time. Look, I know you would make a wonderful girlfriend if you would only give yourself the chance. The problem, my friend, is that you want to be perfect, the best, at everything you do. And there's no such thing as being a perfect girlfriend or having a perfect relationship. Doesn't exist. And it especially doesn't exist while you're trying to be the perfect doctor."

Joss shook her head, refusing to admit Nancy was right. "I know what you're trying to do, but it won't work, okay? I plan to remain happily single for the rest of my life. Or for at least as long as my career lasts. Because my career is what matters most and always will."

"In case you haven't noticed, I have a career and a wife."

"And I'm ecstatic for you." Joss drained her cup and stood. "But you're not me, Nance." What she didn't bother to point out was that Sarah had already made the decision for them. There was nothing she could do.

CHAPTER TWENTY-FIVE

Sarah spent the bulk of three straight days holed up in her tiny studio, other than taking a couple of short breaks to visit Roxi in the hospital. She'd not run into Joss again, counting herself lucky in that department. She didn't want to run into her, not yet, and not while she was so consumed by the sketch she'd made of her, which she'd transferred to a proper canvas and now had decided to turn into an oil painting.

Joss hadn't asked for a painting of herself. But as Sarah worked on completing the sketch in her studio, she found herself wanting to re-create it in full color. And with the texture of oil. It wasn't because she was missing Joss, she told herself, though she couldn't think of any other reason. She was glad in any case for the impetus it provided for getting back to her oils, of being productive in her studio once again. If nothing further came of that, it was fine with her. She'd give the portrait to Madeline once she was satisfied with it.

Sarah studied Joss's eyes, both in the sketch and in the oil. She took her finest brush, dipped it in the light gold she'd mixed and added the tiniest stroke to the green of Joss's left eye. She added a matching speck to the other eye. *Yes*, she thought, satisfied. The sun dancing off the ocean that day had been reflected in Joss's eyes, enhancing the green of them and infusing them with sparks of gold.

She studied Joss's eyes again in a slight rush of dizziness. Joss had been looking at her with unmistakable lust that day. Well, most of the days they'd been together, Joss had looked at her the way a starving person looks at a table of food. But there was more, much more in the shining, luminescent depths. There was vulnerability, need, joy too. There was… As Sarah acknowledged what she saw there in front of her, she felt her body sway a little. She sat down, hard, to collect herself. *Goddammit*, she thought, *I knew it. Joss loves me. Is* in *love with me. It's so fucking obvious in her eyes. Why didn't I see it before?*

Momentarily stunned, she set her brush down and rubbed her forehead out of exhaustion and frustration. She hadn't wanted to see it because Joss hadn't wanted to express it, that was why. It was infuriating. Why couldn't Joss admit the truth? Why couldn't she accept what she surely felt inside? She had been so adamant about her inability and unwillingness to commit to a relationship. But this isn't simply about a relationship, Sarah knew. *Or dating. This is about love. About being in love. And about letting your heart rule for a change. The problem with Joss is that she won't allow herself to love.*

She stood and paced the small space, furious again with Joss and her damned fear. *Yes, that's exactly what it is, fear*, she thought. *Joss is a big fucking coward. It's that simple. And she won't even—*

Her cell phone rang. She half-hoped it was Joss so that she could give her a piece of her mind.

She barked her greeting into the phone.

"Sarah Young?"

"Yes?" Sarah's heart plummeted with disappointment. It wasn't Joss.

"It's Raina Jenstone. Nathan Sellers's executive assistant. Well, former executive assistant. How are you?"

It was good news on the other end, she hoped. She could sure use some. "Good, I'm fine. Former, you said?"

"That's right. As of last week. Look, I know Christmas is only a few days away, so the timing's not great. But can you meet with me tomorrow?"

The hint of excitement in Raina's voice heightened Sarah's hopes. "Of course. Give me the place and time and I'll be there."

They met for lunch the next day, not far from the Vanderbilt district, where the restaurants were small and cozy and offered excellent food. Few tourists found their way to the district, which Sarah appreciated. Nashville was a magnet for tourists, loud and often drunken tourists who stumbled along Broadway from bar to bar. Sarah had had her fill of that scene years ago.

"Thank you for meeting me," Raina said, shaking Sarah's hand before they sat down. "Lunch is on me, so make it good." Her smile was friendly, welcoming, and she was much more relaxed than she had been during their last and only visit in Nathan Sellers's lavish offices.

"I have good news I hope," Raina said after a few more pleasantries and lunch was ordered.

Sarah raised a faint smile. "That's the only kind I'm looking for these days."

Raina explained that Sellers's furniture business had amalgamated with—or rather, been overtaken by—a much larger national chain called The Comfort Zone. The company had outlets in every major city in America and was three times the size of Sellers's company. Raina herself had been not only absorbed into the company but given a promotion. For which, she winked, she was excited.

"That is good news," Sarah said, unsure how she fit into it all.

Raina's smile was warm. Inviting. She was a nice-looking woman—a bit older, refined and sophisticated in her manners and dress—and she seemed to appraise Sarah with more than passing interest. She leaned forward. "Sarah, may I be so bold as to ask if you're single?"

Their food arrived—fish and chips for Sarah, fish tacos for Raina—and it gave Sarah a minute to think about her answer, because the truth was the question confounded her. She chose honesty. "I'm not exactly sure."

Raina raised an eyebrow but said nothing for a long moment. When she did speak, it was with an acknowledging smile. "Well, the lucky lady who hasn't quite managed to sweep you off your feet yet needs a swift kick in the backside. Or else you do."

"You were right on the first count, but I'm afraid a kick probably wouldn't do it." *A miracle was more like it.*

"A pity. And her loss. If you don't mind talking a little business while we eat, I have a proposal for you." Raina leaned down and pulled some papers out of the portfolio case that rested against the table leg.

"I'd like to make you an offer," she continued without seeming to notice Sarah's fork stalling halfway to her mouth. "The Comfort Zone would like thirty-six of your pieces to display at their stores and for staging homes, with the option of adding more later on. You can also offer to sell any of your paintings through us, though we'd take a twenty percent commission."

Sarah's fork clattered to her plate.

"You do have thirty-six paintings?"

"Barely. I mean, I might have to get a couple more done by…by when?" *Holy shit!*

"Four weeks from now."

"All right. I can do that." But only if she hauled ass.

Raina smiled and took a long slow sip of her sweet tea. "Wouldn't you like to know the financial terms?"

Sarah laughed. "Hell yes, though at this point, I'd almost do it for free if you're going to help me sell them too."

"You're not exactly a hard-boiled salesperson, are you?"

"Are most artists?"

Raina shook her head. "Good point. Concentrate on painting, but do me a favor and get a lawyer to look at the terms, okay?"

She set a handful of papers down on the table beside Sarah. A contract. Sarah couldn't resist scanning it quickly, her eyes nearly popping out of her head. "Forty-one thousand dollars to lease my paintings for a year?"

"With an option to renew, yes. I hope you'll find that acceptable."

Acceptable? Jesus, it was more than acceptable. It was like winning the lottery. "If I'm to be honest, this will allow me to be able to focus nearly full time on my work. Well, with a bit of teaching as well." It wasn't lost on her that the money would more than replace what she'd have earned from Joss.

Raina raised her glass in a toast. "That's exactly what I want to hear, more production from you." She winked. "Although if you get too famous, we probably won't be able to afford you."

Sarah slumped back in her chair. "I would love to have that kind of problem."

* * *

Joss cinched her coat tighter around her neck to ward off the wind, which was like a cold steel blade against her skin. The weather wasn't cooperating for such a long walk, but that was fine with her. Wallowing in misery, she wanted the weather to punish her. Wanted the self-flagellation to remind her that she had done absolutely nothing to try to stop Sarah from walking out of her life. Had done zero to try to change her mind, zero to attempt to work out some sort of compromise.

She marched over the footbridge that took tourists and Titans fans from downtown over the Cumberland River toward the stadium. She strode the bank of the river, the only crazy fool out doing so. Tomorrow was Christmas, and she'd never felt more alone. Or at least, more cognizant of being alone.

Her eyes were gritty from lack of sleep. In Florida, she'd never slept so peacefully as she had with Sarah. Now she could barely sleep at all. But Sarah's absence had affected more than her sleeping habits; it had left her with a physical pain that was becoming harder and harder to bear. It hurt to breathe. Hurt to walk. Hurt to just be. The only thing she could compare it to was the depth of loss she had felt when her father died.

Maybe Nancy was right. That she wouldn't give herself permission to be someone's girlfriend because she was afraid to fail. Afraid she wouldn't be able to be both a good surgeon and a good partner. Oh, she'd thought all her life how brilliantly her father had pulled off both, but now she understood how wrong she'd been. He'd been a crappy husband, only managing to fool people into thinking otherwise because her mother had so willingly and so adeptly gone along with the dutiful wife act.

It was with a shrewd sense of competitiveness that she'd followed him into medicine. She'd been none too shabby in competing with his legend in the medical field so far, but she could never replicate his perfect home life. She couldn't ask someone to be a carbon copy of her mother—blindly loving and supportive and willing to settle for very little in return. She didn't even want a woman like that, if she were honest. No. The only kind of woman who appealed to her was the kind of woman who would challenge her, a woman who was her equal in all the ways that mattered. But how on earth could she possibly do justice to her career and a satisfying home life with the kind of woman she wanted to be with?

Joss stopped at the bank of the river, picked up a stone from the ground and tossed it into the muddy water. It entered with a resounding plop and sank out of sight. That was how her heart felt, like it was falling into an abyss, a place that was frightening and lonely and dark. A place where she did not want to spend the rest of her life.

Tomorrow she'd see her mother for Christmas. Maybe Madeline would have some answers to the questions that were caroming around in her head like a pinball. She couldn't stop thinking about Sarah questioning why she'd become a doctor, why she'd wanted to emulate a man whose shortcomings seemed so obvious to her now. She hadn't wanted to think too hard about those questions then, but now she couldn't stop herself. Had she really only gone into medicine to compete for her father's attention? To do the only thing she could think that would make him proud? The mountain wouldn't come to her, so she'd gone to the mountain.

Joss kicked a pebble around like it was a miniature soccer ball, then picked up a stick that'd been well chewed by a dog and tossed it into the river.

She'd been a preteen, maybe twelve or so, when she began seriously thinking about medicine. It was true that her science projects, her toy lab set, were the only things her father seemed to take an interest in. Her basketball playing, soccer...he never once showed up at a game. But oh, he couldn't get to her statewide science fair competition fast enough. And her first-place ribbon, well, he'd acted like the proud father of a kid who'd just saved the world or something. He took her to work one day when she was fourteen, let her watch one of his surgeries a year after that.

Looking back, it was no mystery that her father had strongly encouraged her journey into medicine. It had been the only thing in her life he'd made time for, the only thing that seemed to connect them. And she'd been only too happy to oblige, because his happiness made her happy. But he'd never once asked her if it was what she truly wanted.

What about my happiness? What about what makes me happy? Anger—at him, at herself, at her mother—raged inside until she realized that it was a wasted emotion, that it wasn't helping her decide anything. The life she'd made for herself... It wasn't so bad. It was good, it was satisfying. *Right?* But was she happy? Was it enough? Joss felt her eyes filling with tears. *Goddamn Sarah and all her goddamn questions!*

CHAPTER TWENTY-SIX

A Christmas Eve dinner and a gift exchange was tradition at the Youngs. And while Sarah didn't feel very festive, she needed to see her father and, finally, be honest with him. No matter what the outcome, she would come clean with him. Her newly minted contract with the furniture store giant was exactly the security blanket she needed, although it was Joss who had really started it all. Joss had got her thinking about her father and not in a pleasant way, and it hadn't taken her long to realize that Joss had been right. That she couldn't move on with her life, with her career, couldn't truly begin to believe in herself, until she risked it all and told her father how she felt. It would, she hope, finally set her on the path to success and fulfillment.

Linda greeted her warmly, wrapping her in a hug. The gesture nearly brought Sarah to tears. If she became estranged with her father, of which there was a good likelihood, she vowed to continue her friendship with Linda.

Peter Young's greeting was starkly different than his wife's. He offered an awkward handshake instead of a hug. That was so typical of him. Every time he and Sarah met, they circled each other like strangers in a wrestling ring. Why should Christmas be any different? And worse, why had she hoped he might be different this time? His emotional aloofness was a riddle she'd never solved, but she'd always wondered if the reason was because she reminded him of her mother—the woman who'd abandoned him, leaving him with a young daughter to care for. Or maybe it was because she was so intrinsically different from him—her artistic nature, her easy, outgoing demeanor. For nearly as long as Sarah could remember, there'd been a wall between them, and it had only grown higher over the years when, really, they should have been growing closer. She'd never outgrown feeling cheated, not only of a mother but a father too.

"Drink first?" Linda asked.

Sarah nodded and followed them into the formal living room. She accepted a glass of white wine, hoping it would take the edge off but doubting it would. Nothing was going to make this easy.

The small talk grated on her. Mostly it was Linda who generated the conversation. Her father looked decidedly restless, and Sarah impulsively decided that it was now or never. Screw dinner and presents and all that superficial crap, which meant nothing to her because she didn't want to be here and most certainly didn't want to pretend she was having a good time or that they were a cozy little family sharing Christmas Eve. The idea of spending another minute here made her stomach turn.

She took a deep breath and set her glass down. "Dad, we need to talk."

Color drained from Linda's face, as though she sensed the fissure between father and daughter was about to open much, much wider. "Do you want me to leave the room, Sarah?"

"No. You can stay." She looked at her father, resisting the urge to feel sorry for him. Whatever had been going on between them for years was at least fifty percent his fault. More if you took into account that he was the parent, the adult for most of those years. "Daddy, I can't do this anymore. I can't pretend to be someone I'm not when I'm around you, even if it means…if it means…" She couldn't complete the threat.

Her father's lawyer mask, devoid of all emotion except for condemnation, was firmly in place. She was ten again, being quizzed about a bad grade in math, her most hated subject. "What are you talking about Sarah?" he asked in his deep baritone voice. "What, exactly, are you pretending to be around me?"

Sarah clutched her hands together to keep them from shaking. She felt like an uncooperative witness being grilled on the stand. "I feel like I'm not someone you respect. Like I'm someone you'll never respect until I hold down some kind of nine-to-five job that meets with your approval. I feel like… like…" Sarah's voice began to quaver, and it took a couple of deep breaths to settle herself. "Like a failure when I'm around you. And that can't happen any more."

Peter Young cleared his throat, but his expression did not change. "You're not a failure, Sarah. But neither, to be frank, are you a success."

"No." Sarah pinned him with her eyes. "You're wrong. I am a success, even if my bank account doesn't reflect it." But it would soon reflect it, now that she'd signed the deal with the furniture chain. She bit the inside of her cheek to keep from telling him about her good fortune, because it would never be enough to satisfy him. And it shouldn't be the thing that defined her anyway.

"Hmph, I suspect your bank account doesn't reflect much, except that you have a father who still supports you, and that…I don't know what you call that wealthy doctor of yours, but whatever *she* pays you for—"

"Peter!" Linda yelped.

"It's okay, Linda," Sarah replied, keeping her eyes on her father. "He can say what he wants. I'm going for some honesty here."

"Honesty, huh?" her father continued. "I think you have a lot of nerve, young lady, coming in here and feeling sorry for yourself after all I've done for you."

Heart pounding furiously, Sarah decided she'd have to be the one to keep the discussion from degrading into a slugfest of harmful words. "You have done a lot for me, for which I'm grateful. But you don't respect me, Daddy. And even though I will never accept another dime from you, you still won't respect me, because you don't believe in me. And if you don't believe in me…" She stood abruptly, knowing she needed to let her feet do the talking. "If you can't…" She fought it, but her voice faltered. "If you can't believe in me, then I can't have a relationship with you anymore. Love is about respect and trust. And you don't feel those things for me."

She snatched a last look at her father over her shoulder as she marched to the door. His mouth was moving but nothing was coming out. It was the first time she'd ever seen him speechless. Linda scurried after her.

"Sarah, please. It's Christmas."

"I know." Sarah wiped a tear from her cheek, then busied herself collecting her coat from the foyer closet. "And I'm sorry. But I can no longer pretend that I have any kind of a meaningful relationship with him."

She pulled open the massive oak door and walked out. Expelling a deep breath, she felt, for the first time in years, cleansed. Free. Frightened too, like the ground had shifted beneath her feet. But finally in control of her own life. There was no parachute, no one to be her savior any more. She was on her own.

* * *

Everything about her family home reminded Joss of the South and its more genteel, antebellum era. She'd always loved the hanging tree moss, the azaleas and magnolias in the yard, the large white two-story house with its tall columns, full-length front porch and dark shutters alongside the narrow windows. Rattan rocking chairs provided the perfect place to sit and sip mint juleps, she thought with a wisp of nostalgia that was more fantasy than real. She'd rarely made the time to do things like sip a cool drink on a lazy, sweltering afternoon in the shade of her mother's porch. Her mother, she supposed, often whiled away her afternoons on the porch with a good book, judging by the wear on the faded rockers.

Joss knew all too well that Madeline was a product of a different era, where the subtle but potent power of Southern ladies was shrouded in syrupy charm and cloying manners. Her mother's default, on the surface at least, was to smooth things over with a healthy dose of denial, but Joss wouldn't let that happen today. She wanted answers, wanted the truth about her father and about her parents' marriage. The fact that it was Christmas, well, the timing was unfortunate, but Joss had a heavy schedule at the hospital the rest of the week. She didn't want their talk to wait any longer.

She rapped on the iron door knocker before walking in.

"Merry Christmas, dear," Madeline yelled from somewhere inside. "I'm in the parlor, setting out your gifts."

Guilt washed over Joss. She'd chickened out of contacting Sarah about the sketch she planned to give her mother for Christmas. Now, as she took her time joining her mother, she glanced again at the pathetically impersonal bottle of bourbon in the snowman gift bag she cradled in her arm. It was an expensive bourbon, at least—a limited edition twelve-year-old that had set her back almost four hundred dollars—but not nearly as meaningful as the portrait would have been.

"Ah, there, you are," Madeline said, rushing to give her daughter a kiss on the cheek.

A fire blazed in the parlor's grate. Applewood, by the smell, and it instantly warmed Joss and made her forget about her last-minute gift. Then her eyes were drawn to the painting sitting on the mantel.

"Holy shit," she exclaimed, the expensive bourbon nearly slipping from her grasp.

Madeline smiled proudly. "It's absolutely beautiful, Joss. Sarah dropped it off yesterday. She said the portrait was your Christmas gift to me. It's the best Christmas gift you've ever given me, dear. Thank you so much."

"I, ah—" Joss was rarely thrown enough to be at a loss for words. Sarah, however, always seemed to be the cause lately of her newfound knack for muteness. "I didn't know she was bringing it over. I…We hadn't arranged that part."

"That's all right. We had a cup of tea yesterday, though she couldn't stay long. She seemed, I don't know, in a rush. Preoccupied. Have a seat and I'll bring the coffee in."

Joss set the bourbon under the tree. Sarah was here? Yesterday? They hadn't had any communication in days, but still, why hadn't she let her know she was bringing the painting over? They could have presented it together. Or she could have retrieved the painting from Sarah and brought it over herself. *She doesn't want to see you, that's why.*

Joss stared at the painting of herself. A painting that was supposed to only be a sketch. *God*, she thought, *it looks just like me. Only better. She's made me look almost beautiful.* It was strange, discomfiting, to see her likeness in oil on the wall, and it was a stunning piece of work. She would never have known by looking at this piece that Sarah rarely painted portraits. It was the eyes, she decided, that made the painting. *It's the eyes because I'm looking at her like I'm completely in love with her. Oh God!* The thought made her a bit faint. Had Sarah noticed the same thing? Had her mother?

Her mother clattered into the room, setting a tray on a side table. Joss helped herself to a cup.

"So what do you think of it?" Madeline's eyes again roamed over the painting with appreciation.

"I don't know what to think. I mean, it's very good, but honestly, I thought she was doing a charcoal sketch, not an actual painting."

"Well, she's captured your spirit perfectly. The spirit you rarely show anyone."

Joss did not want to talk about Sarah and her ability to read her so well. If she were lucky, they wouldn't talk about Sarah for the rest of the visit, although that, she supposed, was wishful thinking.

"Speaking of spirits." *Okay, that's a lame way to change the subject.* "I brought you a bottle of your favorite."

"Thank you dear. Are you going home before we go to your Aunt Ellen's later, or will you stay until it's time?"

"I don't know if I'm going to go."

Madeline's eyebrows rose in alarm. "What do you mean? Are you not feeling well? We've been having Christmas dinner at Ellen's for, what, twelve or thirteen years now? Surely you aren't thinking—"

"I don't much feel like celebrating Christmas."

Madeline fixed herself a cup of coffee and returned to the wingback chair opposite Joss. "Does this have something to do with Sarah?"

"Why do you think everything has to do with Sarah these days?" Joss snapped.

Madeline gave her a smile that acknowledged she'd hit the bull's-eye. "You look decidedly miserable. And so did Sarah yesterday."

"She did?"

"Come now, what's going on between you two?"

Joss didn't want to talk about Sarah or about herself. She'd come here to talk about her father. She needed to connect the dots, to delve into the areas of her father's and her parents' life that she'd not been privy to before. But Sarah, like it or not, was the reason she was here pushing for an honest conversation with her mother.

"We're…not together."

"Well, I know that, dear, and I was hoping your little trip south would fix that."

"No, I mean. We were, we did. In Florida, I mean." Damn, why couldn't she form coherent sentences whenever the subject was Sarah? "She doesn't want to see me any more. At all."

Madeline's face dropped. "But why? You two seemed so good together. You seemed so happy with her, Joss, happier than you've ever been. Well, since you were about five, anyway."

Yes, she thought. *That's the problem right there*. A part of her hadn't really been happy since about that long ago. Back before she began trying to prove herself worthy of her father's nearly impossible to earn admiration and attention.

"Mama, I can't do relationships, that's the problem." She took a deep breath, let it out slowly. "And I think the reason I can't is because of Daddy."

There was an interior struggle going on behind her mother's eyes—Joss was assaulting her facade that Joss's father had been perfect in every way. Yet here, in Joss's unhappy admission, was evidence to the contrary. "What does your father have to do with any of this?"

"It started out that I was too busy for a girlfriend. Busy with college, med school, residency. I was busy trying to be the best surgeon I could. I convinced myself I didn't have the time or energy for a relationship."

"Of course you didn't. And that's how it should be when you're starting out."

"No, Mama, you're wrong. High school, college, that's when you start figuring out how to do relationships. It's like an apprenticeship, so that when the right person comes along, you don't mess things up. Like I've done with Sarah."

"I'm sure there's time to—"

"No. I don't know that there is." It was typical of her mother to gloss over things, to diminish problems, to make excuses, and it infuriated Joss. "I was naïve. Stupid. I thought, look at Daddy, he's busy all the time, he's a great doctor, and yet he doesn't have to put much effort into his marriage or family life. He just gets to *be*, and everyone else fits their life around him. But he was selfish, Mama. And I am too, except I have just enough decency and self-awareness to know that it's not right to treat a partner that way. *That's* the reason I'm not with Sarah."

Madeline's frown was her only show of emotion. "You're oversimplifying things."

"Am I?" Joss flew out of her chair and began pacing. "Why did you love him, Mama?"

"What do you mean?" Madeline began shaking out her hands as if they were wet.

Joss stopped in front of her and tried to soften her voice, but the air crackled with tension. "Our not talking honestly about him is hurting me, Mama. I want to know why you loved him, what he brought to your relationship. I mean, what made you stay all those years with a man who made an art out of being absent?"

Madeline's lips pursed so tightly, they were almost white. "Joss, really, I don't think—"

"No. I need for us to talk about this."

"All right, fine." She set her cup down with a loud clink and straightened up as though she were sitting in a church pew. "I fell in love with your father the first time I ever set eyes on him. I was a college freshman. He was in his final year of medical school. He was so handsome, so smart. We went out twice, and then he told me he didn't want to get involved, that he needed to focus on his studies."

Joss winced at how similar to her own life that sounded. She'd acted the same way many times with women.

"It was three years later, when he was a resident, that we met again at a party. I'd never forgotten him, of course. Told him as much. He warned me that his career came first, that it always would. I told him I was fine with it, that he was the most important thing to me. He made us wait years, though, until we got married. Maybe," she said with a self-deprecating laugh, "he was hoping I would get tired of him and leave."

"I suppose," Joss said with a sharpness intended to be hurtful, "you told him something to the effect that you loved him enough for the both of you. That you would make things work no matter what, that you would always stand behind him like the good Southern lady you are."

Madeline's face colored. "It's what you do when you love someone, when you take a vow of marriage."

Joss sat down, rubbed her face in frustration. "That doesn't cut it in relationships anymore, Mama. And maybe it never did. Not with most people."

"Well," Madeline huffed. "I don't care what works for most people. Your father and I, we made it work."

"Did you?"

A vein in her mother's forehead pulsed noticeably. "Joss, my marriage with your father isn't your—"

"It *is* my business. That's what I'm trying to tell you. I learned about relationships from the two of you, don't you see? I learned that one does all the giving, and the other—the world gets to revolve around the other, whether they deserve it to or not."

"That's not fair."

"I think it's an accurate assessment. And while we're talking about Daddy, do you know he only told me he loved me twice? And he never once said he was proud of me?" Joss's voice began to shake.

"Oh, Joss, darling. Of course he loved you. And he was very proud of you. You were the apple of his eye."

"Was I?" Joss had to swallow back tears. "Why couldn't he ever say it? Or show it?"

"He wasn't that kind of man, that's all."

Joss stood, her emotions tangling up inside her, making it impossible to sit still any longer. "Well, it's not good enough for me anymore. And it's certainly not good enough for a woman like Sarah."

"Joss, don't. Please."

"No, Mama, it's the truth. Daddy lived in his own world. We were just the decorations. The afterthoughts. And I spent my entire life until he died trying to please him, trying to make him notice me. Christ, I'm even pandering to his ghost now."

Madeline leapt from her chair and slapped Joss across the face.

The sting of it made her eyes water. She instinctively touched her cheek and watched as her mother's face collapsed in anguish. Her mother had never struck her before. Then again, they'd never before addressed the issues festering below the surface of their family life.

Joss turned and, without a look back, walked out on her mother for the first time in her life.

CHAPTER TWENTY-SEVEN

Sarah had given Roxi her first real set of paints for Christmas, and now, four days later and only nine days after her heart transplant, they were able to try them out together. Roxi was getting a little stronger every day, but she was still fragile. Today's art session lasted only twenty minutes, but to Sarah's delight, it was five minutes longer than yesterday's.

She had told Roxi that she was going to be busy the next few weeks. Busy, of course, being an understatement now that she had only weeks to come up with a few more paintings for The Comfort Zone. She also wanted a few pieces on hand in case a gallery came calling, which all meant twelve-hour days in her studio for the foreseeable future. Roxi took the news in stride, vowing to practice on her own as much as she could.

Sarah kissed the girl on her cheek. "I'll still come by every few days, okay? And hopefully you'll be able to go home in a couple more weeks."

"Okay," Roxi replied, her smile no longer so shy and reserved. "When I go home, can we still be friends?"

"Of course we can, sweetie. You get some rest now."

Sarah collected her things. As she stepped through the door, she crashed into something tall and firm that sent her cloth bag of paint and brushes clattering to the floor.

"Shit." She dropped to her knees and began corralling the paint tubes before they could be stepped on and spill their contents.

The figure she'd collided with crouched too and scrambled to help. Sarah looked up. And froze. It was Joss.

"Sorry," Joss mumbled before Sarah could say anything. "Bad timing, huh?"

Her eyes on the floor, Sarah resumed gathering up her supplies. "I should have looked, my fault. This could have turned into a real mess."

A hand reached out and settled carefully on her wrist. "But it didn't."

Sarah wanted to be angry at Joss. She *was* angry at Joss and had been since their return to Nashville. She was angry at Joss for letting her go, for not coming after her and making her change her mind about them. Angry that she wouldn't fight for them. Angry that she would not allow herself a shot at happiness. But sustaining her fury in Joss's presence was almost impossible. At least, not when she wanted to fall into her arms.

"I meant to wish you a Merry Christmas," Joss said, her voice cracking.

Then why didn't you? But Sarah was every bit as guilty of shutting down contact. "Same to you, Joss."

"Thanks."

For a long moment, a moment in which Sarah felt her resolve crumbling, they gazed into one another's eyes. What she saw there shocked her. Joss looked so sad, so lost, that it nearly made her drop her paint supplies and throw her arms around her. "Are you all right?"

Joss nodded, but not very convincingly. "I've been busy this week, that's all. The sick don't take Christmas holidays."

And neither do you, Sarah thought. She stuffed her supplies back in her case and stood, ready to say good-bye and make a hasty exit. But something about the private suffering behind Joss's eyes made her change her mind.

"Would you like to go for coffee? Or a quick bite to eat? I have a lot of work to do but…" Her confidence quickly deserting her, she was nearly ready to rescind the invitation when Joss quickly accepted.

"Let's do the greasiest, best barbecue ribs in the city," Joss said with a grin that was achingly familiar in its charm and temptation. "Jack's on Broadway in an hour?"

Sarah hadn't honky-tonked or eaten barbecue on the main drag in a dog's age. It sounded fun. And so un-Joss-like that it made her accept before she had time to think about it.

She barely had time to change and get downtown to meet Joss at the appointed time. Well, she didn't need to change out of her jeans and sweater, but she did, switching to her fancier jeans, the form-fitting ones with tiny sequins outlining the pockets, and a butter-colored blouse that was silky to the touch. She was sliding into her turquoise and brown leather cowboy boots when Lauren came bounding into the apartment.

"Ooh, big date?"

"Nope. A quick dinner with a friend, that's all."

"And would this friend happen to be your sexy cougar doc?"

Sarah rolled her eyes. "I told you, Lauren, Joss and I are finished. We're trying to be friends, that's all." She'd told Lauren about their falling out upon their return from Florida, and they'd not spoken of Joss again until now.

Lauren's squint was the kind that said she didn't entirely believe her. "You going to invite her to our little New Year's Eve party Saturday night?"

"No, I am not. Why would I do that? We're not dating, I told you that." Sarah intended on keeping their baby steps to friendship exactly that, baby steps.

"Fine, but there might be other women here who would love to take a crack at your Dr. Hotness. Or is she Dr. Coldness now?"

The idea of someone dating Joss rankled Sarah. It shouldn't, she reasoned, because she had no claim on Joss and vice versa. But it made her want to throw something. Or throw up.

"I'm going to be late," Sarah said, much grumpier than when they'd begun this conversation.

Lauren's eyebrows did a suggestive dance. "Don't do anything I wouldn't do."

* * *

Jack's wasn't busy, which was exactly what Joss expected, given that it wasn't tourist season. She rarely went anywhere near Broadway between May and September, when the place was crawling with out-of-towners carrying their shopping bags of souvenirs and tromping around in shiny new cowboy boots that they'd purchased at one of the ubiquitous boot stores downtown. Broadway was so deserted this time of year that Joss wouldn't have been surprised to see tumbleweeds blowing around.

A sign on the door said a live band would be playing blues music at seven. It was six now. If they hurried through their meal, they'd finish before the racket started. Although Joss didn't want to hurry her time with Sarah. She wasn't sure what she expected, what she hoped for, and she knew better than to hope for much. Sarah had been clear that they were as done as day-long smoked pork, and Sarah seemed like the kind of woman who kept her mind made up. But at least she'd get to spend some time with her. She missed Sarah, and when she contemplated what her life would be like again, the way it had been before, it was awfully desolate.

She licked her lips as the smell of smoke, mesquite and barbecue sauce set her nostrils twitching like a dog on a scent.

She claimed a table—scuffed and worn from years of use, but clean—and took the seat facing the door. She looked too eager, she realized belatedly, as Sarah breezed into the joint. Her boots and faded jeans were sexy, and so was the tight blouse hugging her curves. Her hair was tied back in a functional ponytail and her makeup was light. Joss loved seeing Sarah this way, sexy in a natural, relaxed way. There was nobody more glamorous when Sarah decked herself out in an evening gown, jewelry and makeup, but this, Joss thought with a sense of loss that was like the sulfur that followed a lit match, this was Sarah looking her finest. It made missing her all the more poignant.

Joss stood, but Sarah dismissed the gesture with a wave of her hand. She was smiling at least, but warily. They both had a lot to be nervous about.

"How are you?" Joss asked as Sarah claimed the chair across from her.

"I'm okay, if you balance it all out."

"Balance it out? Like, add the good and the bad and come out even?"

"I'll grant you that you seem to be able to decipher my verbal shorthand better than anybody else."

That was probably true. They'd gotten good at picking up each other's cues and nonverbal signals from all their formal functions, like when to rescue one another from a boring conversation, when to leave, when to stay, when to bail one another out of an awkward moment.

They each ordered a glass of beer and ribs for Joss, pulled pork on a bun for Sarah.

"You don't have to go back to the hospital tonight?" Sarah asked.

"Nope. Tonight I'm all yours." At the slight widening of Sarah's eyes, Joss realized her verbal blunder. "I mean, we can stay as long as you like."

"Are you sure? Cuz that band that's coming up, Lauren says they're really good. And I haven't honky-tonked in ages. But I mean, if you don't want to, I don't mind sitting here by myself for a while."

Oh no, Joss thought, *I wouldn't dream of cutting our time short.* "I'm happy to stay for a while, although I have to be at the hospital by eight tomorrow morning."

"Eight! That must be like sleeping in for you."

"It is. My seven o'clock surgery got canceled, although I have a ten o'clock. So one beer tonight is my limit. Afraid I can't claim drunkenness for anything outrageous I might do or say."

Their beers were delivered, and Sarah leaned forward across the table. "I plan to have a couple of beers. So if *I* do or say anything outrageous, please chalk it up to the alcohol."

Joss laughed. Sarah always made it so easy to laugh in her presence. "You look good, Sarah," she said. She meant it. Actually meant it more than the words could adequately convey. For three months, they'd not gone more than a few days without seeing one another. Before today, it had been two weeks, and Joss had felt every minute of it. Sarah's absence was the stone in her boot that she couldn't get rid of.

"You do too," Sarah said softly, her voice warm and liquid in a momentary letting down of her guard.

"No, I don't. I look tired." *Because I haven't been able to sleep since you dumped me.*

"You look like you work too hard. But you look…" Sarah inhaled deeply as her cheeks took on a faint pink glow, looking, Joss thought, like she was remembering one of their nights together on Sanibel. "Good."

Joss took a sip of her beer, wishing like hell this were a real date, with the real prospect of some hot lovemaking at the end of it. But she'd take whatever she could get if it meant spending time with Sarah. "So. Tell me the good and the bad you've been dealing with."

Sarah took a slow sip of her beer and watched as their waiter set their food in front of them. It smelled divine, and Joss tucked a napkin into the collar of her shirt.

"This might be messy" was her explanation to Sarah.

"Hmm, if a surgeon says it's going to be messy, then it's really going to be messy."

Joss laughed and dove into a rack of ribs. "Start with the bad, so we don't have to end on a downer."

Sarah summed up her Christmas Eve confrontation with her father and how she'd not spoken to him since.

"That sucks, but I'm glad you did it. He needs to know how you feel. You're not a kid, you're an adult, and he needs to treat you like one."

"I'm an adult now, but I wasn't. Not when I was still accepting money from him."

"It might take him some time, but he'll come around, don't you think?"

Sarah shrugged. "Linda thinks he will eventually, but I'm not so sure."

"And you're okay with it if he doesn't?"

"For now. But it kind of makes me feel like an orphan."

"Well, don't. You can go keep my mother company since we're not really talking to each other either."

Sarah stopped chewing. "You're not? But that's, that's…"

"Shocking?"

"I thought you two were extremely close."

"We are. I mean, as close as two people can be without being completely honest with one another." Joss told her about their disastrous conversation on Christmas Day and how it'd ended with a slap. "Denial is my mother's form of Prozac."

"Oh shit. I'm sorry, Joss."

"Well, what the hell. I figured if I could give you advice about coming clean with your dad, I could put on my big girl pants and do the same with my mother."

The band began setting up, but Joss barely noticed because she couldn't keep her eyes off Sarah. She remembered how her attention only ever vaguely and briefly wandered from her when they were in a room full of dozens or sometimes hundreds of people. No matter how much effort she'd spent trying to convince herself otherwise, she knew Sarah was the sun and she was a planet that revolved around her. She'd take whatever Sarah could give her, even a superficial friendship, because it was better than nothing.

"That painting you gave to my mother. The one of me. It's stunning, Sarah, and I don't mean the subject. Thank you for that."

"You're welcome. Your mom really likes it, doesn't she?"

"I suppose. Or she did before I pissed her off."

"She will again. And you're a spectacular subject to work with."

Joss doubted that. "You have sauce on your chin," she said, then reached over with a spare napkin and tenderly wiped it away.

Sarah's blush made Joss tingle inside. She saw how her touch affected Sarah, and it gratified her to no end. *She still cares about me.*

Pointing at her glass, Sarah said to the waiter, "I'll have another please."

"We need some good news," Joss said. "Please tell me you have some."

"I do." Sarah's smile was contagious. "Finally. Someone wants my paintings in a big way." She described in detail the deal with The Comfort Zone and how she was now under the gun to produce more paintings to meet her quota and to have more stock on hand in case a buyer or a gallery came calling. "And you're a big part of it all, Joss."

"I am?"

"I know why you wanted me to sketch you. And it did help get me back in my studio, and it gave my confidence a boost, so thank you."

Joss clinked glasses with Sarah and congratulated her. But her smile felt chiseled in place. She was pleased for her. Of course she was. She wanted her to succeed in the worst way, because her talent and dedication deserved no less. But it wasn't lost on her that the more Sarah succeeded, the less she needed Joss. Or at least her money.

Not that their arrangement was back on or ever would be again. Sarah had made that perfectly clear. And anyway, Joss no longer wanted Sarah to need her like that, didn't want to be Sarah's sugar daddy. *Sugar mama*, she corrected herself. Benefactor. Whatever. It was all so confusing. Whatever the hell she was or wasn't to Sarah, she missed her, as the ache in her chest so painfully reminded her.

The band started up. They were Canadian, Sarah had explained, and they began singing about being sent down to a bone cage—some dark, dank place of punishment. Joss could relate. She settled back in her chair and nursed her warm beer. She could see Sarah's boot tapping in time as the band next struck up a tune called "Don't Let the Devil Get on Your Train."

"They're good, aren't they?" Sarah said over the noise.

You're good, Joss wanted to say. What she said was, "Come back to my place with me."

In silence, Sarah studied her for a long moment. "To talk?"

"No. Not to talk."

It was slow in coming, but when Sarah finally smiled her agreement, it was like the warm sun breaking through the clouds after a long, dark storm.

CHAPTER TWENTY-EIGHT

The contemporary décor of Joss's fifth-floor condominium surprised Sarah a little. Given Joss's mother's old Southern home, which overflowed with nineteenth-century charm, Sarah wasn't prepared for the sleek furniture, the recessed lighting, the textured concrete flooring, the exposed duct work. But it suited a busy professional like Joss.

"Drink?" Joss called from an open concept kitchen that shone with lots of chrome and stainless steel.

Sarah sauntered closer and leaned against the granite-countered island, trying hard to pull off a casual attitude, but her insides roiled with nervous energy. There was little sense in disguising what she was here for, what their intentions were. "What I want," she said in a voice husky with want, "is a night with you."

The idea of making love with Joss consumed her like a fire rampaging across a tinder-dry pasture. The only reaction from Joss was in her eyes, which turned a deep, sea green. Joss wanted her too, and Sarah didn't wait for her to say it. She reached for her waist and pulled her into her. Their bodies came together and so did their mouths, as Sarah kissed her with a ferocity that surprised her and yet was inadequate in expressing how much she wanted Joss. She wasn't normally like this, didn't ever throw herself at a woman with such relentless carnal need like this. She was a freight train and Joss was the penny on her track, about to be flattened. She needed to feel Joss's body, naked, against her own, needed to feel her skin sliding against Joss's. She wanted the soft wetness of her mouth, her lips, raining down on her, possessing her. Yes, she decided, these things and more were exactly what she needed from Joss, and she was not to be derailed.

Joss pushed against her with her hips and planted her hands on the counter on either side of her. Sarah moved against her, pushing, locking them together, grinding against her, signaling that she wanted to be captured and conquered. *Oh, God, I'm so wet*, Sarah thought as the air rushed from her lungs. Physically, she wanted Joss even more now that they were no longer… whatever it was they were no longer a part of. She missed her. Badly.

"This doesn't mean…" Sarah pushed out the words before they were crushed in another kiss.

"I know."

She expected Joss to kiss her again, but she didn't. She gazed into her eyes instead.

"What?" Sarah finally asked.

"Nothing, just savoring the moment. The way your eyes darken when you're turned on. The way your neck and your cheeks turn pink." She popped another button on Sarah's blouse. "Those things don't lie."

No, Sarah supposed, *they don't*. This was what she wanted. Absolutely. They kissed again, engaging in a spirited duel with their tongues, then separated long enough to gasp for air before joining in another searing kiss. Joss reached behind her, grasped the ends of her sweater, and began sliding it up her back. Without breaking the kiss, Sarah released the rest of the buttons on her blouse and let it float to the floor.

Joss's mouth slid down her throat, sucking softly, leaving what Sarah pictured were tiny little imprints. Hands cupped her breasts, cradling, then squeezing firmly as though Joss were measuring their heft and shape, committing every detail to memory.

"God, I missed this," Joss said in a voice strained with lust. "My bedroom. It's down the hall."

She tugged Sarah by the hand, and they practically sprinted, landing on Joss's bed with a hard bounce. They laughed together in each other's arms. With her touch, with her voice, with her expression, Sarah tried not to reveal anything that might give Joss the idea that this was more than simply a convenient fuck. They could ill afford to tangle up any emotions in this one-night stand. Or at least, Sarah couldn't. She knew Joss cared for her, and judging by the way she'd looked at her when she had sketched her portrait, might even be in love with her. But if she was, it was a closely held secret, one that Joss wasn't about to share, let alone act on. And she probably never would. *No*, Sarah thought, *we can't make this complicated. This doesn't mean anything has changed.*

Enough, she finally decided. She slid her jeans and underwear down her legs and kicked them off. Because she could wait no longer, she roughly took Joss's hand and thrust it between her legs.

Joss's eyes widened with the evidence of Sarah's desire. "You're so wet."

Sarah leveled her with a challenging grin. "So what are you waiting for?"

"Not a thing."

Joss pushed Sarah's bra aside, settled her mouth delicately on first one nipple, then the other. She sucked hard then soft, licked, sucked again, alternating the pressure, and it drove Sarah wild. With her thighs, she locked Joss's hand in place. Joss was palming her back and forth, and it was all Sarah could do not to come. She bit her bottom lip as a groan pushed past her throat. There'd been other women in her past, but the sex with them had never been like this, never this intense, this *good*, this *hot*.

Joss unleashed a desire in her that Sarah barely recognized as her own, and it came with a razor-sharp awareness of every nerve ending in her body.

Two fingers, three, pushed inside her, thrusting fast and hard like the pounding sea in a raging storm. Sarah could no longer hold back the tide of her desire. She came on a moan that was very nearly a scream, gripping Joss's hair, furiously rocking her hips against Joss's hand to absorb every last vestige of pleasure. She could never get enough of the exquisite pleasures Joss was so expert at giving her. If it weren't so damned risky, she'd consider a weekly rendezvous with Joss, exactly like this.

"You needed that," Joss said with a self-satisfied grin. The kind that said, *I'm the cowboy who just fucked you like you've never been fucked.* Sarah would be indignant about that if only it weren't true.

"I did." Sarah gasped for breath, ripples of pleasure still coursing through her. Joss was still as sexy as ever with her hair flopping rebelliously over her forehead, her eyes twinkling with I'm-just-getting-started mischief that came across as a dare. Or a promise, more like.

Sarah's heart cartwheeled until she ground her teeth and forced the flurry of inappropriate emotions back into submission. *Goddammit, it's more than sex. It's always more than sex with this woman.* She needed to exert control before her heart ran away on her. She rolled herself on top of Joss. *Time to take control.*

* * *

Joss came faster than she wanted. When Sarah touched her like that, she couldn't help herself, even though she didn't want it to end so quickly. If she could have, she would have ridden the crest of her desire for hours, enjoying and committing to memory every last second of the bone-shattering pleasure.

They lay on their backs collecting their breath and their thoughts. Joss had no idea if Sarah planned to spend the night, though she hoped so. Everything about this evening had been a surprise to her. A pleasant surprise. She never thought Sarah would agree to her bold proposition so easily, but then, she never thought she'd actually proposition her the way she had either. Seeing Sarah at the restaurant, laughing with her, feeling the sexual chemistry between them crackle in the air like distant lightning, Joss knew there could have been no other outcome but to come back here and screw their brains out.

"I need to taste you," she whispered to Sarah.

"Yes."

Joss slid down Sarah's body, smelling the sweet tang of her skin along the way, brushing her thumb along the inside of her thigh where it was softest. She knew Sarah's body as well as her own now. Knew every indentation, every curve, every sensitive spot, the smell of her skin, the scent of her desire. She knew where and how Sarah liked to be touched. Knew exactly how to access the very core of her pleasure, which was no small thing. Joss had never gotten to know a lover's body as intimately as she had Sarah's, and yet she knew instinctively there were still many places she could happily explore. Probably a lifetime of explorations.

Her mouth slid further down Sarah's body, down her belly, licking a playful trail as Sarah squirmed with pleasure beneath her. With her tongue she parted Sarah's lips, slowly painting circles, ever so surely closing the distance to her clit. With the first hard stroke of her tongue, Sarah cried out, pushed herself harder against Joss's mouth, and Joss lapped her hungrily, greedily. She took her with her fingers too, felt Sarah's desire curl into itself before exploding outward in a violent shudder and a high-pitched cry.

As Sarah spent herself with slow, endless spasms, Joss held her tightly. When she crawled higher to look into Sarah's face, she saw tears on her cheeks.

"Sarah, baby, what's wrong?"

Sarah shook her head, crying softly, turning away from Joss.

"What's going on? Please tell me." She kissed her neck until Sarah violently pulled away.

"Don't, Joss."

Christ, what did I do wrong now? Joss wanted to scream out. Sarah was a riddle she couldn't ever seem to solve, and every time she tried, she got it wrong.

"I want to help," she said lamely, but it was true.

Sarah swung her legs over the side of the bed and hurriedly pulled her clothes on. "I thought this could work, but I was wrong."

"No. You weren't wrong. We have a good time together, Sarah. The best. This..." She spread her hands outward, encompassing the bed. "This isn't wrong."

"It is for me." Sarah's eyes looked tortured in the dim light. "I love you, Joss, but you don't or...or can't love me back. I can't make love to someone who doesn't...I mean, I thought I could. With you. But I don't need another person in my life who can't love me for who I am."

Ouch, Joss thought. *That hurts*. Exactly as Sarah intended, she supposed.

"Wait," Joss pleaded, having no idea what to do now. "It's not like that."

"It is like that. To be with me, you have to be all in or you're out." Her eyes turned hard, uncompromising. "You taught me the power—the *empowerment*—of an ultimatum, remember?"

Sarah rose hastily, her top missing because it was somewhere in the kitchen or maybe the hallway.

Joss wanted to argue, to make her stop, to make her come back to her. But what would she say? Sarah wasn't wrong, and Joss felt the sting in her eyes as she repeated her words in her mind. *I love you, Joss...but I don't need another person in my life who doesn't love me for who I am...You have to be all in or you're out.*

Sarah left the bedroom, and a moment later, Joss heard the soft click of the front door opening and closing. She'd done nothing to stop Sarah from leaving because she was a coward, a loser, a fucked-up, half-assed girlfriend who couldn't give Sarah what she wanted. And she wanted to give it to Sarah. If only she had *it* to give. It was hopeless. *She* was hopeless.

She rolled over and let the tears flow onto the sheet, where they mingled with the dampness of Sarah's tears.

CHAPTER TWENTY-NINE

Covered in paint after pouring herself into her work for ten straight hours, Sarah barely made it back to the apartment in time to shower before guests were set to arrive for her and Lauren's New Year's Eve party. She was no more in the mood for a party than she was for a trip to the dentist, but Lauren had nagged her about it nonstop for two days, accurately sensing that Sarah was trying to work out excuses in her mind to skip the festivities. *I'm only doing this so I don't get a reputation as a party pooper*, she'd told Lauren.

Since her evening with Joss, she'd been moping around, pissed off at herself. She wasn't angry with Joss for what had happened. Joss was simply being, well, Joss—happy to oblige sexually but offering nothing deeper. Sarah knew it would end up that way before she'd accepted the proposition, but her hormones had happily agreed before she could give it much deliberation. Oh hell, who was she kidding. Deliberation or not, she would have accepted Joss's offer because she'd been unable to resist the lure and the promise of the hot sex that only Joss could provide her. Which all would have been fine had she not freaked out after her second electrifying orgasm—when it hit her how much in love she was with Joss. And what a huge mistake it was to be in love with someone who couldn't love her back. Aside from the instant gratification of sex, landing in Joss's bed was nothing but trouble for her fragile heart, and she *knew* it, dammit. Knew it would make her want Joss even more.

What a fucking mess. She sipped watery beer from a stubby bottle and felt like spitting it right back out, the way she wished she could expel Joss from her system. Something stronger, much stronger, was in order if she were going to get through this party, she decided. And probably the next three months, for that matter.

"You look like a woman who needs some of what I got."

The butch—about Sarah's age—was stocky and athletic looking and had short sandy hair that reminded her of Joss's. Minus the blond highlights. She was leaning against the kitchen doorframe and eyeing Sarah with more than passing interest. In her arm she cradled what looked to be a bottle in a paper bag.

"That's not a very original come-on."

"I know, but if it flops I can always pretend it's the bottle I was trying to sell you and not my irresistible body."

Sarah laughed and nodded at the bag. "What've you got in there, partner?"

A James Dean smirk. "Does it matter?"

"Hell no."

The apartment was packed. Sarah figured she only knew about half the people here. The other half were Lauren's friends or they were friends of friends who were borderline party crashers.

It was too cold to go outside, too jammed even to find a corner from which to sip whatever life-saving nectar was in that bottle.

"Follow me," Sarah said before she could think about what she was doing. Well, she knew what she was doing. It was the *why* she didn't want to think about as she led Bottle Girl to her bedroom and closed the door behind them. "I'm Sarah, by the way."

"I'm Annie." The woman looked like it was Christmas morning all over again, and Sarah was the present she was about to unwrap.

"You don't look like an Annie." Sarah held her hand out for the bottle.

"Everyone says that, which is why they usually call me A.J." She pulled the bottle out of the bag—Jim Beam—and handed it to Sarah, who immediately took a healthy glug. It was nothing like Joss's expensive bourbon, but what the hell, it'd do the trick.

A.J. made herself at home, flopping onto her side on Sarah's bed and doing her best to look alluring in a bad boy sort of way. "I don't usually get invited to a pretty lady's room so quick. Why don't you come on over here and keep me company?"

Sarah laughed. She didn't mean to laugh quite so loudly and so sarcastically, but she couldn't help herself. Defeat etched itself onto A.J.'s forehead.

"C'mon," Sarah said. Out of pity for A.J., she lightened her tone. "Sit up."

A.J. obeyed, and Sarah, standing beside her, clutched the bottle between them. "We're not going to have sex, okay?"

A.J. rubbed her chin thoughtfully. "You sure? Cuz, like, I'm pretty good in bed. I mean, so I've been told."

Sarah stifled another laugh, though she had to bite the inside of her cheek to do so. "I'm sure you are, and yes, I'm sure about the not having sex part. Here, have another sip."

A.J. took the bottle from her and raised it to her lips. When she finished, she said, "How about we make out then? Like, it doesn't have to be too hot and heavy."

Sarah raised an eyebrow, her curious nature wanting to see where A.J. was going with all this. Sarah hadn't dated much over the past couple of years, and she wondered dismally if this was what dating had come to. "What do you consider not too hot and heavy? Hypothetically speaking, of course."

A.J. smiled, raking her eyes boldly over Sarah. "Kissing, feeling each other, you know, over our clothes. I mean, unless you want to go under our clothes. That'd be, like, more than okay too."

Sarah smiled and shook her head. It was high school all over again on dates with boys—oh, and one girl—trying to feel her up in the back of her father's Mercedes. "Thanks, but I think I'm done with women for a while."

A.J. smiled hopefully. "You might change your mind after we get through this bottle."

Sarah lifted the bottle and drank from it. "I doubt it. I don't seem cut out for one-night stands."

"Ah, so you're one of *those*, huh?"

"One of what?" She didn't like A.J.'s tone.

"Can't have an orgasm without love." A.J. drew out the word *love* like it was something distasteful.

Sarah thought about that, took another sip of whiskey. That wasn't entirely true, but with Joss it certainly seemed to be. She wanted no distinction between love and sex with Joss. She wanted the lines to blur and roll into one another, the pleasures of her mind, body and heart indistinguishable. She wanted nothing short of their hearts' longings and their bodies' desires to fuse like clouds, growing into something bigger and heavier and more powerful. A few rain clouds converging into a mighty storm. She shrugged at A.J. "Maybe I am."

A.J. sat back against the headboard, drawing her knees up to her chest. To complete the picture, she only needed a long piece of grass stuck between her teeth and a cowboy hat on her head. "So tell me about this asswipe who broke your heart."

Jim was loosening things up inside Sarah. She told A.J. a little bit about Joss, but she changed the name to Jess and altered her occupation to a business executive.

"That's your first mistake," A.J. said, her words beginning to slur too. "Falling for one of them business types. You should fall for a musician, like me." She flashed another cocky grin.

Sarah rolled her eyes playfully. "I already have a musician in my life, my roommate Lauren."

"Yeah, Laur's cool." A.J. spread her hand out and patted the other side of the bed. "Come here and tell Uncle A.J. how you plan to get your revenge on this Jess dumbass. Cuz she is a dumbass if she won't give you the time of day."

"Oh, she gives me the time of day all right. For certain, um, things. But not when it comes to commitment and not…" Sarah blew out an exasperated sigh. God, it all sounded so juvenile when she encapsulated it the way she had, but it really did come down to one simple fact. "She doesn't want to be my girlfriend."

"Crazy motherfucker," A.J. mumbled. "Who wouldn't want to be your girlfriend?"

Emboldened, Sarah took another swig of whiskey. *Oh what the hell*, she thought. A.J. was harmless, and even if she wasn't, Sarah could handle her if she got out of hand. She scooted over to the space beside A.J., let A.J.'s arm dangle loosely over her shoulder. "I guess she's not the girlfriend type," Sarah acknowledged. "Which I knew going into it, but I thought…I don't know."

"You thought you could change her, huh?"

They each took another sip, the bottle nearly empty now. Sarah nodded.

"Fuck that," A.J. proclaimed. "Changing is for diapers, not people."

"I guess so," Sarah said. It wasn't easy letting go of the idea that Joss would come around to her way of thinking eventually. She was a good woman, with so much to give and so much that was worth loving in return. It was mystifying that she would not give them a chance.

Sarah's thoughts drifted to what Joss might be doing right this minute. Probably working. At least, that's what she'd told Lauren when Lauren had invited her to the party. Invited her behind Sarah's back and then didn't fess up about it until this afternoon. Thank God Joss wasn't coming. Sarah wasn't ready to see her again, because if she did, she knew she'd start blubbering away like a crybaby or fold like a house of cards and fall into bed with her again. Neither scenario held much promise.

She was tired, so tired. And A.J. was warm. And softer than she'd expected. She leaned into A.J.'s shoulder, felt her eyelids droop. "Sorry to dump all over you, A.J. Thanks for listening."

A.J. pulled her in tighter. "You change your mind yet?"

Sarah's mind was growing fuzzier by the minute. "Change my mind about what?"

"Fooling around. It would take your mind off things. Relieve some stress."

Sarah smiled into A.J.'s shirt, which smelled of Gain laundry detergent. "No, I haven't changed my mind."

"Your loss, my friend."

"I'm sure it is," Sarah said before drifting off to sleep.

* * *

Joss maneuvered around people like they were pylons in a parking lot. She wouldn't have believed Sarah's and Lauren's apartment could hold so many people. She wondered if they were breaking some sort of fire code or something.

Someone tried to press a bottle of beer into her hand, which she rejected.

"Have you seen Sarah or Lauren?" she asked. The reply was a head shake and a smile.

She moved on, asked someone else, who impatiently jerked a thumb toward the kitchen. It would take her a few minutes to make her way through the swarm of people, she realized. She swallowed back her nervousness, having no clue what she would say to Sarah. Her decision to come to the party was purely last minute, entirely spontaneous and probably insane, but screw it. She missed Sarah, needed to see Sarah again, even if it meant having her yell at her and tell her to get lost.

I'll tell her I love her, she thought suddenly. *Which I do. Except I don't know what happens next. I don't know what that's supposed to mean, how I'm supposed to act now, but I'll tell her, dammit.* She wondered if such an admission would mean they would start fitting their lives together. Start sharing calendars, asking each other's permission to do things or to go someplace, hitting Crate and Barrel together, sharing changing rooms at Nordstrom's. Christ, moving in together? It was all so overwhelming. And scary as hell. Maybe, she thought with desperation, there was a book, a how-to manual, that explained what being a girlfriend meant. Maybe Sarah would allow her to learn as she went along.

Fuck, she thought. *I'm thirty-eight years old and I don't know the first fucking thing about being anybody's girlfriend. How pathetic is that?*

She told herself to slow down, to simply tell Sarah how she felt. They'd take it from there, work things out together. Baby steps and all that.

Lauren was pulling a tray of some sort of bacon-wrapped hors d'oeuvres from the oven. "Hey, Joss, glad you could make it. Your work schedule change?"

"Hi. Yeah, something like that. Have you seen Sarah?"

"She disappeared an hour or so ago. I think she went to bed early." She pointed down the hall. "She'll be glad to see you. Why don't you go wake her up?"

"I'm not so sure about that. She's not exactly thrilled with me lately."

"Then it sounds like you two have lots to talk about. Go ahead, it'll be fine."

Joss hesitated, thought about fleeing while she could, but she'd come here to see Sarah, and she wasn't going to leave until she did. Especially now that she was ready to confess her love. *If I don't do it now, I might never do it.* "Okay. Thanks."

"Good luck."

I'm going to need it, Joss thought, as she made her way down the poorly lit hall and past two women groping each other up against the wall. "Excuse me," she muttered, halting at the door she knew to be Sarah's. She knocked lightly once, twice, a third time. She tried the handle, which was unlocked. She'd pop her head in, and if Sarah was sleeping, she'd leave her alone and call her tomorrow.

Slowly, she opened the door and let her eyes adjust to the dim light of a tiny lamp on the night table. There were two people in the bed, two sleeping forms molded up against one another, fully clothed, but looking intimately cozy, like they were resting up before they got down to business. Or maybe the business between the sheets had already happened and they were sleeping it off before rejoining the party. She stepped closer, her stomach in her shoes as she prayed one of them wasn't Sarah.

Fuck! It was Sarah, all right, her long red hair fanned out on the stark white pillow. She was snoring softly. As was the short-haired woman in a flannel shirt beside her. The stranger's arm was around Sarah's waist and her right leg was wrapped around Sarah's left in a display that looked far too intimate for Joss's liking. For a moment she couldn't breathe. And then it was like someone had delivered a kick to her stomach. She doubled over, backed up against the door, and forced herself, with considerable effort, to stand up straight.

So that's it, she thought. *Forty-eight hours after we make love, she's fucking somebody else!* Anger shattered the shock. *She says she couldn't have meaningless sex with me, but she can screw somebody else at the drop of a hat? That's rich*, she thought, as her heart hardened into something impenetrable and into something irreversible.

Well, fuck you, Sarah Young, and the cowgirl you rode in on.

She didn't bother to close the bedroom door as she stomped away.

CHAPTER THIRTY

Now that the holidays were well past and her social obligations met, Sarah hoped she could start putting the drama and heartache of the last few weeks behind her and throw herself completely into her work. She'd finished two small paintings over the past few days. Her freshman class started later in the week—she'd successfully dropped the other from her teaching load—which meant she needed to get another piece painted before then. She aimed to have at least two more paintings done by the end of the month.

Her phone chimed from a pocket in her coat, which was hanging on a stand in the corner. Someone was texting her. She ignored it. She'd given up hoping it was Joss. She'd texted Joss on New Year's Day, after Lauren told her Joss had showed up at the party after all. Sarah had missed Joss, but then, she'd missed most of the party, thanks to falling into a drunken slumber next to that A.J. woman for a couple of hours. She shook her head in dismay, but smiled anyway. A.J. was a hoot. Nice, in a down-home, cowpoke sort of way. After they'd rejoined the party,

A.J. kept asking Sarah out, failing to be discouraged in spite of Sarah's firm rebuffs. "But we already know we're good in bed together," A.J. had said with a sly wink, and it made Sarah laugh. She'd needed laughter that night. And a friend. But she'd never go out with A.J. or any other woman in the foreseeable future. Joss had ignored her text, reaffirming in Sarah's mind that there was no room for her in Joss's life anymore, especially if there wasn't sex involved and certainly not if there was to be gooey love and commitment expectations.

Her phone chimed again. Then it began ringing insistently. *Goddammit!* She tossed her brush in a can of paint thinner and wiped her hands on the nearest paint-spattered rag.

"Hello?" she said, anxious to get rid of the caller as quickly as possible.

"Oh, thank God I caught you, Sarah." It was her stepmother Linda, her voice sounding like rubber bands pulled tight.

"What's wrong?" The fine hairs on the back of Sarah's neck sprang to attention.

"It's your father. He's been rushed to the hospital."

Great, he's trying to be dramatic to get me to come slinking back to him, was Sarah's first thought before she realized how cynical that was. "What's wrong?"

"I don't know, his heart, I think. He came down with bad chest pain and was really short of breath. Right after lunch. I called an ambulance, though he didn't want me to. Said he could tough it out, but he looked awful. Sarah, I'm worried about him. I think he's having a heart attack."

A million thoughts raced through Sarah's mind, but one stayed with her: *My father's going to die while I'm not speaking to him.* She'd have to think long and hard about whether she could live with that if the worst happened. "Where are you now?"

"Vanderbilt's ER, though I think they're moving him to the cardiac unit any minute now for more tests."

Sarah would go see her father. Then it occurred to her that he might not want to see her. "Linda, do you think he'll want to see me? Or should I stay away?"

"Of course he'll want to see you."

Sarah's hand trembled. "I'm not so sure about that, but I'll come sit with you. I should be able to get there in about twenty minutes. Can I bring you anything?"

"No," Linda said, relief in her voice. "Just bring yourself."

* * *

Joss looked over the results of the echocardiogram. With the press of another button on her computer, she pulled up Peter Young's electrocardiogram graph. She hadn't examined him yet—she'd left that to the ER doctor and her second-year resident—but she was sure it was the same Peter Young who was Sarah's father. His records confirmed he was the right age, and the workup said his wife Linda had accompanied him in the ambulance.

Joss strode down the hall to the cardiac ICU, where her resident had admitted Peter Young. She would examine him for what she felt sure was acute mitral valve regurgitation, and then she'd discuss her findings with Peter and, she supposed, Linda. Sarah too, if she was here, although Sarah had said she'd had a falling out with her father. Would she show now that he was having a health crisis? She thought about her own chilly relations with her mother, how they'd barely spoken since Christmas Day. If her mother turned suddenly ill, she would do all she could to help her and be there for her, no matter what disagreements they were having. Nothing mattered more than family when someone's health was threatened, Joss had learned through experience. Family could really help or hinder a patient's recovery, both physically and mentally. She also knew how much people regretted not mending fences before it was too late—she'd held the hand of many a distraught survivor who'd lamented an estrangement after it was too late to do anything about it.

"Mr. Young," Joss said, extending her hand. "I'm Dr. McNab, the attending physician."

He was pale, and there were dark smudges beneath his eyes, but he was indeed Sarah's father.

His hand was limp as a rag. He wheezed when he spoke. "I remember you. Sarah's...Sarah's..."

"Yes," Joss said thinly. "I am." Or was, but she didn't know how much he knew. Or cared to know. "You're not feeling very well, Mr. Young?"

"Took you all those years of training for you to reach that conclusion, did it?"

Yup, same old cantankerous bastard, Joss thought. She'd heard it all before and could only be amused by such comments now, not insulted. "Well, you can't be feeling *that* bad if you're going to smack me down with a line like that."

Peter Young's sheepishness was short-lived. "Something's sitting on my chest, doc, and I can't breathe."

Joss popped the ends of her stethoscope into her ears. She listened to his heart and lungs, asked him to take deep breaths, palpated his abdomen. They went over his history and his symptoms, even though he complained he'd already gone through it all with two other doctors.

"What's wrong with me, doc? Give it to me straight. I can handle whatever it is."

God, his blue eyes were exactly like Sarah's, and she marveled at that which still had the power to shatter her. "I'd like to bring your wife in so I can go over things with both of you. And Sarah, if she's here too."

"Sarah won't be here," Peter croaked.

"I'll get the nurse to bring in whoever's in the waiting room for you, okay?" She patted his shoulder. "I'll be back in ten minutes."

Joss hustled back to her office, closed the door and leaned heavily against it. She couldn't decide whether she wanted Sarah to be there or not when she spoke to Peter and Linda. If they were to see each other again, what would they say to one another? Well, nothing in the presence of her father and Linda, of course. But even if she got Sarah alone, was there anything left to say? Evidently she had moved on with someone else, having run out of patience with Joss and her solitary, perpetually single ways.

And right when I was ready to try to figure out how to make things work with her, Joss thought grimly. Well, it figured that the fickle finger of fate was fucking with her. With them. Nancy told her it probably wasn't meant to be, that there were other fish in the sea. "Right," Joss told her, "like that worn-out old line is supposed to make me feel better?" She didn't want any other fish, didn't plan to ever go fishing again. If there was one thing the experience with Sarah had taught her, it was that she'd been right all along. She simply wasn't cut out to be in a relationship. They were simply too hard and too much of a mystery to her.

Joss retrieved her iPad. She'd use it to call up the echocardiogram results and other diagrams to show her patient and his family exactly what was wrong. And what she could do to fix it. She took a deep breath, straightened her lab coat and marched back to the Cardiac Intensive Care Unit, doing her best to prepare herself mentally in case Sarah was there.

CHAPTER THIRTY-ONE

Sarah's father had avoided looking at her when she entered his cubicle in the CICU. It went both ways. She too had had a hard time settling her gaze on him, especially because she'd begun to question whether their estrangement had played a part in his being sick. Had the stress led to a heart attack? Well, even so, she reasoned, she refused to take all the blame the way she would have in years past. His health was his own responsibility; he worked too long and too hard, and his temper had undoubtedly impacted him too. Still, their recent confrontation couldn't have helped and for that she felt bad.

"It's not good. Not good at all," Peter said, directing his attention to his wife. He was acting like he'd lost a case before it reached the jury.

"The doctor didn't say that, did he?"

"*She* and not exactly. But I can tell."

Joss breezed into the cubicle, and Sarah's knees buckled.

"Not you too!" Linda clutched her arm and pulled her up. "Are you all right?"

"I'm fine," Sarah mumbled, chagrined that seeing Joss still had this dizzying effect on her. She couldn't see Joss and not think about her mouth, about the fire in her eyes, about the soft touch of her hands. And about that damned stubborn streak of hers that would never allow them to be together.

Joss didn't glance her way, for which Sarah was grateful. But that meant Linda was the only one in the room who was acknowledging her existence. God, it hurt to see Joss again. Far more than she would have expected and almost more than she could handle. Tears were not far from the surface, and she had to quietly clear her throat to hold back the tide.

"Did Peter have a heart attack?" Linda asked, preempting Joss.

"No."

"It sure as hell felt like one," Peter replied in a tone that seemed to imply Joss didn't know what the hell she was talking about. "And you'd better not tell me it's all in my head."

"It's not all in your head, Mr. Young. I'm afraid you have a serious problem with your heart. But I can help you, all right?"

Sarah's father seemed to relax at this last bit, but his expression remained tense, worried.

"What you have," Joss continued in a commanding, even tone, "is acute mitral valve regurgitation. It can happen when the valve or the tissue near it ruptures suddenly. Instead of a slow leak, blood builds up quickly in the left side of the heart. Your heart doesn't have time to adjust to this sudden buildup of blood the way it does with the slow buildup of blood in the case of chronic regurgitation."

"And this is what caused my chest pain and shortness of breath?"

"Yes."

"What would suddenly cause this to happen?" asked Linda, her face still pale from the shock of everything that had transpired over the last couple of hours.

"In your husband's case, probably an undetected case of endocarditis. Which results from an infection."

"How the hell would I get an infection in my heart?" Sarah's father asked.

"Have you had any dental work lately?"

"No."

"Probably a virus then. Have you been sick at all during the last couple of months?"

"Early December," Linda answered. "Peter had a bad cold, but nothing that kept him down more than a couple of days."

"That could have been it. Sometimes these seemingly run-of-the-mill viruses cause all kinds of damage to our bodies, even though it doesn't seem so bad at the time. It can take weeks before it becomes apparent. But I'll order some blood work too."

Joss proceeded to show them grainy images of Peter's heart on her iPad, then swiped to diagrams of the heart and its valves and explained everything to them in a way that they could understand. She was calm, so calm, Sarah thought. Reasoned and confident too, but not emotionless. She managed to convey knowledge and competence but also sensitivity and patience, waiting until every question was answered, and often answered in multiple ways. Sarah hadn't doubted that Joss would be good at this, and she was relieved more than anything. When Joss had suffered the loss of her sixteen-year-old patient a month ago, Sarah worried her confidence might have been shaken. If it was, there was no evidence of it now.

Joss explained that regardless of the cause, surgery would be necessary and that she was quite sure she could repair the valve instead of replacing it, for now. "But you may need a new valve in five, ten years. It's hard to predict at this point. But if that needs to happen, it's nothing to worry about." She smiled at Linda and Peter. "I replace valves every day, all right?"

"When will I need this surgery?"

Sarah thought she saw, for the first time since she was a kid, real fear in her father's eyes.

"Tomorrow. I feel you're stable enough, and if we don't repair the valve soon, it could continue to degrade and quickly, forcing us to do a complete replacement. That would be a much more intensive surgery. I'd rather take the repair approach first. If that doesn't work or the repair doesn't hold up for very long, we can then do the full replacement."

Joss patted Sarah's father's hand to reassure him. The gesture, small as it was, stunned Sarah a little. She knew Joss had little respect for her father, given the way he'd treated Sarah all these years. And she was the one who'd encouraged Sarah to give her father an ultimatum. But Joss was in doctor mode, Sarah reminded herself, and it was impressive the way she so effortlessly separated her work from her emotional involvement or from any personal judgments she might harbor. It didn't matter whether she liked Sarah's father or not. He was her patient, and she would do the best job she could for him.

"I'll let you talk things over for a piece, but I'll need consent forms signed shortly."

Linda nodded, and Joss, finally, looked at Sarah. Her face, her voice, had not veered from her professional demeanor, but her gaze settled over Sarah like the warm glow of a light. She took a step closer to Sarah. "Can I see you privately?" To Linda and Sarah's father, she said, "I'll check back with you guys in about an hour, okay?"

* * *

Joss became hyperaware of the sterility evident in her office. Sarah, artist that she was, would surely take note of the lack of personal photos, the absence of plants or paintings or mementos of any kind. It could be anyone's office, now that Joss took a quick look around. Her only defense was that she was here to work, not entertain people. Besides, the OR was her second home, not her office.

She tossed her stethoscope onto her desk, shrugged out of her lab coat and draped it over the back of her chair, though she wasn't about to sit there. This was not a one-on-one with a patient, though it felt like something ominous and final, the kind of conversation in which she told a patient there was little she could do for them.

She motioned for Sarah to take one of the four chairs around a small, round table, like they were going to sit there and consult over a report the way Joss might do with a colleague.

Maybe that's what they needed to do. Maybe they needed to go over the autopsy of their dead relationship, because resuscitation certainly seemed out of reach now. Or maybe they should forget about discussing what went wrong and skip the blame game and simply agree to move on. She should say something to demonstrate that she was okay with Sarah moving on, because she certainly didn't want to play the role of sore loser or the rejected lover who remained bitter. But seeing Sarah in bed with another woman had been far harder to bear than it should have been. She had no claim on Sarah, no right to her body or anything else that was Sarah's, but damn, did she have to move on so quickly? So easily?

Joss felt her jaw tightening and the acid in her stomach fire up like rocket boosters. *I'm not big enough to be okay with this*, she thought with quiet alarm. She knew then that seeing Sarah with someone else would always bother her, even, she supposed, years down the road.

"Your father," Joss said, too cowardly to confront Sarah about her new girlfriend. "Have the two of you reconciled yet?"

Sarah's eyes widened perceptibly, but her voice remained flat. "Is he going to die from this? Is that what you're trying to tell me?"

Heat shot up Joss's neck. What the hell was she doing bringing up Sarah's relationship with her father in the context of his health crisis? She'd simply wanted to get Sarah alone, that was the problem, and because of it she wasn't thinking straight. She was grasping at any subject to talk about, and her father's health was common ground. "Sorry, I didn't mean to alarm you. I expect him to recover fully from surgery. What I meant by my question was that it might be more helpful to his recovery if there wasn't the stress of, well, your estrangement."

Sarah's face seemed to clamp shut before her eyes. "You were the one who encouraged me to be honest with him, to stop accepting the way he was treating me. And you were right. It was something I should have done a long time ago."

"I know, I...We couldn't have known that he was going to get sick, that's all. Look, I'm sorry. It's your business and your father's. And I'm not sorry I gave you that advice, Sarah. You were right to do it."

Sarah looked away, and there was the glint of tears in her eyes. She spoke in a whisper of frustration. "Maybe so, but I seem to be fighting with everyone right now."

"You're fighting with your new girlfriend already?" The small opening was too much for Joss to resist. It might be her only chance to get back at Sarah for the pain she had caused her.

"What are you talking about?"

Joss winced. It was too late to back out. "At your New Year's Eve party. At your apartment. I saw you with someone."

"Lauren told me you showed up, but I missed you somehow."

"I came later, hoping to talk to you. But you were... indisposed. With someone else."

"Indisposed? Come on, Joss, I'm having trouble deciphering whatever it is you're trying to get at." Sarah's voice had an edge to it. "What is it that you think you saw? And why didn't you answer the next day when I texted that I heard you came to the party?"

Joss swallowed against her dry throat, remembering the image of Sarah lying in someone else's arms. Remembered too how she'd felt like she'd been kicked in the stomach by a steel-toed boot. She'd been too raw with hurt to try to discuss it in a text. "I couldn't talk about it in a text," she said, even now finding it tough to draw breath. She'd never be able to chase that image from her mind. "I saw you. You were in bed with another woman."

"What?" Astonishment played across Sarah's face, then anger, then something that resembled recognition. "Oh no. You saw me with A.J., didn't you?" She pursed her lips, shook her head lightly, but there was no apology in her actions. "So that's what this is all about."

"You're not denying it?"

"I'm not denying what you saw, but it wasn't what you think. If it's any of your business." Sarah stood abruptly, nearly knocking over her chair. "Look, you had your chance, Joss. And you made your choice. There really isn't anything else to say that wouldn't be going around in circles."

Joss stood too, still smarting, still wanting to hurt Sarah the way Sarah had hurt her. And still wanting to kiss her madly. "Apparently you made your choice too."

As Sarah stalked out the door, anger accentuating her strides, Joss knew this thing between them was a long way from being over. She'd never be able to leave Sarah behind, to banish the sweet pain from her heart. No matter how many women she slept with or spent time with, laughed or argued with, nothing and no one would ever come this close again.

She slumped into her chair, inadvertently knocking her stethoscope onto the floor. She wondered, as she stared at the snake-like object near her feet, if it had the power to detect a broken heart. *Her* broken heart.

CHAPTER THIRTY-TWO

Sarah waited with her stepmother while her father underwent surgery. The hours dragged and the buckets of coffee did little to keep her energy up. It was exhausting, the way Joss and her father tugged at different parts of her, separate and yet intertwined like a ball of string. It was also ironic that Joss was the one performing life-saving surgery on the man Sarah had not been able to forgive for not loving her enough. For it was Joss who had given her the strength and determination to accept nothing less than full acceptance from her father. And it was Joss who, like the flipside of the same coin, couldn't seem to love her quite enough. Who couldn't quite get out of her own head enough to give herself to Sarah. They made quite a pair, Joss and her father, Sarah thought. Both stubborn, both afraid to love and be loved, both seemingly paralyzed in the face of letting Sarah go.

Sarah and her father had hardly spoken since his arrival in the hospital. The air was so frosty between them that she could have scratched her initials in it. Her father had given no sign that he was ready to apologize, that he was ready to begin treating her differently. And Sarah had chosen not to take the first step toward reconciliation either. It was up to him to make this right, she'd decided, even though he was lying in the operating room now and faced weeks of recovery. She'd always been the one to give in, to go to him, to compromise her feelings, her values, to do whatever was needed to make his life easier. It was always she who wanted to keep the peace, who was afraid to ruffle too many feathers, mostly because she'd felt sorry for him having to raise her alone. It was up to him now to show her that he loved her and maybe even needed her.

The day Sarah's mother left was the first and only time Sarah had ever seen her father cry. She was just a kid, but she'd put her arms around him, tried to comfort him in his anguish. He'd pushed her away, preferring to be alone, and they'd never bridged that distance, had never been close, even when they were all the other had. For all intents and purposes, it was as though both parents had abandoned Sarah that day nearly two decades ago. But her father's emotional abandonment had cut the deepest.

Linda knew better than to interfere between Sarah and her father. But she felt no such compunction when Joss was the subject. She asked Sarah during the long wait what had happened between her and Joss, and Sarah told her, using broad strokes to describe the honeymoon atmosphere on Sanibel Island and then the quick disintegration upon their return to Nashville. It had been her decision to end things, she explained, because she was no longer willing to stand for people in her life who weren't prepared to give her what she needed.

"Maybe it's selfish," Sarah admitted, self-doubt shadowing her. She hoped that her father's health crisis and Joss's role as his doctor wasn't some kind of sign for her. A sign that they were both meant to be in her life and that pushing them away had been a mistake. Maybe they, in spite of their faults, deserved to be loved too. "I don't know, Linda. Maybe I'm too demanding. I mean, why should I make her change for me?" And for that matter, should she bother trying to make her father change too?

"That woman's in love with you."

No way, Sarah thought. *Joss cannot possibly be in love with me.* Then she remembered the way she'd looked at her while she sketched her. And more recently, the hurt in her eyes when she'd described seeing Sarah in bed with A.J. It was the haunted, injured look of someone betrayed, even though nothing had happened between Sarah and A.J. And even if it had, it wasn't Joss's concern. But deep down, it felt as though Joss did in fact have every right to feel betrayed. "I think she's more into keeping score than anything else. And she has absolutely no intention of falling in love with me."

"Too late."

It must be the stress of her father's surgery that was making Linda so smug and sure, Sarah thought. And maybe, just maybe, she had a small fraction of a point. But it was a moot point because Joss had no intention of giving into her feelings. "I know you mean well, Linda, but look. Joss has made it very plain to me that she does not want to be in a relationship with me. And as I know all too well, it takes more than one to make a relationship work."

"She probably doesn't know how. You two are so good together, Sarah. Don't tell me you're giving up on her. Can't you work with her on this?"

"You know what? I'm so tired of being the one doing all the work when it comes to relationships. I can't do it alone anymore." *I won't do it alone anymore.*

Linda patted her hand knowingly. "I know, sweetie, I know. Some people need more time than others, that's all."

Yeah, like about a century and a half, she thought morosely.

Joss entered the waiting room and motioned for them to join her in the hall. She looked satisfied, on top of her game, and the reassurance it gave Sarah was immeasurable.

"How is he?" Linda asked in a voice pitched high with worry.

"He's doing fine. The surgery went well. I was able to repair the valve, and I think it will actually be stronger than it's been in years. It should hold, but we'll need to guard against infection for the next few days."

Linda expelled a long-held breath. "Can I see him?"

"Soon. He's in recovery right now. We'll keep him in CICU for a good twenty-four hours, then move him to his own room for a few days so we can monitor him."

Nearly collapsing with relief, Linda hugged Joss and thanked her repeatedly.

Sarah exchanged a subtle look with Joss, a silent thank-you, and it confirmed they were no longer furious with one another, no longer accusatory and raw with hurt the way they'd been yesterday. Maybe, she thought with fresh hope, they could be friends after all. But not yet. Right now the bruise on her heart was too fresh.

Sarah turned to go. She had work to do in her studio.

"Sarah…"

She kept walking because there was nothing else to say. If she never set foot again in this hospital, it would be too soon.

* * *

Joss poured herself a rare glass of wine—it was technically her day off, discounting the fact that she'd gone to the hospital briefly to check on Peter Young. She was satisfied with yesterday's surgery but needed to sign off before he was allowed to transfer out of CICU to the medical floor. She'd just set her glass on the coffee table and was about to pick up the novel that she'd begun weeks ago on Sanibel when the buzzer announced company.

"Mother?" Joss said into the intercom, staring in surprise at the security camera's grainy black-and-white image of Madeline McNab, awkwardly shifting from foot to foot. Joss could count on one hand the number of times her mother had visited the condo in the last four years. Reasons were scarce, excuses plentiful. "I'll buzz you in. Come on up."

Joss hoped her mother's surprise visit meant she was extending some kind of olive branch. The coolness between them was worrisome. And unusual. Madeline had her faults, to be sure, but she'd never before kept Joss at arm's length like this.

"Wine? Coffee?" Joss offered, but her mother shook her head and sat down, clutching her purse to her like a shield.

"We need to talk," she said in an uncharacteristically meek voice. She looked small, fragile, and not at all like the fierce woman Joss had known all her life.

"We do." Joss sat down next to her mother on the long, comfortable sofa. One or two hairs were actually out of place on her mother's head. "It's all right, Mama. We'll get through this."

"Not necessarily, dear. Not after what I'm about to tell you."

Oh shit, Joss thought, mentally steeling herself for her mother to trash her father, to tell her he was a horrible husband and that she should have left him years ago or perhaps that she shouldn't have married him at all. None of it would be surprising, but it wouldn't make it any less difficult to hear.

"It's true," her mother finally said, "that your father wasn't around much. That he didn't have a lot of emotional energy for you and me at the end of the day. It wasn't his fault, it was the job. And he was good at his job. People needed him."

"We needed him too," Joss said quietly.

"Yes, we did. But you see, it was I who ultimately failed your father and not the other way around."

"How could you say that? You stood by him. You supported him in every way possible. You raised me practically single-handed. You did your part and then some." The anger she now directed at her father was all the more acute because she'd so seldom verbalized it. And never this intensely. He'd always been her hero, in spite of his shortcomings on the home front. She didn't want to hate him.

Madeline nodded slowly, even as her eyes scanned the room as if searching for an escape hatch or for something to swallow her up. After a moment, she squared her shoulders and was instantly the brave and stoic woman Joss knew.

"I stayed with your father for many reasons, but the biggest was guilt."

"Guilt? Guilt for what?"

Madeline's eyes shone with unshed tears. Her chin quivered ever so slightly, but she kept her gaze locked on Joss. "For eight years, I had an affair behind your father's back."

Joss's lungs sucked for air that was no longer there. She could not move or even speak. Her mother? An affair? *For eight years?* She shook her head, wanting to expunge what she'd just heard, wanting, if only she could, to stuff the words back into her mother's mouth. But everything in Madeline's voice, in her words, in her eyes, said that it was the truth, and the truth was what she'd been begging of her mother. If her mother was brave enough to speak it, then Joss would have to be brave enough to hear it.

"It was with one of his colleagues, doesn't matter to you which one. The man—and his wife—don't live around here anymore. It was a long time ago, you were still a kid. But for eight years we—" Madeline closed her eyes briefly. "We snuck around. For a while we even thought we were in love, but it would have been a scandal then to leave our marriages."

"Did...did Daddy ever find out?"

"Yes." Tears began to trickle down Madeline's cheeks. "He walked in on us once, right here in this...this...Your condo."

Oh, God, Joss thought, her head spinning. *No wonder she never visits me here.*

"And that was the end of it. We—your father and I—agreed to stay together. We both felt guilty. Me for what I'd done and him for making the conditions ripe for a neglected, lonely wife to wander into another man's arms."

Joss closed her eyes. Her parents' marriage had been a train wreck and not at all what she'd thought it was. Not even close. The ground that had once been so firm beneath her feet, so reliable, no longer was. Much of her own history, at least as far as she knew it, was a sham. "Jesus, Mama, I don't even know what to say."

"You don't have to say anything. Just don't hate me, Joss."

"I don't hate you." It was hard not to judge, though. Why had her mother put herself in the position of straying in the first place? Why had she let her father neglect her the way he had? Why had they both been so weak as to let guilt propel them through more years of a lousy marriage? They were questions for another day.

"Good. Then do something for me."

Joss looked into her mother's eyes, which had grown fierce with resolve.

"Don't end up like your father and me. When I say I want you to be happy, I mean it. I want you to have it all. And I don't want you to let your career blind you to the rest of what's important in life. Your job is *not* a substitute for love, Joss. It cannot take the place of a happy home, of a happy relationship. Trust me, I know that lesson all too well. And your father did too, even though it came too late."

Joss let her mother's words sink in one at a time in a gradual reckoning until something began to shift and give way inside her. Her parents had been human after all, had been something far less than perfect. Perfect, she realized, was a fallacy. She'd been striving all this time for something that didn't exist and had been so damned afraid of falling short of perfection. She didn't need to be perfect, because they certainly hadn't been. They'd never taught her, never allowed her, to be less than perfect. Well. Maybe it was time for her to be her own woman now.

Her voice came out in a strangled whisper. "I don't know how to do it, Mama."

Madeline squeezed her hand. "That's the thing, my dear. Nobody knows how. You just put one foot in front of the other and move forward, all while hoping for the best. The key is in taking a chance. And in realizing what you have."

Joss thought about that. She knew what she had with Sarah, but was she brave enough to risk the heartbreak that might come with pursuing it? Was she brave enough to risk needing Sarah so much? And would Sarah even allow it?

CHAPTER THIRTY-THREE

Sarah clutched Roxi's small, brown hand in hers and led her into the Frist Center for Visual Arts, Nashville's hippest and most happening art gallery. The girl was growing stronger every day and had promised Sarah that she was up to spending a couple of hours at the gallery. They were here to see an exhibit on nineteenth-century American art, but Sarah had a funny feeling that Roxi would be drawn like a magnet to the Martin ArtQuest Gallery upstairs, where people of all ages could make use of interactive stations that allowed the participant to produce instant art. She'd ask Roxi and her mother later about signing the girl up for the gallery's upcoming summer art camp for kids. If money was an issue, Sarah was happy to pay for it.

They studied a couple of the oil paintings in glass cases, one a scene of a Plains Indian camp, the other portraying a family's summer stroll through a park. Next they stopped before a barn scene on oil, and Sarah had Roxi point out all the animals and then discuss the techniques the artist had used.

"Hi Roxi, Sarah."

She would recognize that voice anywhere, especially its low, intimate timbre that sent pleasurable shivers up and down her spine. She turned around, and there stood Joss with that damned home-run smile of hers.

"What are you doing here?" Sarah asked. She hadn't invited Joss to join them. Hadn't, in fact, seen her since her father had come out of surgery three days ago.

"Nancy, er, I mean Dr. Nancy told me y'all would be here, so I thought I'd drop by and say hello. That okay with you, Roxi?"

"Sure." Roxi beamed, her eyes taking in both women. "Dr. Joss, is Miss Sarah your girlfriend now?"

"Um, well…" Joss began blushing, which gave Sarah some secret satisfaction. It was a rare thing to see Joss put on the spot. But her blush quickly evaporated, replaced by the cocky grin. "What do you say Sarah, are you my girlfriend yet?"

It was Sarah's turn to blush. She wouldn't play this little game with Joss in front of Roxi, even though she was tempted to say something cutting and sarcastic, like, *Don't ever get yourself a girlfriend, Roxi. They're a pain in the butt.* "Roxi, what do you say we go check out some of those interactive stations upstairs?"

"Okay," the girl said, making for the staircase with the typical attention span of a nine-year-old.

"Very clever," Sarah mumbled to Joss, who was half a step behind her. "Deflecting Roxi's question onto me."

"You could be, you know."

Sarah nearly tripped, but regained her balance quickly. "Could be what?" *Fine.* If Joss wanted her to play this little game, then so be it. She'd make her spell it out. Or spit it out, as was more likely the case.

"What Roxi said."

Yeah, right, Sarah thought. Joss had no more intention of having a girlfriend than Sarah did of working an office job, like her father wanted her to. She walked on in silence until they caught up to Roxi, who'd made a beeline to one of the wooden sit-down easels designed for kids. She picked up a colored pencil and immediately began drawing.

"I've learned some things recently," Joss said gravely, the playfulness gone. "Things that have made me reflect differently on the way I've felt about…you know, things. Everything, really."

"You're speaking in riddles," Sarah said, knowing she was being cruel, but she couldn't afford to open the door to her heart. Not even a crack. If Joss had something to say to her, she could damn well come out with it. "And this isn't the place for it."

"All right." Joss brushed lightly against her shoulder. "Let's go somewhere we can talk."

"No, Joss." Sarah took a step away. Being this close to her ignited a slow burning fire in her belly. "I don't want to talk. It's too late for talk." Talk hadn't got them anywhere, and there was no reason to think it would now.

"But, Sarah—"

Sarah set her jaw and speared Joss with a glare, trying to convey that she would not relent. Getting together to "talk" would only lead to another fight. Or sex. And either way, it would end with Sarah's heart breaking all over again. "Talk is cheap, Joss. And I've had all the cheap talk I can stomach."

* * *

On her iPad, Joss read over Peter Young's chart with his latest scan and ECG before taking out her stethoscope and listening to his heart, moving it gently over his chest. There was only a slight murmur, which had been receding, and his heart sounded strong. His recovery was going well, and she told him he should be fit to go home in a day or two.

"I guess I need to thank you for everything, doc."

"No thanks necessary, Mr. Young. Just doing my job."

"I thought…because you're a friend of Sarah's, that maybe… maybe you took special care."

Joss looked into the eyes that were so much like Sarah's. Anger pulsed through her. She didn't respect this man for the way he treated his daughter, especially the way he'd behaved toward her at the Christmas fundraiser, belittling her in front of others. It had since taken every ounce of her experience and professionalism to treat him with dignity and respect. But now she could hardly contain the bitterness, the near hatred that coursed through her veins for this man who seemed so utterly contemptuous of a woman who…a woman… Joss took a deep breath. Her chest hurt, as though there were vise grips around it. She'd lost Sarah, and it was not something she'd ever forgive herself for. But this man had thrown Sarah away over and over again.

It took great effort to keep her voice equable. "Mr. Young, I need to talk to you about your daughter."

Joss pulled up a chair and ignored the look of surprise and discomfort on her patient's face. Too bad. Peter Young needed to hear what she had to say, even if it meant crossing a line and going outside professional boundaries. If it was too late for her and Sarah, it wasn't, perhaps, too late for him and his daughter.

"You," she said, steel in her voice, "need to treat Sarah like an adult. And not just any adult, but like a woman deserving of your respect. And your thanks."

"My thanks? Thanks for what? For the tens of thousands of dollars she's cost me over the years?"

"Money? That's all you care about? I would give Sarah every last penny I have if she'd…if she'd…" *Oh hell.* Sarah wasn't a woman whose affections could be bought. "She stood by you, Mr. Young, even during all the times you treated her like crap. She's your daughter, your only child. Are you punishing her because her mother left you? Is that it?"

His face beet red, Peter Young began to stammer that Joss didn't know what the hell she was talking about.

"You're right, I wasn't there and I don't know the whole picture." She needed to get back to what she did know. "Have you ever thought that maybe she let you support her as a way to get your attention? To remain close to you? And did you ever stop to think that maybe your disdain for her art has been what's held her back? That maybe she would have been successful a whole lot sooner if you'd shown her the respect and approval she wanted and deserved?"

"What do you mean successful a whole lot sooner? Don't tell me she finally sold a painting!"

"Oh, she's done more than sold a painting." Joss wouldn't tell Sarah's father about her good fortune with the furniture chain nor the news that a gallery in Louisville had offered her an exhibit, something which Roxi had let slip at the Frist Center the other day. "Sarah's financially independent. Which should worry you, Mr. Young."

"Worry me how?"

It was tempting to twist the knife a little, but Joss was careful to avoid sounding like she was enjoying this turn in the conversation. "She doesn't need your money anymore. But what she does need and will always need is a father. Don't make the mistake of your life by letting her go."

Joss thought about the absence of her own father. What hurt more than anything was that they'd never really taken the time to get to know one another. She'd never had a heart-to-heart with the man, and if she could go back now, she'd pepper him with a million questions. And not medical questions. She'd ask him about his regrets, about what she meant to him, about how he really felt about her mother and their marriage, and if a stellar medical career had been worth the cost of almost losing his wife and never truly knowing his daughter.

Peter Young was silent for a long time, and Joss watched an aggregate of emotions flicker across his face—anger, resentment and, finally, resignation.

Joss stood to go. The rest was up to him. "Just love her, Mr. Young. That's all she wants. It's all," she said in a voice sandpaper rough with her own anguish, "any of us really wants."

In her office moments later, Joss sat behind her desk and let her eyes wander the room. Four large framed certificates on the wall lauded her medical and educational accomplishments. Near them was a framed photo of her and her father at her med school graduation right here at Vanderbilt, standing below the sign that featured his name in big letters. Joseph McNab's legend still loomed large here, following her wherever she went on campus and in whatever she did at the hospital and at the medical school. The only time she'd been out from under his shadow were the two years she'd spent at Stanford and then the few years following his death.

Maybe, she thought, tapping a pen on the felt blotter of her desk, it was too late for her and Sarah, but it wasn't too late to remake herself, to start over, to live in her own light, to live without her father's ghost sitting on her shoulder. All that remained was convincing herself that she deserved to take the first step.

CHAPTER THIRTY-FOUR

Sarah sipped champagne from a crystal flute and tried not to let her father's presence at her Louisville gallery opening throw her any worse than it already had. When he and Linda had walked in, wanting it to be a surprise, they'd said, Sarah had nearly fainted from the shock. Even more shocking was that her father acted like he actually wanted to be here. He was congenial to the curator and other guests, and his smiles actually involved his mouth for a change. Sarah marveled at how effortlessly he seemed to be pulling off the proud father routine, considering she'd never seen it before. She had to admit the act didn't seem disingenuous. There was a real twinkle in his eye, a lightness to his step that was brand new. He'd even asked Sarah pointed questions about her paintings and tilted his head to listen keenly to her answers.

"Okay," she later whispered to Linda. "Where is my father and what have you done to him?"

Linda fixed Sarah with a mischievous smile. "I'm wondering if Joss did more to him than fix his heart valve."

"If she did, I owe her big-time. He's almost human now."

Linda gave her a warning look. "Sorry," Sarah said. "I'm just not used to seeing him this way."

"I think maybe he's beginning to appreciate the important things in life after his health scare. And I know he still has a long way to go in repairing his relationship with you, but tonight is a start, don't you think?"

Sarah's father had never attended one of her exhibits before—her student showings during college and graduate school. He'd not even shown a cursory interest until now, but Sarah wasn't about to look a gift horse in the mouth. "You're right. I think he and I need to have some serious conversations, but for now, I'm going to enjoy this."

Linda leaned closer and lightly dug her nails into Sarah's forearm. "Hmm, I think things just got a lot more interesting around here. Look who's walked in!"

Not sure she could handle any more surprises tonight, Sarah flicked a glance at the door. Three couples had come in, clustered together, but Sarah didn't recognize them.

"No, no," Linda whispered in excitement, "over by the sculpture."

Sarah's stomach bottomed out at the flash of short blond hair and the tall, slender build of the woman in the well-tailored suit. "Oh my God, it's Joss. What's *she* doing here?"

Linda shrugged, but her grin made Sarah highly suspicious. "Did you know she was coming?"

"Actually, no, I didn't. But I wish I'd thought to invite her."

Sarah rolled her eyes. "I might not survive this evening, you know. First Daddy, now Joss. I think I need another drink." An entire bottle, more like.

"Good idea." Linda winked and snatched her empty glass from her hand. "I'll go get you one."

Joss circled the perimeter of the room, but there was no doubt where the focus of her attention lay. She kept glancing at Sarah—nervously, Sarah thought. But once she materialized at her side, she was maddeningly cool and breezy, affecting an I-was-just-in-the-neighborhood air that Sarah didn't buy for a single minute.

"Hello, Sarah. Congratulations on the show." Joss smiled, but it was lacking the tiniest shred of confidence, Sarah realized happily. She liked having the ability to throw Joss off balance.

"Thanks." Sarah narrowed her eyes at Joss. "You drove all the way to Louisville to tell me that? You could have sent a card or a text."

"No. Telling you in person was definitely worth the five-hour drive."

"Uh-huh. And the real reason you're here? Besides that?" Sarah didn't want to hope against hope that Joss had somehow come to her senses about them, because she knew the odds of that happening were about the same as her work fetching Warhol-like prices. Nothing had come close to convincing her that Joss was anything more than a lost cause.

"Dr. McNab." Sarah's father stepped between them and practically embraced Joss. "How wonderful to see you."

There was a flash of surprise in Joss's eyes before she blinked warmly at Peter Young. "Nice to see you here too, Mr. Young. And please call me Joss."

Sarah's father squeezed Joss's elbow, the affectionate gesture sending another wave of shock through Sarah. "Sure thing, Joss, as long as you call me Peter. It's so nice that you could come to Sarah's showing."

"I could say the same to you," Joss replied, not unfriendly, but the dig wasn't lost on Sarah or her father.

"Well, let's not beat around the bush," he said, his hand still on Joss's elbow. "It's thanks to you that I'm here at Sarah's exhibit. And I don't just mean because of my health you helped me regain. Your...conversation with me helped me see things differently. And appreciate certain things."

Sarah looked from Joss to her father, having no idea what the hell was going on between the two, but her senses had sharpened to a new level of alertness.

"That wasn't a one-way street," Joss said quietly. "I needed to take some of my own advice."

Growing more impatient by the second, Sarah finally implored them to tell her what the hell was going on. But Joss shook her head lightly and took Sarah's arm to steer her away. "Will y'all excuse us for a few minutes?"

"Of course." Peter winked at Joss, ignoring Sarah. "Take all the time you need."

"What the hell was that all about?" Sarah hissed as Joss guided her to a darkened room that was roped off to visitors. She unclipped the rope to allow them to pass, then clipped it behind them. Light spilling from the hall illuminated a cushioned bench, which Joss led her to.

"Sit, please," she said, and Sarah did. "There's something I need to know first. Are you with someone else right now?"

"With someone? I'm here with Linda and my dad, if that's what you mean."

Joss's breath came in rapid bursts. "No, I mean, you're not… Do you have a girlfriend, Sarah?"

"A girlfriend?" The worry on Joss's face was almost comical in its intensity. "Why would I have a girlfriend?"

"Well, that woman you were with at your New Year's Eve party. You never really told me if she's…if you and she…"

"Oh God, Joss, she is not. And never was. Jesus, is that what you think of me?"

Joss collapsed onto the bench beside her. "Oh, thank you Lord. And no, that's not what I think. But I've been a little, I don't know, insane since Christmas."

"Insane? Joss, you're one of the sanest, most methodical, reasoned people I know."

"Which is why I've been such a complete idiot these last few weeks."

"What are you talking about?"

"Come to my hotel room tonight and let me explain."

Sarah drew in a deep, unsteady breath. She would not be able to keep her hands off Joss if they ended up in a hotel room. Nor would she want Joss to keep her hands off her. Alone together, Sarah knew their bodies would mutiny and take over the ship. "You know that would mean trouble."

With a featherlight touch, Joss cupped Sarah's chin and let her eyes roam over her face. "God knows, I'll want to make love to you until my dying breath. But it's not about that, Sarah. Not this time. Please."

A voice in her head screamed at her not to do it, not to believe Joss. But her heart knew different because there was something about Joss that told her things had changed. That Joss had changed. Sarah stood, unsure and a little frightened. As resistant to change as Joss had been all this time, she too had resisted giving Joss a chance to change. She didn't know if she could survive her heart ending up in a million pieces again, but she also knew she was lonely without Joss. And sadder than she'd ever been, and she was damned tired of it. "All right."

* * *

"Would you like a drink?" Joss asked, stalling so she could steady her nerves. Being alone in a hotel room with Sarah was almost more than her body could handle, but she had things to say to Sarah. Important, life-altering things.

"Thanks but no. Any more alcohol tonight and I'll probably end up throwing myself at you."

There was no humor in Sarah's voice, but there was a hint of challenge in her eyes, and it was all Joss could do not to rush to the empty place beside her on the sofa and take her into her arms. It'd been so long since she'd held Sarah, yet Joss remembered distinctly the scent of her, the way her skin felt beneath her fingers and her lips, the way she precisely shifted to fit herself to Joss's body. There were certain memories in life that never faded, and the solid feel of Sarah against her was one of those.

"Was it you," Sarah asked, "who somehow got my father to realize what an ass he's been to me?"

"Not really. But I did tell him it would be the mistake of his life if he let you go."

Joss got to her feet, wanting to stand for what she was about to say next, even though dropping to her knees and begging Sarah's forgiveness wasn't a bad idea either. She did want Sarah's forgiveness, but not before she said what so desperately needed to be said.

"Sarah, your father isn't the only one who would be making the biggest mistake of his life if he let you go." She grasped Sarah's hands. "I don't want to be without you in my life. I don't want to do any of what I'm doing if you're not here to share it. Letting you go would be the one thing in my life I would forever regret. And that I could never recover from. Please..." Her voice shook from the sob that had amassed in her throat. "Please come back to me. I love you, Sarah. So much."

Sarah leapt off the sofa and into Joss's arms. They rocked together for a long moment, and then their mouths found one another in a dizzying kiss that was meant to solemnize an agreement Sarah had yet to verbalize.

"Will you?" Joss asked between rushed kisses. "Will you come back to me? Will you stay with me? Will you forgive me?"

A tear slipped from Sarah's eye. She looked at Joss in a way she never had before—with awe, with reverence, and with, Joss was relieved to see, unbridled joy. "Yes, yes, and yes, Joss. Being with you is the only place I've ever wanted to be." A trace of a smile formed on her lips. "Well, there is one other place I'd like to be right now. Before we go anywhere else."

Joss laughed, Sarah's eyes having told her where her thoughts had already wandered. "Show me?"

Sarah raced to the bed, shedding her clothes along the way. Joss did the same, falling on Sarah in a hail of kisses and affectionate murmurings.

"There's so much I want to tell you," Joss whispered, but Sarah stopped her with a finger against her mouth.

"Later. I can't wait another second, Joss. I need you to make love to me. Now. God, I need you to take me as hard and as fast as you can."

Sarah didn't wait for Joss's reply, grabbing her by the wrist and forcing her hand down and against her wet, soft flesh. "Oh, Joss, I need to feel you inside me. Please."

Joss needed the physical connection too. Feeling how wet Sarah was, she thrust her fingers inside her, hard. She thrust until Sarah moved rhythmically with her, demanding Joss fill her, demanding it deeper and faster and harder until she came with a loud guttural groan. She clenched herself around Joss's fingers, her body trembling with spasms that seemed to emanate from her very core.

"I love you, baby," Sarah blurted, her breathing still coming in short bursts. "But I'm not above using you for the next couple of hours before we talk again."

"I love how much you love sex with me."

"And I love when you make me come. Please make me come again."

"You mean use my mouth for something other than talking right now?"

Sarah nodded, biting her bottom lip to keep from screaming as Joss's fingers found her again. She was so wet again, so insatiable for what Joss could give her, that it made Joss wet too.

* * *

The first stroke of Joss's tongue immediately drove Sarah to a place higher than she'd been before. Sex with Joss had always been wonderful, had always left her fulfilled and wanting more, but now that she knew Joss loved her, her heart had joined her body in this state of pure ecstasy. Something deep and needy had now been answered in her, something that went far beyond her body to encompass her heart and soul too. She was, she realized, with the woman she needed to be with for the rest of her life. She was with the woman who would dream with her, who would soar with her, who would laugh with her and cry with her, who would comfort her and love her.

Sarah rode the waves of pleasure Joss's mouth gave her, and when she came again, she began to cry.

Joss scooted up beside her. "Sarah, honey, are you all right?" She covered her face with tiny kisses. "I love you, baby, and I won't let anything happen to you, I promise."

"I waited so long to hear you say that, Joss. It almost feels like it's too good to be true. Please tell me it isn't."

"It isn't too good to be true." Joss turned on her side, leaning on an elbow. "You were right. At the Frist Center, when you told me it was too late for talk. That talk was cheap. And that's when I realized I needed to make some real changes in my life if you were ever going to come back to me. That I needed to show you that I meant it. And…" Joss leaned down and kissed the tip of Sarah's nose. "If I was ever truly going to be happy. Which I wasn't before I met you."

Sarah felt her heart lift. "I always felt you were so happy with me, and yet it was like you wouldn't allow yourself to be."

"No. Because I didn't trust it. I didn't trust that I deserved it or that I would know how to keep that kind of happiness going. God, Sarah, you were right about so many things. My parents, everything."

"What about your parents?"

Sarah listened wordlessly but with rapt interest as Joss told her of her mother's confession.

"Now that I know what a disaster their relationship was on so many levels, I know that I want so much more than that, something better. With you."

Sarah began to pull Joss to her, but Joss held her back. "Wait. There's more."

"I'm not sure how many more confessions I can handle tonight." She wasn't entirely kidding. Her emotions, and her heart, hadn't yet settled from the roller-coaster ride Joss had taken her on over the last hour.

"I know that to do this right I have to make changes. Big changes. Because I know I can't have the kind of relationship I want with you if I don't. I can't just tweak a few things and fit you into my life the way it is."

With mild trepidation, Sarah watched as Joss held her breath for a moment, then let her words rush out of her in a stream, as though she couldn't wait to get them out. "I've handed in my resignation at the medical school, effective this June. Teaching was my father's great passion and his legacy, not mine. But that's not all, Sarah. With your okay, I'd like to hand in my resignation at the hospital too."

"What?" Sarah felt herself go still. "Joss, you're a gifted surgeon. Don't tell me—"

"No, I'm not quitting medicine."

She was smiling, and Sarah began to breathe again. "Good, because if you wanted me to support you on my artist's salary, we wouldn't exactly be living the high life."

"You mean I can't be *your* kept woman this time?"

Sarah pretended to consider. "Well, all right. But I'll need you for sex three times a day. At least."

"What? That's hardly fair. I didn't demand sex from you at all when we had our little agreement."

Sarah pushed Joss onto her back and lay on top of her. "Maybe you should have."

"Hmm, and you would have complied?"

"Absolutely. Your own personal mistress, at your sexual beck and call. Would have been a turn-on, actually."

Joss laughed at her, and Sarah couldn't help but join in. "Yeah, you'd have beaten the crap out of me if I'd even suggested such a thing."

"Maybe, but let's pretend right now that I'm your mistress," Sarah said, dropping her voice an octave. "Tell me what you'd like me to do."

Joss smiled and let her head sink into the pillow. "All right."

* * *

It was after Joss's second electrifying orgasm that she finally pulled Sarah to her. The hour was late and her strength was waning, but she needed to ask Sarah the one question that would change both their lives.

"There's more I need to tell you. To ask you," she said as her mouth left a tiny trail of kisses along Sarah's temple and down her jaw.

"I think you've softened me up enough now to know I'll say yes to anything."

"Good. Then how about saying yes to moving with me to Chicago."

"What?" Even in the dim light, Joss could see Sarah's eyes become huge orbs of surprise.

"I've been offered a job in the cardiology department at Northwestern. Remember Dr. Jeff Billings from the Chicago conference you attended with me? The guy who gave me the concert tickets?"

Sarah nodded.

"Well, he's offered me a job there doing valve replacements."

"You really want to leave Nashville? What about your mother?"

"My mother's encouraging me to do this, if you want to know the truth. Says I need to strike out on my own, get out from beneath my father's shadow. And she says I need to quit being such a mama's girl and focus on being Sarah's girl."

"Well, your mother is a very brilliant woman, as you know."

"You could start over there too. They have some wonderful galleries there, and you went to college there, so you know lots of people, right? And—"

Sarah shushed her with a kiss on her lips. "You don't need to work so hard to convince me, you know."

"I don't?"

"No. Joss darling, I'd go anywhere with you. And I love Chicago."

A tremendous weight fell away from Joss. "You'll do it?"

"Of course I will. But I expect you to make an honest woman of me one of these days."

Joss winked. "You sound like your father."

"Well, I'll never tell him this, but he was right about that part."

Joss laughed and let fantasies of Sarah in a wedding dress parade through her mind. There wasn't anything stopping them from whatever it was they might want to do now. Not their families, not their jobs, not the ghosts from their pasts.

Joss kissed Sarah, a soft fluttering kiss that soon turned into a deep, soulful kiss. "Let's plan a Christmas wedding."

"Seriously? Oh no, no, no. No, you don't, Joss McNab."

Oh shit, Joss thought. "What did I do wrong now?"

Sarah firmly cupped her chin. "You will not ask me to marry you like that."

"Oh, you're right. What was I thinking?" A woman like Sarah would expect champagne, candlelight, roses, a diamond ring. "What are you doing next Saturday night?"

Sarah kissed her and smiled against her mouth. "I have a feeling next Saturday night we will be doing something very romantic."

Joss pulled Sarah on top of her. The rest of her life, she knew without a doubt, wouldn't be long enough to be with this woman. The tragedy would be if they didn't start now.

"I love you, Sarah Young."

"I love you too, Joss McNab. Now, make love to me again."

Bella Books, Inc.

Women. Books. Even Better Together.

P.O. Box 10543
Tallahassee, FL 32302

Phone: 800-729-4992
www.bellabooks.com